BULLETS

A novel by
Elijah Drive

Professional poker player Jon "Big Slick" Elder was minding his own business in a diner when an Arizona sheriff walked in and killed the man sitting next to him, a Mexican day laborer accused of murder. The law officer then arrested Slick simply because the sheriff didn't like the color of Slick's skin.

Slick knew the stranger who had been sitting next to him at the diner was no murderer because, in addition to cards, Slick also kills people for money. The poor man didn't have the look, but Slick does, and with the help of a beautiful assistant district attorney, a Navajo state trooper and a homegrown federal agent, Slick sets out to prove the dead man's innocence. What he discovers, as he digs deeper, is a deadly mystery that threatens not only him, but his new-found friends as well. But Slick hates to have anyone… ANYONE… toss him his shoes and tell him to get out of town.

BULLETS – a novel by Elijah Drive.

1

"WAIT, WHAT? YOU never eat meat?"

"Nope."

"Nothing, no burgers, no ribs, not one fucking hot-wing?"

"Nah man."

"No fucking barbecue, ever?"

"Never," Slick said.

Stutz stopped digging and stared up at Big Slick, wanting to comment further upon the irony of a black man refusing barbecue, but struggled with how to communicate said irony without offending the six foot four, very dark-skinned man helping him dig a hole in the desert.

Stutz usually never hesitated to air his opinion on the worthlessness of non-whites and whoever was inflamed by it, well fuck 'em, but that was when backed up by four or five of his skinhead buddies, armed boot to belt.

At that particular moment, however, Stutz was all alone in the desert with Big Slick, who was at least a head taller, fifty pounds heavier and holding a shovel. Stutz had longed to say something funny about a spade holding a spade for the past half hour as it was, it was torturing him, but he couldn't take the chance of pissing the big bastard off, at least not until the job was over and done.

Stutz finally just said, "I don't fucking believe it. God-damn vegetarian."

"I'm a vegan, actually."

"Vegan, not vegetarian? What the fuck does that even mean?"

"No meat, no fish, no dairy."

"No dairy? Like, like…"

"Eggs, milk, anything made from eggs or milk—"

"No ice cream? No milkshakes?"

"Nope. No pasta either."

"Sweet Jesus jumped, I don't fucking believe it."

Stutz tossed down his shovel and hauled himself out of the hole, huffing. He dug into a cooler and pulled out a brew. Beer dribbled down his ratty beard as he watched the other man sweat and finish the hole. Slick could read his mind and knew the redneck fucker was thinking that this was the proper order of things anyway, that the black man labored while the white man supervised.

Stutz was one of those white guys with a barrel chest and outsized gut offset by skinny arms that he unsuccessfully tried to draw attention away from with a series of prison tats, swastikas that he hadn't tried to hide. When Slick approached the truck earlier for the meet, Stutz had been unsettled, to say the least.

"They never said you was … was…" he stammered.

"Wasn't from around here?"

"You can say that again," Stutz finally allowed. "You the fella Hadenfeld sent?"

"Yeah. I'm the contractor. You put up a deposit, you got the rest of the cash?"

"I got it, but you get it only when it's over and done, boy."

And that was it for talking over the next few hours as they drove to the designated spot in the Arizona desert and got to work. Stutz hated blacks and couldn't believe he'd gotten stuck with one on this job, but it'd been known to happen. A referral for a hitter was just that, a referral. The broker never asked or cared for the color of the contractor's skin, and usually the client didn't either. It was the hit that counted. And usually the hitter was insured for his own protection. But that didn't mean Stutz had to make nice conversation with the bastard. He held his tongue as they toiled in the hot sun.

Finally, the boredom of the work and afternoon hunger pangs got to Stutz and he announced that the best steak he had ever eaten in his whole goddamn life was at this shithole diner in South Texas and he'd give his left nut for it right at that moment. When Slick said he didn't eat meat, it shocked Stutz so much he forgot about not talking to him.

"No meat, no dairy? How can you live like that, man? What do you even eat?"

"Fruit, vegetables, nuts and grains. Anything that grows from the ground up or down, I eat. I don't eat anything with a face."

"But that ain't even natural or healthy."

"Sure it is, it's very natural."

"No it ain't, we need meat, we're carnivores, have been since the fucking caveman days, clubbing fucking mammoths and making Flintstone fuckin' burgers outta their ass, you know? We're carnivores, man."

"We're not, actually. We're omnivores."

"What?"

"We're not carnivores, we're omnivores."

"Omni-what? What the fuck is that? No fucking way, we eat meat, so we're carnivores, like wolves, you don't know what you're talkin' about!"

"Carnivores eat meat, but they can only eat meat, they can't eat other shit. Lions, tigers, wolves, all carnivores, a vegetable diet will fuck them up. Herbivores eat only vegetables, they can't eat meat, when they do, it fucks them up. Mad cow disease came to be as a result of feeding cows beef product. Cows, sheep, horses, all herbivores. Omnivores eat both vegetables and meat. They need the vitamins from veggies and the protein from meat. Pigs, bears and humans, all omnivores."

Stutz had to think hard about that for a minute, and thinking hard wasn't something he was used to doing for any extended length of time. Then he got it.

"Hold on the fuck, you're sayin' humans need to eat meat, 'cause we're whatever you called it—"

"Omnivores, yeah. We need the protein."

"So if we're SUPPOSED to eat meat, how can you stand there and say ya don't!"

"We need the protein, we just don't necessarily need it from meat. I get it from beans, nuts and soy. But, yeah, meat is one source for all omnivores. Bears eat fish."

"So hell, boy, you're making my argument for me. If eatin' meat's good enough for bears an' pigs, why ain't it good enough for you?"

"Because of how they died—the animals."

"What's that even mean?"

"You ever been on a chicken farm, a ranch or a slaughter house?"

"I look city to you, boy?"

"So you know, then, how the animals in those places live and die. They live in torment, often never leaving a tiny cage, never moving, just planted there in their own waste in a dark factory barn and pumped full of chemicals and steroids and then they're slaughtered. It's beyond sick. Every time I look at a steak or a chicken wing, the only thought that goes through my head is how awful this creature's life and death was, and if I eat it, I contribute to that bad karma, and I won't do that."

"But ... but they're fucking animals, what do you expect?"

"Humanity." Slick stopped digging and wiped his brow. "From humans, I expect humanity. I expect compassion. It's not that the animal was killed and eaten, that's part of the natural order of things. That's life. It's HOW it happened that's wrong. If I eat a fish that I caught or a deer that I hunted because I had to eat them to live, that'd be different, that's the natural order of things. But as it is now, where we put living things on a factory belt of torment, it screws the deal."

"Deal? What fucking deal?"

"Look, cows and chickens and goats evolved, right? They evolved a coping mechanism for survival. Their strategy was to partner with humans through domestication. They give us their skin and meat in return for protection from their predators like wolves and shit like that. That's the deal.

"The problem is now that we've become worse than wolves, we don't respect the deal anymore, we don't let the animals live right, we treat them horribly, we give them chemicals and shit and we raise sick food, which, in turn, makes us sick. I don't eat meat because we don't honor the deal. We start honoring the deal, I'll reconsider my position."

Slick climbed out of the hole.

"Hey boy, whatta doin'? That hole ain't big enough yet."

"It's big enough."

"Listen, it's gotta be big enough for three men, they told you, right? I know we're gonna be planting beaners in there and they's really small compared to you brothers, but it ain't big enough for three men. They told ya, right?"

"They told me. The hole's big enough, trust me. I've been doing this awhile."

Slick stuck the shovel into the ground, opened the cooler and rooted through it. Nothing in there but Pabst Blue Ribbon, which figured. He was so thirsty that he didn't care, cracked one open and drank. He could tell Stutz didn't like Slick putting his hand into a white man's beer cooler, much less sharing any beer with him. Stutz was biting back a ton of words and sooner or later he was going to burst.

"They told ya? So you know how this is supposed to go?"

"Sure, but feel free to refresh my memory, if it makes you feel better."

"There's gonna be three of 'em, they're gonna meet me over by that cactus grove there, next to them rocks, see it?

They think they're only gonna be meeting me, no one else. You'll be in the brush, behind 'em, and when I say so, you step out. Two of the Mexs are big and they'll probably be armed, but they ain't shit, fucking farmers with shotguns is all. You take those two out right away. Got it? That's your job.

"The third one, you'll know him because he's a short bastard, that's Esteban, you don't kill him. He's mine. We tie him to the truck bed. He ain't gonna die quick, I'm gonna have fun with him first. It's gonna take a long while 'fore he dies. They told you that, right?"

"Yep."

"You fine with this, then? You don't like it when chickens is tortured, you might not have the sack for what I'm gonna do to this fuckin' beaner. You gonna be cool?"

"Sure. He deserves it, right?"

"Yeah, he deserves it, boy. Trust me. Let's go set up, we only got an hour."

"What'd he do?"

"Who?"

"This Mexican, what did he do?"

"Raped a white girl. Fourteen. Only fucking fourteen years old and he raped her ass bad, she's in the hospital. Some sort of technical bullshit keeping his ass out of jail, but he knows we're after him. He's coming out here to pay my boys off for protection. That's what he thinks, anyway, and he's bringing his brothers as backup. Only it ain't gonna go as planned for their sorry asses."

"Raped a fourteen-year-old girl? That's terrible."

"Yeah, it's a fucking disgrace. Fuckin' Mexican gang-banger, this Esteban. They do that shit all the time. The beaner gangs around here, they ain't no joke, you know. Fucking cold, remorseless killers, wanna kill our sons and rape our daughters, we have to protect our borders from the Mexican horde before we're overrun and it's too late."

"Keep America white, right?"

"Yeah, and…" Stutz nodded in agreement before he realized what'd just been said and by who. "You fuckin' with me, boy?"

"Nope. Not at all."

"You think this is a goddamn joke. Where you from?"

"I live in New York City."

"Fuck. Figures. You don't know what we have to deal with here. We got Mexicans swarming over the border every fucking day and night. Take our jobs, our land, our women, our fucking natural resources. You think it's fuckin' funny, I can tell, and maybe you even sympathize 'cause you're dark like them, but don't make the mistake of thinking you'll be welcomed with open arms by the beaners, they hate the blacks just as much as they hate white people. There's a race war going on down here and it ain't the one you think you're fighting. You want to end up with Spanish as the official language of our country?"

"*Dios nos Ayuda!*" Slick said.

Stutz spat on the ground. Damn Hadenfeld for sending him this fucker. If he could've have done this alone, he would have, but he didn't dare fuck this job up.

"All right, boy, enough of this jawin', let's get set up."

"Wait, one question."

"What? And there'd better not be anymore of your lip,

neither."

"Just a question, you said the two Mexicans that are with this Esteban, they'll be armed with shotguns but not to worry because they're farmers, right?"

"Yeah, and?"

"But you also said Esteban is a gang-banger. So why would a gang-banger bring a couple shotgun-toting farmers to a meeting with a badass like you?"

"They're his brothers, his blood. So what?"

"So it don't make sense, a banger, he'd bring some old school gang hard cases, right? Some Uzi-carrying blooded killers. Not a couple of farmers with shotguns."

"Hey, we just do what—"

"Not only that, why would I get hired to help out a pure white native like yourself in some simple racial cleansing? Seems to me you got enough boys in your crew who'd be more than willing to knock off a few Mexicans with you, right? Why am I even here? Something ain't right, don't you think?"

"You ain't getting paid to think. You're getting paid to back me up, kill who I say to kill, bury bodies where I tell you to bury 'em, and that's it. You got that, boy?"

Stutz glared, putting a hand on the pistol tucked into his pants for good measure. He was gonna plant this mother-fucker alongside the Mexicans when it was all over, insurance or not, and anyone who didn't like it could go fuck themselves.

Slick smiled, tossed his empty can and picked up the spade.

"Sure boss, whatever you say. Hey, I'm just asking, that's

all."

Slick trudged in Stutz's direction, voice and manner calm and relaxed.

"You don't ask nothin', you don't say nothin', you just do as you're fucking told and nothin' else, you hear me you goddamn yappy nigger?"

"She wasn't fourteen," Slick said as he got close.

"What'd you say?"

"I said she wasn't fourteen, and she wasn't white. She was twelve and Mexican."

"What? How did you—"

"Esteban's her older brother and he didn't rape her. You did. They can't go to the law because she's an illegal. Esteban beat the shit out of you for it a few days ago, might have killed you if his friends hadn't pulled him off. You have to kill him before word gets out that your ass was kicked by a Mexican half your size—and also why.

"So you had a message sent to him that your gang would deliver you to him for a price and you plan to kill him yourself without any of your people finding out, because, as nasty as your gang is, even they ain't down for raping twelve-year-old girls. Since you're on your own, you reached out to a broker for help, and they sent me.

"Thing is, I ain't down for pedophile rapists, either. So it's my distinct pleasure to tell you that Esteban and his friends, they won't be showing up. It's just you and me out here and I should tell you up front that—"

Stutz broke out of his stupor and went for his pistol. Slick grabbed Stutz's pistol hand, squeezed tight, leaned close and finished his sentence.

"—I ain't your boy."

Slick yanked Stutz's hand up and out of his belt, twisting it hard. He kicked the inside of the redneck's knee, hard, and he went down. Slick still held the spade in his other hand, and he brought it up and down on the other man's shoulder, breaking his collarbone. Stutz screamed in pain.

"I bet you've just been dying to say something about a spade holding a spade this whole time, right?" Slick said.

He snagged the pistol from the fallen man's belt. Tossed it. Turned back just as the fallen redneck yanked a wicked dagger from his boot with his good arm.

Stutz swiped at Slick, who caught his wrist easily. Twisted until it snapped and the knife fell. Slick turned Stutz over on his stomach, grabbed him by the belt, picked him up and hauled him over to the freshly dug grave. With a grunt, Slick swung the other man into the pit. He fell hard, gasping in shock when he landed on his broken bones.

"I told you this hole would be big enough."

Slick picked the pistol back up, chambered a round.

"Listen, my man, this ain't right, I didn't kill her and besides, she was just a—"

"Just a Mexican?"

"Yeah! Come on! It ain't the same, you're an American, you gotta understand—"

"I do. You screwed the deal. You fucking raped a kid."

Slick shook his head. "Now karma's come to collect on your ass."

"Fuck you, you fucking cocksucking nig—"

Slick raised the pistol and fired three times. Hit Stutz once in the chest, twice in the head. Classic double-tap.

"Your hate was your undoing, friend," he said to the dead man.

2

S LICK WAS ON his third cup of coffee when the cops walked in, and they came in with a definitive purpose beyond breakfast that everyone in the diner could sense. Conversation came to a complete halt as folks waited, expectant.

There were four of them, hands on their pistols, confident enough they didn't pull the weapons but clearly looking for someone. Slick eased back on his stool and took a last sip of coffee just in case he didn't get any more for a while.

He didn't usually drink coffee, organic tea was his beverage of choice, but he was exhausted and had had trouble staying awake while driving.

After dumping all the stuff—the cooler, the pistol, everything—down into the hole with Stutz, he poured gasoline into the pit and lit it up. The only thing he kept was a dirty roll of cash, which was, he assumed, what Stutz had intended to pay him with.

He then drove Stutz's truck to where he left his rental car, which wasn't too far away—he'd known in advance where Stutz was planning the ambush and planted a rental—but wasn't too close either, as he had to dump the truck afterward and didn't want it to be found anywhere near the body. He then burned the truck and hit the road, hoping to catch an earlier flight if he made the four-hour drive to Tucson in three.

When dawn broke, Slick caught himself nodding off, tires rumbling on the edge of the freeway, and he knew he'd have to do something if he wanted to make it home at all. So when he spotted a sign for a town, he decided to pull off and grab some real coffee.

The sign had read: "YOU ARE NOW ENTERING THE CITY OF BENDIJO, POP 14,201."

Bendijo was Spanish for blessed, Slick recalled from somewhere in his youth. *Population fourteen thousand, two hundred and one,* Slick had mused as he pulled into the city proper, *wonder who that last one is?*

An hour and two and a half cups of very strong coffee later, Slick stopped wondering about the population of Bendijo and started worrying why four white cops with attitude were eyeballing the customers, one of whom was Slick.

It was after eight and the diner was half full, a mix of people, mostly truck drivers, construction workers and laborers and a couple of guys dressed for desk jobs. Everyone was friendly, everyone pleasant, lots of Spanish spoken on both sides of the counter.

Slick was clean, he had scrubbed himself good after the job, even washed the cash. No weapons, no drugs. He was careful. But here were four cops with obvious bad intentions and a lifetime of traveling while black had taught Slick that he was in a potentially dangerous situation just for being who he was.

The lead cop, a big bastard with the name RAWLINGS on his nametag, scanned the diner. He had requisite mirrored sunglasses, a crew cut and a hard gut, which seemed to be the way of white folks down in this part of the country. He chewed gum, which made Slick dislike him almost immediately. *Gum isn't for grownups, it's for kids.*

Slick slid his hand into his pocket, pulled out his smart phone and pretended to check for text messages. Chance favored the prepared mind.

Rawlings finally found whomever it was he was searching for and swaggered forward, pulling out a police baton. His uniform told Slick that Rawlings was a sheriff. The other three, deputies, followed him. Bad procedure, one should have stayed by the door, another in the back. If they were here to arrest someone, they should have their guns out and ready. Sloppy.

Sloppy or not, they headed right for Slick. He rehearsed his reaction in his mind, got his story right and tight. Took a deep breath, got into character.

And Rawlings walked right past him, not even sparing him a glance. He stopped at the man sitting next to Slick at the counter, a Hispanic man in blue jeans and a denim shirt. He'd been sitting there with two friends, chatting up a storm in Spanish.

Rawlings, with his baton, tapped the man on the arm.

"Let's go, Pedro, on your feet."

"What for?" Pedro asked, fear in his eyes. "I am arrested?"

"Let's go, on your feet." Rawlings tapped him again with the baton. Slick lowered his phone, tucking it out of sight under the counter. He didn't want to be involved, now that he knew they weren't looking for him.

"What charges, why?"

Rawlings reacted instantly and swung the baton hard. It connected with Pedro's face, breaking the man's nose and probably several other bones in his face. He fell straight down to the floor. Rawlings kept swinging the baton, bashing the man's back and legs, cursing a blue streak. The rage came at a flip of a switch, which told Slick that Rawlings was not only ready to lose his shit, he welcomed it with open arms.

Pedro's two companions got to their feet, hands in the air, and just watched, helpless. The other three cops chewed gum, weapons out but relaxed, and waited for the beating to end. Finally Rawlings stopped, nodded, and two of them stepped forward, cuffed the unconscious Pedro, picked him up by the armpits and dragged him out. Pedro's face was basically caved in. *He'll be lucky to live,* Slick thought.

Rawlings stared at Pedro's companions then turned to the waiting officer.

"Take them in, too."

The remaining cop nodded, stepped forward, told the men in Spanish to slowly turn around and put their hands on their heads. They complied without a word or sudden movement. The cop cuffed both as Rawlings watched. One hand on each cuff, he waited patiently. *Sloppy,* Slick thought again.

After a moment, the other two deputies returned, having evidently dumped the bleeding and unconscious Pedro in the back of a patrol car, took the cuffed Hispanic men from the third deputy and marched them outside.

Rawlings glanced around at the other customers in the diner. A few, all white, smiled at him with apparent approval. Other folks, however, just looked away, concentrated on their food or coffee—same as Slick. He'd followed everything out of the corner of his eye, but his plan was to stay out of it.

He felt Rawlings stare at him. Slick did his best to mask emotions, but a man next to him just had his face cratered, ignoring something like that was far from natural. After thinking about it, Rawlings finally tapped Slick on the arm with his baton.

"Hey, boy. You see something here you don't approve of?"

Slick didn't approve of white men calling him boy. But he swallowed that and just shook his head in answer.

"Look at me when I'm talking to you, boy."

Rawlings tapped him on the arm with his baton again. There was still blood on it from Pedro's skull, and it colored Slick's shirt. The sheriff didn't seem to care.

Slick sighed, set his coffee down and turned to face Rawlings, who took his sunglasses off and gave what had to be his official version of a badass stare.

"What you doin' here, boy?"

Slick thought about that, glanced at his coffee as if to answer, *"Isn't it obvious?"*

"I meant, smartass, what you doing in Bendijo? You ain't from here."

"Just passing through."

"Passing from where and to where?"

"I'm driving to Tucson."

"Why?"

"Catch a flight."

Rawlings eyeballed him more. Slick could read people, it was one of his specialties, and he could tell Rawlings didn't like Slick sitting there as witness to what had happened, didn't like it at all.

"What you got in your hand there, boy?"

Slick had a real bellyful of being called boy, but he swallowed it again and opened his hand, revealing his smart phone. Rawlings took it from him. The keypad was locked. It had his nickname scrolling across a screensaver of an Ace-King of Spades.

"Big Slick. That you?"

Slick nodded again. He saw Rawlings come to an internal decision.

"On your feet, let's go."

"Hey, Ted, come on now," a man chimed in from a back booth, smiling but concerned. "He's obviously just a tourist having coffee. Give him a break. Remember, it's good for the local economy."

The man wore a suit and tie, both expensive. Slick put him as either an insurance salesman or a banker. Rawlings didn't look back, just stared at Slick, still wary.

"That right? You a tourist, boy?"

Slick was exhausted. He hadn't slept in twenty hours. He usually held tight to his emotions but when he was this tired he occasionally slipped and let them loose.

"Jon."

"What?"

"My name is Jon Elder. My friends call me Big Slick, my lawyer and my accountants call me Jon, my bank calls me Mr. Elder because that's my name. Jon Elder. It's not boy, nigger, coon, jungle bunny, porch monkey, blackie, nappy, darky, spade, melon-head, or negra, none of the above. My name is Jon Elder, you can call me Jon or Mr. Elder or Sir, but you don't call me boy. Got that, Ted?"

Rawlings swung his baton, hard, right for Slick's head. Slick caught it before it landed and held it, a few inches away from his face.

"And this ain't the way to run a chicken farm. You're screwing the deal, Sheriff."

Slick lost consciousness when the deputy hit him on the head from behind and was completely out, thankfully, for the very severe beating that followed.

3

WHEN SLICK WOKE up, his whole body hurt. He'd gotten one of those cop beatings, the kind where they hammer at your arms and legs with a baton while you're cuffed. He stretched, muscles complaining. Didn't seem to be any broken bones, just deep bruises everywhere. His neck creaked and cracked. So far everything moved as it was supposed to, the joints and tissue screamed at him for it but did as they were told.

He was in a holding cell, a brand spanking new one. No graffiti, no dirt or grime, clean cement painted yellow, a coat that was shiny and new. He lay on a metal cot and there was a metal toilet, sans seat, on one side. No mirror. He felt his face; swollen and bruised, dried blood but, again, no broken bones. He was barefoot and his belt was gone. The three cells next to his were empty.

He had no idea how long he'd been unconscious. He could see sunlight so he knew it was daytime, but that was about it. A clank as the hall door opened and a deputy walked in. Slick figured they had cameras on the cells, which was how they knew he was finally awake. The cop, one of the four from the diner, stepped close, jangling cuffs.

"Stand up. Put your back to the bars, hands together."

The nametag on the cop's uniform read BROWER. Slick

recognized him as the deputy who stayed in the diner with Rawlings the whole time. That made Brower the one who knocked him on the back of the head. White, of course, younger and in better shape than his boss and wore the same coat of entitlement, though it fit him much better. Slick stared at him, not moving. Brower tapped the bars.

"Let's go. Don't make me beg. If I have to go back and get help, we'll come in here with batons and pepper spray and it'll get ugly. Be a sport, let's do this friendly."

Slick considered that and decided to cooperate, seeing as Brower was speaking to him like an adult. He stood, backed up to the bars and put his hands through them. Brower cuffed his wrists, tight. He was being more professional and careful with him than he had been with the Mexicans earlier, something else to consider.

Brower waved up at the camera and the cell door clicked up. He kept his hands on the cuffs, tight but not painfully so, and led Slick through the door and out of the holding area. They passed through a hallway and Slick noted an open office area of desks and a front door to the outside. A few cops lounged, doing paperwork or just farting around. Brower kept going, past the office area and into an interrogation room with a table and a couple chairs. He pulled a chair out for Slick, raised an eyebrow.

Slick sat. From the cast of the sun through the front door, it was afternoon, but it didn't feel like the same day to him; despite his aches and pains he actually felt rested. And thirsty, he was thirsty as hell, which would mean he'd been unconscious for a day and a half at the very least. Could he have been out that long?

Brower cuffed Slick to the chair, which was bolted to the floor, and walked out of the room, whistling. Slick glanced around. Big mirror on one wall, figured to be one-way and likely to have a camera on the other side. Everything was clean and pristine. New paint, new furniture, everything polished and buffed to a high shine, simply glistening.

Brower returned, plastic bag in one hand, computer notepad in the other. With him was an elderly man with white hair, lots of wrinkles and a smoker's rasp in a western shirt and a bolo tie. The old fellow carried a doctor's bag. He set the bag on the table, pulled out a light and stethoscope. He began examining Slick. A fair examination, despite his tobacco cough, the old doctor knew what he was doing.

"Got a headache?"

Slick nodded, with a wry smile. Of course he had a headache. A baton to the back of the skull tended to do that. The old doc checked his eyes.

"Double vision, nausea?"

Slick shook his head. "Just thirsty. Real thirsty. Could use some water."

"Later," Brower said. He had parked himself against a wall, admiring his manly pose in the mirror.

The old doc glanced over at Brower. Held it. Brower sighed and left the room. Doc continued his examination, short but thorough.

"You're banged up pretty decent, but you'll live," he said by the end.

"This the first time you've looked at me?"

"I checked you when they first brung you in yesterday, real quick. You were out."

Slick shook his head. He HAD been unconscious for a day and a half. Motherfucker. He had a thought.

"What happened to the other three guys?"

"What other three guys?"

"They arrested three other men, Mexican, I think, same time as me. What happened to them?"

"Friends of yours?"

"Nope, never saw 'em before I walked into the diner. I'm not from around here and don't know anybody, just wondering who they are. I mean, if not for them being arrested, I wouldn't even be in here."

"Far as I know, two of them went up to Yeardly. That's the men's prison, eighty miles north. We send our prisoners up there once they're officially charged."

"What about the third, the one who had his face dented in?"

The old doc didn't answer right away, tucked everything away in his bag.

"Yeah, that one. Intensive care, ain't woke up yet. Might not."

"What were they arrested for?"

"Murder, far as I know, least the one in the coma was. Other two aiding and abetting, that's the word around the campfire."

Slick thought about that. Brower returned with another deputy behind him, one Slick hadn't seen before, another big white man, this one with arms round and swollen, a weightlifter, and from the look of the acne on his face, on the juice, too.

Brower stood in the doorway, holding a plastic bottle of

water, other hand on his pistol, as the juiced deputy unlocked Slick's cuffs from the chair, brought them around to
his front and cuffed both hands to a handy ring on the table.
The juicer was none too gentle about it, but it could've been
the 'roids. He glared at his prisoner the whole time like he
was a stain on his khaki uniform pants.

Brower nodded and the juicer, whose nametag read
COLLINS, stepped back, leaned against the wall. Brower set
the bottle of water on the table, just out of Slick's reach. He
looked at the doc. Doc coughed, took a small piece of paper
out of his pocket and laid it in front of Slick.

"So far you check out, take it easy if you can. Just watch
for these symptoms on the list here, they pop up, means you
have a concussion. I also recommend that, if or when you
get the chance, you see your own physician and ask him to
do a CT, okay?"

"Will do. Thanks Doc." Slick held his right hand up as
far as the cuffs would allow. Doc took a moment before
giving him a quick handshake and ambled out.

Slick looked at the bottle of water then up at Brower.
Raised an eyebrow. Brower nudged it over within reach.
Slick grabbed it, cracked it open. He couldn't lift it up all the
way to his mouth, had to bend down to drink. Demeaning,
but that was the purpose, probably. Slick drank half of it and
stopped. Didn't want to drink too much at once.

Brower sat opposite him. Opened the bag, rooted
through it and pulled out Slick's wallet from the personal
effects inside. He glanced at the ID briefly, but it was
obvious he'd already examined everything. He tapped on
the notepad, looked up at Slick.

"Now then, MISTER Elder, would you like to give a statement?"

"Yeah. This has got to be the cleanest fucking police station I have ever seen. I mean, you could do surgery on the floor in here, it's that clean. In fact, even Mr. Clean himself would go, 'Damn, this place is CLEAN,' that's how fucking clean this room is."

"Thank you. We try. Now, how about a statement regarding your arrest?"

"Arrested? I was arrested? Funny, I don't recall being arrested. I recall being assaulted without cause by two men, both wearing law enforcement uniforms, one of whom was a sheriff named Rawlings, the other man a deputy named Brower. You."

Slick smiled a winning smile. Brower had no reaction, just tapped something into his notepad. "Anything more to add?"

"Yeah. I would like to have my phone call. Now."

"We have a few questions, first."

"Phone call, first. Lawyer first."

"Answer a few questions then we'll see."

"No, we won't, that's not how it works, deputy. I ask for a lawyer and then you don't get to question me until said lawyer appears. That's how the system works."

"That's not how we do things down here."

"So I've noted. I don't know about you, but in the country I live in, it's against the law to arrest citizens without cause, without telling them what they're charged with, without reading them their Miranda rights. I still don't know what I'm charged with."

Brower smirked at that, and dug into the plastic bag. He took out the roll of cash, bound tight by a rubber band. Held it out between them.

"What's this?"

"Hard cash money."

"Where'd it come from?"

"Read what's written on it. Says it's the official currency of the United States of America. That's where it came from."

"Uh-huh. That's all you got to say?"

"I have a lot more to say, you don't even wanna know, but I'm holding it in."

"You know, Jon, can I call you Jon?"

"No."

"I have to tell you, Jon, you're in a big heap of trouble here. The judge in this district hates, HATES drug dealers, I mean just despises them. This roll of hard cash money right here? This is a drug roll."

"I say no to drugs, officer."

"I'm a deputy, actually. It's a drug roll, I've seen them before, I know what it is. You know it, too. This roll right here is evidence enough, just on its own, to throw the book at you, not just the book but the whole set of encyclopedias. You're going inside, hard time. You could get life without parole. Your only bet is to try to cut a deal. Let me help you. Tell me who you're working with, where the operation is, give us some information and we can go to the judge and get you a fair deal."

"Lawyer. Now."

"You have to give some information first. That's how it works. Give me a little something, just a bite, so I can go to my boss and tell him you're cooperating, that you're a good guy and genuinely want to do the right thing here."

"I got something your boss can bite. My ass. Lawyer."

Brower sighed. Glanced up then back down. Slick knew it was coming, but that didn't make it any easier. Collins stepped behind him and hooked a hard punch into his kidneys. Slick yelped in spite of himself. Another blow and yelp. Pain flooded him.

Slick put his head down on the table, did some deep breathing, trying to control it. Wasn't easy and sweat beaded on his forehead. The deputies just watched him. After a moment, the deep breaths turned into deep chuckles. Hard ones.

"What's so funny?" Brower asked.

"You two guys. Pegging me as a drug dealer. Worst police work ever!"

Collins hooked another hard punch into Slick's side, curling him up. He followed that with a hard pop on the chin. That dazed Slick and he saw spots. He worried he might upchuck the water he drank, which would be bad. He needed the hydration. Collins stepped back. They waited. Slick shook his head, clearing the cobwebs out, and sat back up. Stared at them.

"So where'd the money come from, if it's not drugs? You steal it?"

"Wow. You are piece of work, you really are. You are so amazingly bad at your job I'm kind of in awe of it, seriously."

Brower didn't like that, he leaned forward, eyes hard.

"I happen to be very good at my job and you'd better

keep that in mind. The arrest-conviction rate in this county
is the best in the state. We catch scumbags like you, we bust
them and send them to jail. That's where you're going."

"Two minutes."

"What's in two minutes?"

"Two minutes is all the time it would take for a real cop
to figure out who I am and where that cash came from. You
have my ID, my name, and I'm assuming you have the
Internet even here in the sticks. It would take a real cop less
than two minutes to figure out who I am, where the money
came from and what I do for a living. It's been a day and a
half and you still haven't figured it out—ergo, worst police
work ever."

Collins stepped forward again, but Brower waved him
off. Tapped into his computer notepad, smirking.

"Yeah, we're nothing but backward ass redneck fucks
down here, right?"

"Hey, if you want to make the case for that, I won't argue."

"Fact is, Jon, I did do some research on you. I know
you're a professional poker player, I know you travel for
your work, made some money at what you do, you think
you're a big shot with cards, I know all that. It's a good
story, but, at the end of the day, that's all that it is. A story.
Doesn't matter what the facts are, it's the story that matters,
and I have a better story in mind than the one you got.

"It's about a drifter with a huge wad of cash and suspicious behavior who, when questioned by law enforcement
officers, reacted by physically attacking them in front of
multiple witnesses. Must be drugs. I can sell that story to a

DA and he, in turn, can sell it to a judge and jury and send your black ass straight to jail without passing go.

"Now Jon, I get that cops in New York might do things a little different, but you're not in New York, you're in Arizona. We care about our community, we care about our women and children and we decide who goes to jail here and what they go to jail for. Get me? You read drugs to me and I don't have to prove it, I only have to make folks believe it. Face it, you're already a statistic. You're going to jail. The only questions are where and for how long?"

"Fine. Charge me and get me my lawyer. Now."

"You'll get a lawyer. First I want a confession."

"Yeah, right. Uh-uh. Lawyer."

"You don't have to say anything, you only have to sign this."

Brower slid a sheet of paper over to Slick, along with a pen. Slick didn't even look at it. He leaned over the table edge, searching for something on the floor.

"What are you looking for?" Brower asked.

"The crack you dropped at some point, because you must be smoking serious crack if you think I'm signing a confession to anything. You're nuts, it won't even hold up in court. I asked for a lawyer and you refused, that's enough to throw everything out as is. Shit, I still haven't been Mirandized. None of this will hold up."

"If it won't hold up in a court of law then there's no reason for you not to sign it, right? So sign it, we'll get you a court-appointed lawyer and you can make your case before the judge."

"I'm not signing anything, I'm not confessing to anything. Fuck you."

Another hard hook to the kidneys from Collins and this time Slick yelled out loud. Brower just shook his head, packed up his stuff but left the sheet of paper on the table. He stood and stared at Slick a moment, waiting for him to catch his breath.

"Let me explain something to you, Jon, in simple words so you'll understand. I'm stepping out of this room for a few minutes. While I'm gone, you're gonna have a choice before you, and it's this. You either sign that confession or Wally here is going to beat you to death. I'm not exaggerating or speaking metaphorically, he will kill you with his bare hands, he's done it before, he likes it.

"You'll die here, in this room, and no one will bat an eyelash about it. Trust me on that. Your only out is to sign that confession."

Slick thought but a moment on that. Nodded. "Everyone's gotta die at some point, here is just as good as anywhere."

Brower shook his head in mock sadness, nodded to Collins and opened the door. Loud shouts echoed out in the main office area. Heated, angry words peppered with colorful profanity bounced off the walls. Slick smiled when he heard them.

"You know who's doing the shouting, deputy?" Slick asked.

Brower stopped. Stared at Slick.

"You don't, but I do, I know exactly who it is. And if I were you, I'd put a leash on this steroid freak of yours here, at least until you find out what's going on. It'd be in your best interest. Just my advice, of course, the choice is yours. We all have choices."

Brower listened to the shouting and considered it.

Finally, he jerked his chin at Collins, who stepped back, glowering. It was true, the pimple-scarred bastard had wanted to beat Slick to death, Slick could see it. Brower grabbed the unsigned confession and stuffed it into his pocket.

Slick let out a deep, deep breath of relief. That had been far too close.

4

"LISTEN TO ME, you piss-eyed bunch of inbred colicky pig-fuckers, if you don't bring my friend Jon out here right fucking now, we're gonna have a situation, I mean it!"

Thumper brought his fist down hard on the counter, cracking the glass. The well-fed deputy behind the counter flinched, unsure of what to do, and looked for help.

"Answer me, motherfucker! Where's my friend?"

Thumper was not tall. That was the first thing most people noted. He wasn't a tall man. Five-foot five or thereabouts, but his chest and arms were corded with hard muscle, he walked light on the balls of his feet and the scar tissue around his eyes and nose suggested he'd done a lot of fighting on a professional level, which he had. Anyone just glancing at him could sense the danger as Thumper held himself as a man capable of handing out a considerable amount of physical damage to anyone at any time.

And he was supremely pissed. The fat deputy, named Moore, looked around for salvation, but no one wanted any part of this problem. What was shocking to all the uniformed men in the room was that Thumper had absolutely no fear of them whatsoever. They weren't used to that, even from a fellow white man. Moore cleared his throat and tried to take control.

"You need to calm down, your friend is being processed—"

"Bullshit, save that horse-hockey for the cheap seats. He was arrested yesterday, fat boy, so he was processed yesterday. Don't fucking lie to me, asshole. Bring him out here, pronto, before I force feed you that cheap tie you're wearing."

Moore didn't know how to respond to that. Or rather, he did know how he'd usually respond, but Thumper's two companions, standing silent, intimidated him. One of them was a lawyer in an expensive suit with a fancy leather briefcase in hand. Moore didn't recognize him but he knew a pricey lawyer when he saw one.

The other fellow, a massive bronze man in a highway patrolman's uniform, Moore knew all too well, and he was the real reason everyone else in the office had found something else to do rather than skullfuck Thumper for having the balls to raise his voice to any of them.

"Answer me, motherfucker, where is he?"

Brower stepped into the office area.

"What seems to be the problem?"

"The problem is that Jon Elder was arrested in this shitburg yesterday, that's the fucking problem. He's in here somewhere and we want to see him right fucking now."

"Well, have a seat. It'll be a while yet."

"No it won't, Sparky, we'll see him right now or you'll see my foot go up somebody's ass, pronto."

The lawyer stepped forward, "Deputy, my name is Melvin Hayes, I'm Mr. Elder's attorney and I demand to see my client without delay or haste."

"Your client waived his right to counsel."

"Bullshit!" Thumper said. "Pure corn-fed bullshit!"

"Do you have the signed release?" Melvin asked.

Brower shook his head. "He stated it expressly, in my presence. Deputy Collins was also present for the statement. He refused to sign anything but verbally waived right to counsel."

"Then it's not official," Melvin said.

"As far as we're concerned, it is. You doubt our word?"

"Fuck yeah, we doubt it. Slick would never waive right to counsel!" Thumper said, hammering the glass counter with his fist once again. It shattered and the cops jumped.

"What the hell is going on out here?"

Rawlings stormed out of his office, face beet red and jowls flaring. "I'm on the phone with the governor's office and I can't hear myself think! What the fuck—"

Rawlings stopped on a dime when he saw the three men at the counter.

"Navajo Joe," he said to the huge state trooper. "It figures, whenever I get a pain in my balls, you show up. What do you want?"

"Sheriff Ted. What do I want? Gun control, socialized medicine and world peace, among other things," the big man said. "The list goes on and on."

"You mean you don't get all that on the reservation as part of your government handout package, along with the free smokes and scotch?"

"Not yet, anyway, maybe someday, but what I want is beside the point. I'm here in an unofficial capacity, strictly as an observer," Navajo Joe said.

"Then do me a favor and unofficially observe somewhere else."

"Be happy to. Let this lawyer see his client and we'll be on our way."

"Who's his client?"

"Jon Elder, as I told this fat fucking moron behind the counter," Thumper said.

"Wait, who the hell are you? You don't talk to my deputies like that—"

"My name's Tommy Olson and I talk how I want to who I want whenever I want, last I checked, this was still America and we have free fucking speech!" Thumper said.

"Keep it up and I'll arrest you for disturbing the peace—"

"And I'll be happy to appear as witness before the judge," Navajo Joe said, "and tell him I saw that Tommy, the defendant in question, wasn't disturbing the peace."

"In other words," Thumper said, "go fuck yourself, Sheriff."

Rawlings stared at Navajo Joe and Thumper, plainly furious. Melvin was a smart enough lawyer to know when to keep his mouth shut and stayed out of it. Rawlings looked to Brower, asking a silent question.

"Defendant waived his right to counsel," Brower said.

"Without a signed waiver, it's not official," Melvin said. "So, unfortunately, I cannot accept that."

Brower and Rawlings exchanged another look. Rawlings nodded.

"Okay, but it'll still be a minute, Doc Johnson is checking him," Brower said.

"No, he's not, we saw Doc driving down the street not

ten minutes ago," Navajo Joe said. "Can we dispense with this happy horseshit and get this lawyer to his client, please? Some of us actually have to work for a living."

Rawlings didn't want to give in, but he was trapped. "Lawyer only. You other two stay here, where I can see you."

Brower snapped his fingers and led Melvin on back. Rawlings turned to Moore. "Call the DA's office, have them get someone down here."

"Already did, Sheriff, but…"

"But what?"

"The only ADA currently available was Dubya De—" Moore stopped himself before finishing. Navajo Joe heard the slip and laughed.

"Camilla 'Dubya Dee' Leon, the one and only brown person working in the DA's office. This ain't your day, is it, Ted?"

Brower returned, stood next to Rawlings as the sheriff seethed.

"What about bail? You gonna cite him out?" Joe asked.

"Not a chance, violent offender."

"What? What's he charged with?" Thumper asked.

"Obstruction of justice, assaulting a law enforcement officer, resisting arrest."

"My ass. Who'd he assault? Who arrested him?" Thumper said.

"He assaulted me," Rawlings said. "And the two of us arrested him."

"That's a goddamn fucking lie. If Slick assaulted you, you'd be walking in plaster, if you could walk at all, and if he decided to resist arrest, you wouldn't even have gotten the cuffs on him. You're a bald fucking liar, Sheriff," Thumper said.

Rawlings involuntarily put his hand on the baton at his belt, his intent clear. Navajo Joe slid between the two.

"For an assault victim, you have nary a blemish, Ted," Navajo Joe said.

"He's also suspected of drug trafficking."

"What! That's a hot crock of shit, you fuckers!"

Navajo Joe held up his hand to keep Thumper at bay, glanced at Rawlings.

"You find drugs on him?"

"No, but there were other indicators—" Brower began.

"Then you've got nothing on that, you're reaching," Navajo Joe said. "I'd be happy to call the state's narco specialist to help you figure that out, if need be. He owes me a favor. All that's left is the assault and resisting arrest charge."

"And obstruction of justice."

"If you're not gonna cite him out, what about bail?"

"Not up to us, up to the judge."

"That's another crock and you know it. Think I just got off the reservation? Try again. You can bail him out now if you want to. You got cash, Thumper?"

"I got cash, I got bond, security, I got it all."

Thumper plopped a bag on the counter. Unzipped it. Loaded with money.

"So why not take the way of less stress, Ted? Bail our friend out and then we'll be out of what little hair you have left on your head," Navajo Joe said.

"I'll think about it."

"While you think about that, also think about this. I might ask a few of my fellow troopers to join me for lunch here in town at the diner every day. You remember Mohammad Jones, played tackle for the Chargers for a few years? He's a trooper now. He remembers you, Ted, and none too fondly. You pulled him over for a busted taillight one night, years ago when he was driving back to college after winter break, except it wasn't busted until after you stopped him. Like I said, he remembers you none too fondly. There's quite a few fellows I know like that, big, dark and unreasonable when the subject turns to Sheriff Ted Rawlings. We can congregate here every day, for lunch.

"You know they have a size requirement for the staties, right? You gotta be a big bastard to be considered for State Patrol, not like being a deputy where the sheriff hires whoever he wants regardless of qualifications or their physical condition or mental capacity. You actually have to be able to do the job to be a trooper."

None of the deputies in the room liked that one bit. Brower took a step in the trooper's direction, eyes glittering. Rawlings stopped him. He took a moment, popped a fresh stick of gum into his mouth.

"I don't like threats, Navajo Joe. You think you're immune, untouchable? Think you can walk in here and say whatever the hell you want to my people and there will no consequences? Times change, Joe, Arizona's changing, even for your people on the reservation, you should think about the future."

"The red man has no future, Ted. I've been told that ever since I was a tiny papoose. Funny thing is, once a fella accepts that about himself, it makes everything else in life so much simpler."

Nothing was said. Moore finally piped up.

"Dubya Dee is here."

Rawlings glared at Moore for again slipping up verbally, and he dropped his eyes. Rawlings cursed silently and ground his teeth.

"There's paperwork. Fill that out, leave a cash bond and we'll release him, but only after the ADA signs off on it."

Navajo Joe glanced outside at the woman headed up the sidewalk and grinned. "I have a feeling she'll see things our way."

5

S LICK WAS HUDDLED with his lawyer, exchanging whispers, when she walked into the interrogation room. Slick didn't really hear much of what Melvin said after that. He was charmed, almost immediately, and by the very woman whose sole purpose was to send his ass to jail.

She had that type of energy that he always responded to. She charged up a room like a tuning fork hit hard and the air vibrated with her presence. She looked good, and she was one of those women who knew she looked good, was comfortable with that fact and didn't make a big deal out of it. Dark, gleaming hair, black eyes that snapped, he could tell, olive skin and enough curves on her body to make for careful navigation but not so many that one would get lost in them.

She sat opposite them, file folder in hand, and looked Slick in the eye.

"Mr. Elder, I'm Assistant District Attorney Camilla Leon, I'll be handling your case. Counselor, I don't believe we've met before. Camilla Leon."

"Melvin Hayes, how do you do. I'm out of Scottsdale."

"You're a ways from home, Mr. Hayes."

"Evidently even farther than I thought, seeing as my client was denied his phone call, denied his right to counsel, was abused during questioning and told that if he didn't sign a confession to crimes that he didn't commit, he'd be beaten to death. I seem to have wandered into a third world country where the Bill of Rights is an afterthought."

Camilla considered that for a moment and Slick saw a flicker, somewhere deep inside, she hid it very well but it was in there. She was angry and not at them. Slick liked her more and more. She kept her professional face on, allowing herself just a glance at those behind the observation glass, and leaned forward.

"If your client was denied his phone call and right to counsel, how do you explain your presence here? Did he not call you?"

"His friend Tommy Olson called and retained my services. Mr. Elder was booked for a flight in Tucson yesterday morning. He missed the flight and didn't call Mr. Olson when he was scheduled to do so. Mr. Elder is a professional poker player and often carries large amounts of cash on his person, so when Mr. Olson didn't hear from him when he was supposed to, Mr. Olson, a former police officer, grew understandably concerned and used his contacts to track him down. He discovered that his friend had been arrested in Bendijo and that's how we ended up here."

Camilla thought about that, looked at Slick for a moment then back to Melvin.

"What's a professional gambler doing in Bendijo?"

"Sight-seeing," Slick said. "Great town you got here."

"It has its charms. Well, in this situation I can probably knock off a few of the charges, go down to simple battery, and—"

"For who, for me or for the deputies who illegally assaulted me?"

"For you. It's a good deal, I recommend you take it."

"I appreciate your recommendation but no. Hell no."

"You can't be serious about this, my client was grievously assaulted—"

"I understand that but you understand that's not my purview. My job is to pursue the charges against your client. I have sworn statements from the deputies and Sheriff Rawlings himself, stating that he assaulted them."

"My client is, I was informed on the trip here, a black belt in karate, trained for years in something called Muay Thai—"

"Muay Thai, it's a form of kickboxing, I'm familiar with it."

"And he also has a purple belt in Brazilian jiu-jitsu, which is, I'm told, equal to a black belt in nearly any other form of combat. That's what I read online. Anyway, what do I know from belts? In essence, if he were to assault someone, one would think there'd be some small sign or physical evidence of said assault, hmm?"

Camilla thought that over while she gave Slick another studied gaze. Usually he didn't like being examined so closely, but he had to admit to himself that, in her case, not only did her scrutiny NOT bother him, he actually kind of enjoyed it. She sighed and shuffled more paper.

"I also have sworn statements from five other witnesses in the diner who support the sheriff's version of events. It's your word against theirs."

"What color were they?" Slick asked.

"What color were who?"

"The witnesses. They were all white, right? Anyone who was there and wasn't white, well, they didn't see anything, right?"

Camilla let that comment cook a bit, pulled her folders together and leaned back.

"Look, it's not that I'm not sympathetic to the position you have, I am, it's simply that if you have a grievance of that nature, you need to contact the state AG or file a civil suit. It's not my purview, as I said before. I'm here on a criminal matter. That's my job. That being said, in light of the circumstances, I'm prepared to do a deal."

"What deal?" Melvin asked.

"Drop it all down to obstruction, he gets off with a desk ticket and a simple fine along with time served. Our esteemed sheriff will be most unhappy with me about that, but it won't be the first time I've disappointed him. You take that deal and promise to leave town immediately, I'm sure I can get my boss to sign off on it."

"No," Slick said.

"No? What is it you want, you want all the charges dismissed?"

"No."

"You WANT to go to jail?" Camilla asked. Even Melvin looked perturbed by this.

"No. I want a trial. I want your sheriff, his deputies and every one of those good citizens who are on record as witnesses to take the stand and testify, under oath, everything they claim to have seen. That's what I want."

Camilla pushed back in her seat, thinking hard. Glanced

at the glass again.

"And then what?"

"And then, after my lawyer gets through with them, you'll be able to charge each and every one of the lying bastards with perjury."

Camilla smiled. For the first time since she came into the room, she smiled and she had a real good one that filled the entire room. Even Melvin was touched by it.

"Cool," she said. "Sounds like a good time."

"There's something else we should mention," Melvin said.

"What's that?"

"There were three other men arrested the same day and time as my client, one for murder, the other two for aiding and abetting. I don't have their names yet, but…"

"That's not my case, but I'm familiar with it. What about them?"

"My client asked me to also represent them."

"He asked you to represent them?"

"Yes. Providing they agree to it, of course. It's up to them, in the end, and I understand one of them is in intensive care. Pedro is his first name."

"Pedro Garcia, yes, he's in a coma."

Melvin wrote that down. "Yes. Mr. Elder has retained me, in their behalf, to represent them in court if they agree, and he seems certain that they will, as it's likely they only have a public defender."

Camilla stared at Slick, hard now.

"Let me get this straight. You're paying your very expensive lawyer here a whole lot of money to represent a

Mexican day laborer charged with capital murder?"

"And his two friends."

"You don't know them?"

"Nope. Never saw them before yesterday."

"You never talked to them before yesterday?"

"Didn't even talk to them yesterday, he just happened to be sitting next to me at the counter of the diner. Didn't even say hello. Don't think he speaks much English and my Spanish is limited."

"But you're picking up the tab for his defense in a capital murder case?"

"Yep."

"Why?"

"Because"—Slick leaned forward—"he's innocent."

"And you know this how?"

"Sheriff was wrong on me, odds are he's wrong on Pedro, too. That's my bet and I like to gamble when the odds are in my favor. Either way, Pedro gets good representation in court and who doesn't deserve that? We all do. Melvin is very, very good at what he does."

Melvin handed her his card. Camilla took it, nodded and stood.

"It's not mine, I don't get the big, juicy murder cases, but I'll let my office know and send you the files. Mr. Hayes, pleasure to meet you. And Mr. Elder—"

"Call me Jon."

"Mr. Elder, a word of advice. Anyone who works long enough in law and order knows it can get screwy and unfair. We do our best, but there's no such thing as a perfect system and while there are more successes than failures, failures do happen. It happens. But don't take that fact of life as a license to jerk me around, I won't appreciate it."

"Wouldn't dream of it."

6

"JOE, HOW ARE you? Been some time," Camilla said when she came out. Brower and Rawlings were nowhere to be seen. Neither was Collins. They hid at the sight of her.

"Good to see you, as always, Camilla," Navajo Joe said. "What do we have?"

"The usual weirdness. Is he a friend of yours?"

"A friend of a friend. Thumper, ADA Camilla Leon, she's good people. Camilla, this is Tommy 'Thumper' Olson."

"Thumper? Your name is Thumper?"

Thumper was not disposed to jokes or comments about his nickname even on a good day, and this had been a long way from a good day thus far. He glowered.

"What about it?"

"Didn't you used to box? In Texas?"

Thumper hesitated, not sure if he was being put on or not.

"Yeah. Texas and a bunch of other places. Who told you that, Slick?"

"No, actually, I'm pretty sure I saw you box once. In El Paso, about twelve, thirteen years ago or so? You were on the same card as Diego Nunez?"

"Yeah. Diego, they called him Danger, he fought after me. He was a bigger name, I was in the prelims, he was main card. Seriously? You remember that?"

"Diego's my second cousin, he's from here and we all traveled as a family to El Paso for the fight. I remember you because, let's face it, Thumper is a memorable nickname. I remember you won by a knockout in the second round."

Thumper smiled in spite of himself, proud. Nodded.

"It was a good fight. How's Diego these days, he's out of the fight game, right?"

"Unfortunately. He's dead. Drive-by shooting, about six years ago."

Thumper shifted, uncomfortable. "I'm sorry. He was a good fighter."

"He was. But I thought … the lawyer told me you were a police officer?"

"Was. Got out, did other things. Now I run a gym, in Chicago."

Navajo Joe watched deputies pretend to do paperwork while listening in. Former cop, former boxer, it was all very interesting, and when they brought his name up on their computers they would also discover that Thumper had served four years in Joliet for manslaughter. He'd beaten a man to death with his bare hands, in a locker room after a match. Navajo Joe knew they'd run right to Rawlings with that nugget of information.

"Where are we at, you drop the charges again?" Navajo Joe asked her.

"No. No deal, all charges still stand, as per the defendant's wishes. He wants a trial, can't wait for it, it seems. So

I'll do what I can. You'll bail him out?"

Thumper nodded. Melvin stepped out of interrogation, looking for them. He walked over and leaned in to whisper.

"Mr. Elder requested that Mr. Olson leave before he comes out."

"What? Why the fuck for?"

"He thought it for the best."

"They worked him over, didn't they? Motherfuckers! You cowardly cocksuckers! I swear, you're gonna pay for this—"

"Thumper, come on," Navajo Joe said, "let's do what he asked. We got him out, that's the thing, right? No need to get yourself arrested for beating up some sorry sack of shit in a deputy's uniform, let's go."

"Mr. Elder also asked that you find a suitable place for him to get something to eat. He said, and I quote, 'It better not be fucking Red Lobster or Outback Steakhouse, either, it has to be food that I can eat.' That's a direct quote. Find a good place and he said that he'd meet you there. I can drop him off in my car."

"He's a vegetarian?" Camilla asked. "There's that new organic Indian place off of Main, they have a vegetarian menu. Joe, you know it?"

"I know of it. Never been there. Always felt a bit too complicated, me going to an Indian restaurant and not finding buffalo or maize on the menu."

"I'll bet," Camilla laughed. "Go on, I'll wait with Melvin here until your friend is released. He'll be okay. My word."

They shook hands and Navajo Joe led Thumper out of the station, the short man glaring bloody murder at the deputies as he left. Melvin went to the back to get Slick and Camilla checked her phone for messages.

"Pretty chummy. You're supposed to be on our side, aren't you?"

She turned. Brower appeared, leaning on the counter with both forearms, working on a stick of gum. Camilla just looked at him for a moment and then hung up.

"I'm on the side of law and order. People who obey the laws, I'm on their side. People who enforce the laws, I'm on their side, provided said laws meet constitutional scrutiny and requirements. People who break laws? I'm not on their side."

She stepped closer, leaned in.

"People who abuse positions of authority and break the law? Definitely not on their side. If you did beat him while he was in custody and I find evidence of it, I'll bust you so fast you'll have atmospheric burns on your ass. The defendant seems pretty confident he can prove without a doubt that THAT'S what happened to him. If he can, and you go before a judge and jury and perjure yourself, I'll make it my business to see you do time, deputy, you and anyone—ANYONE—who does the same. I'll be spreading that word around town, by the way. I'll make it my mission. That's my word."

Brower shook his head, chuckling.

"Funny. I know you're speaking but damned if I can follow a word you're saying, all my eyes wanna do is follow the bouncing balls," he nodded to her chest. "Pretty damn distracting, can't imagine what it's like down in the DA's office. Have to make it hard to get things done down there, you and your tits getting in the way of everything.

"Gotta think that at some point George is just gonna have to clean house, if only in the name of efficiency and teamwork. 'Cause that's what it's about, right? Teamwork. My boss and your boss, they go back, all the way to kindergarten. Me? Same with all these boys here. You? Where do you go all the way back to? It's obviously not the same place we come from, and at some point that's gonna bite you in the ass, sweetheart. Go ahead and tell your boss I said that, and George will call up my boss, one of his best friends, to 'complain' about it, and then they'll have a good, long fucking laugh together."

Camilla stared at him, her eyes burning, and bit a profane response back when Slick shuffled out of the back with Melvin and stepped up to the counter. Brower slid back and let Moore take care of it. Slick's eyes went back and forth between Camilla and Brower, not missing the obvious tension.

"Ms. Leon, look forward to seeing you again," Slick said.

She nodded. Slick glanced at Brower.

"Look forward to seeing you again, Brower, but for entirely different reasons."

Brower ignored that as Slick signed the papers and Moore handed over his plastic bag of valuables. Slick took his shoes and belt out, dropped the shoes on the floor and slipped them on. He tucked his wallet into his pants and pocketed the cash after eyeballing it to make sure it was all there. He felt eyes on him as he searched the plastic bag, not finding something specific that he needed.

"So where's my phone?"

"What phone?" Brower asked.

"My cell phone. The one the sheriff took off of me. Where is it?"

"You didn't have a phone, sir."

Slick smiled, he'd hoped they'd do this. "You mentioned that you know what I do for a living, right, Brower?"

"I do, and you can call me Deputy Brower."

"So you remember that I'm a professional card player. I sit at a table all day and analyze whether or not someone is lying to me. I'm good at it, I trained for it, learned everything there is to know about it from a former FBI interrogator who was a master at catching lies, truly. He saw everything. No one can hide all their lies, not completely, no one, our bodies give it away in very specific, personal ways. I learned the craft of reading them very well. So let me ask you again, where's my phone?"

"You didn't have a phone, sir. I'm sorry."

Slick turned to Camilla. "See that?"

"See what?"

"His left eyebrow, catch it? It bounced up just a hair when he lied. That's his tell. Let's try again. Brower, did you or did you not have me beaten during questioning?"

"Look—"

"It's a simple question, was I or was I not beaten in custody? Yes or no?"

"I don't have to answer to you—"

"You do, however, answer to me, deputy. Answer the question, was he beaten while in custody?" Camilla asked.

Brower took a breath, opened his mouth to speak but before the words even came out, his left eyebrow jumped up.

"Hah! See, didn't even need to say a damn thing and there it is. Bingo!" Slick grinned at Camilla, who only glared at the deputy, now supremely pissed.

"You have an issue with your treatment in custody, take it up with the sheriff. I don't answer to you or anyone," Brower said. "End of story."

"Fine. Give me my phone and I'll go."

Brower caught Moore staring at his forehead and pushed him aside.

"Get back to work, Moore, stop fucking around. Listen, I don't know what happened to your phone, this is all you had on you when you were brought in."

The eyebrow bounced up and down and it was next to impossible for everyone not to notice. Even Melvin enjoyed the show. Camilla stepped forward.

"Where is it?" she asked.

"If it's not checked in then it's not here. Everything else is here, including the roll of cash. Why would I take a phone? He didn't have one on him when I processed him."

"Hah, now you're getting it, you have to parse hairs to get by," Slick said. "I didn't have the phone on me when I was processed because Rawlings took it away before I was allegedly arrested. Good work, you're figuring the game out. But that doesn't mean you don't know where my phone is. You do."

"Your phone is not here. That's all I can tell you."

"Sure it is. You know it's a smart phone, right Brower? Look at me," Slick leaned on the counter. "It's got a built-in GPS chip. Phone doesn't even need to be on for me to track it. It's how Thumper found me. All I have to do is step outside, use my lawyer's cell to trace it and find out EX-ACTLY where my phone is. I could do that, you know. I could stand out there with your ADA and PROVE to her, beyond any shadow of a doubt, that you're a lying scumbag, I could."

Brower swallowed, but held his gaze steady. Slick grabbed the rest of his items.

"But I'm not going to do that," Slick said. "I'm not. Keep the phone, I don't need it. And I want you to think about that right up until my trial. Let's go, Melvin."

Slick walked out, lawyer in tow.

7

"HOLD ON," CAMILLA said as she caught up with them outside the station. Slick and Melvin waited for her on the steps. Slick blinked in the sun.

"Ms. Leon, we've answered all your questions, and my client—" Melvin began.

"Cool your jets, counselor, this is off the record."

"It's okay, Melvin, I got this. What do you want to know, counselor?"

"If you can prove they're lying about taking your phone, Mr. Elder, then why don't you? Why let them keep it?"

"Call me Jon."

"Mr. Elder—"

"Jon."

"Okay, Jon. Can you really GPS your phone and prove it's inside?"

"Absolutely."

"So do it. Right here, right now. Do it and let me go in and wipe that big shit-eating grin off of Brower's face."

"First of all, that phone is at this moment probably fast on its way out the back door of the station and into an incinerator. But really, that's not the question you should really be asking. The question you should be asking is the same one Brower asked. Why would he take the phone?"

She thought about that. Nodded.

"You recorded your arrest. That's why you wanted them to take the stand and testify under oath. You have it recorded. And when they heard you say you wanted them to perjure themselves in interrogation, they figured it out and yanked the phone."

Big Slick just smiled at her, but said nothing more.

"Or maybe that's only what you want them to think. You could be playing them, too. And me. If you had it recorded, why let them keep it then? If it's destroyed then there's no evidence against them, it's still your word against theirs. Why?"

"Why indeed?"

"Are you playing me?"

"No more than anyone plays anybody else."

"Listen, no one has time for these games. This is taxpayer money, time and expense that could be used elsewhere—"

"Then get a better sheriff and department. I didn't ask to be arrested."

"He's an elected official. I'm not and therefore have a responsibility to my office and the people who depend on it for fairness. I don't like being played like this."

"Come on. You played me, to a certain extent, offering to drop the charges down to battery then to obstruction. That's not playing? You know who these guys are, what they do. That makes you part of it."

"Don't you fucking dare lump me in with them!"

"Why shouldn't I? You're telling me you've never sent someone to jail who you knew was innocent on the word of those men in the station? You're telling me that you've never seen people falsely arrested, falsely charged and sent to jail in the name of law and order?"

Camilla didn't speak at first, didn't trust herself not to scream, but she was pissed. She took a deep breath, let it out, and then let him have it in measured tones that gained momentum until her words flamed at the end.

"You know what they call me, here and in my office? Dubya Dee, which is short for Window Dressing. To my face. My boss doesn't do anything, he's a basically a decent man but to him I'm only a quota fulfillment, so he can point to me and say, 'Hey, I love brown people, I even have a Hispanic on staff.' I know he's full of shit, show me a politician who isn't and I'll sign up for his or her staff immediately. I don't have that option, I only have George and his good old boy network here in Bendijo.

"They don't let me near the questionable criminal cases because they know I won't send an innocent person to jail, they know I won't put up with cops perjuring themselves on the stand, they know I care about my professional ethics, so the answer is, no, I've never sent anyone to jail who I didn't, on some level, believe deserved it. So I get the bullshit cases, close them and they put up with me because I take good picture. I put up with it because I was born here, it's my home and I love it and the old man won't live forever and when he goes, I'll be in a place to actually do something about things."

She took a break and moved her hair out of her eyes. Slick really dug that motion of hers, so natural and yet so real and beautiful.

"I don't play, I never have. If I find evidence of any officer of this town breaking the law, I'll do something. They know that. That's why they don't like me, because I'm a huge pain in the ass and I refuse to fucking play! Have I made that perfectly clear for you? So now that I've established my bona fides, what about you? Why did you let them keep your phone?"

Slick gloried in the tantrum she just so elegantly threw at him. It was clean and clear and passionate. He liked this lawyer, and he rarely liked any lawyer, even his own. This one, though, she was a piece of work. He nodded.

"Okay. I hear you. I believe you. So let me ask you this. What are they afraid of?"

"Evidence. That you have recorded evidence that proves your innocence and their malfeasance. That's why they kept your phone, right?"

"Right. Now, what are they afraid of?"

"I don't know."

"Exactly."

"Exactly? What does that mean?"

"It means they thought they had it figured out, had me figured out, now they don't have it figured out. Maybe I'm playing them, and you, or maybe I'm not. They don't know. And fear of the unknown, it's a real bitch, grinds at a person's guts. Those boys, inside? They're killing themselves right now, trying to figure out what I have over them. It's gonna make for some sleepless nights. It's gonna be fun."

"So you are playing them?"

"Of course. But that doesn't mean I don't have bullets in the hole."

"Bullets?"

"Bullets, it's a poker term, stands for pocket aces. In the hole, that means cards they can't see. Bullets in the hole, a pair of aces, in the pocket where they can't be seen."

"You're holding aces then."

"Maybe, maybe not. It wouldn't be in my best interest to state one way or the other. They'll have to go to court to see the cards in my hand and, personally, I'm looking forward to it. You may not like to play, but you're at a gaming table whether you like it or not and if you won't play, then I'm gonna have to."

She considered that, took a deep breath and let it out.

"I believe that you've been wronged, and if I do come into evidence of such, you won't find a bigger champion. However, let me warn you that if, in the course of whatever 'game' you think you're playing, if you break any law, I'll come down on you as hard as I'd come down on them."

"I'd expect no less. Have a good day, Ms. Leon."

Slick and Melvin left her there and went on their way.

8

"**D**ON'T SAY IT," Slick said to Thumper, before he could go off, "I get it, I'm pissed off too, but all I want to do is eat some really good food and find my bliss first."

Slick sat down at the table, grabbing a menu with one hand, holding his other out to the trooper. "Hi, I'm Jon but everyone calls me Big Slick."

"Joe Stormcloud, everyone calls me Navajo Joe. Nice to meet you."

"Damn those motherfuckers…" Thumper began, furious. Slick moved gingerly, like every muscle hurt, which it did.

"Dude, seriously, it's not that I don't appreciate it, but I'm fucking starving and all I want to think about is eating. Besides, I could hear you tearing those cops a new asshole from the holding cell, so I already saw that show."

"And a fine show it was," Navajo Joe said. "Where's your lawyer?"

"He went to meet up with his other clients, so you guys will have to give me a ride to a hotel. And Thumper, may I compliment you on a fine choice of restaurant? You've surprised me."

"Wasn't me that chose this place, it was that lady lawyer, she recommended it," Thumper said. "Wait, what other clients? You should be his only focus—"

"He's doing what I asked, it's complicated, I'll explain later."

The waiter came and Slick ordered a lot of food, along with a pot of herbal tea. Thumper tapped on the table, full of energy and anger; Slick recognized it.

"What's this shit about a hotel?" Thumper asked. "Ain't you headed back home with us? You can come back for the trial, or not at all, don't matter, the bond ain't no problem either way."

"I'm sticking around for a while, bro."

"What? What for?"

Slick glanced at Navajo Joe, appraising him. The trooper took it, nodded.

"Go ahead, ask me whatever you want," he said.

"How do you know Thumper?" Slick asked.

"We go back a ways, me and him. I owed him a favor from back in the day, so when you didn't turn up, he called me to help track you down. When I found out where you'd been arrested, I knew what must have happened and figured it was better to come down in person, otherwise both your asses would be in jail right now. Everyone in Arizona law enforcement knows about Bendijo."

"Which is what, exactly?"

"Sheriff Ted's got a reputation, one he's had for awhile, which is that if you ain't white, you ain't all right. He doesn't say it that baldly, course, but he ain't that far from it, either. It's the same protecting-our-borders shit we've heard since the dawn of time.

"He's making political hay off of demonizing brown

people, but enough folks respond that there ain't much we can do about it. The past year or so he's been getting a lot of attention for it in the national media and I think he figures he can ride this all the way to either the governor's office or a reality show, one or the other, and make some real money. Hear tell he's even got a book deal."

Navajo Joe took a sip of water and shrugged.

"It's all a scam, of course, but a pretty good one. Make folks afraid, tell them what they're afraid of, whether it's true or not, and make them believe that you're the only one who can keep them safe. It's a scam he's played ever since first running for sheriff and folks bought it. Too many white people are gullible like that, sorry Thumper."

"Hey man, I'm with you… White folks be too crazy, my extended family, you don't even wanna know, bunch of freaks on a stick."

"So let's say some of the local American patriots were to find themselves in harm's way, it wouldn't matter to you how said harm came to be?" Slick asked Navajo Joe.

"I'm always amused when I hear white people go on about how they're the one hundred percent natural born Americans, myself," Navajo Joe said. "But it's tricky. On an official level, I've pledged to serve and protect everyone, regardless of race or creed or place of birth. That's how I see it. But the truth is, in some situations I'm less inspired than others, on a personal level. That's the most I can say."

"I can understand that."

Food came and Slick dug in. Thumper made a face at it.

"Dude, how can you eat that? Looks like paste."

"Delicious, my man. You want some?"

"Get it away, stop it, you're gonna make me gag. It looks like hurl on a plate."

"So you're planning to stay in town for a while?" Navajo Joe asked.

Slick nodded, kept eating.

"You don't mind me asking, why?"

"Fellow sitting next to me at the diner, minding his own business, got his skull caved in by Sheriff Ted. He's in a coma now."

"Yep. Murder suspect, I'm told. Killed Roger Carlson, they say."

"They also said I was a drug dealer. Thing is, I didn't know this guy, didn't talk to him, but I sat next to him for at least a half hour. And I'm telling you, there's probably a lot I don't know about the guy, but the one thing I do know is this—he's no killer. And they knew it, too. They knew it, came in and dented his head in anyway and dragged him out and arrested anyone else who looked at them cross-eyed for it. And well…"

Slick took a bite, swallowed. Sipped some tea and stared at Navajo Joe.

"That ain't right."

The trooper leaned back in his chair, scratched his head.

"Okay, well. I make it my business not to tell folks what to do with their lives, everyone's got their own path to follow. That doesn't stop me from offering a word of advice, if you've a mind to hear it."

"Sure."

"If Ted thinks you're a threat or even an annoyance, it could be more than just uncomfortable for you here, it could be dangerous. You could get pulled over and a substantial amount of drugs might be found in your car or on your person. Or you could just end up shot by a cop, with a handy pistol close by to justify the shooting. It's been known to happen. I'll drop word around that you're a friend, but the reality is people like us, we don't have many friends around here, you know?"

Slick nodded again. Navajo Joe stood, took out his card and gave it to him.

"There's my cell number, you get jammed up, call me. If I can help you, I will. Any friend of Thumper's is a friend of mine."

"Appreciate it and the same to you from me, Joe."

The trooper put out his hand, shook with both men and walked out.

"Seems like a good man," Slick said.

"He's good folks, no doubt."

"He know what we really do for a living?"

"He's probably figured it out, though he's never said. But he's smart as a whip, so probably. That don't mean he'd be down with it. He's an unusual guy."

"Dude."

"Yeah Slick?"

"Thanks."

"Shut up. Don't even have to do that, but…"

"Go ahead, say it."

"Slick, you want to clean house here, fine. I'm all right with that, you know how I feel about people like those assholes, but why not let them drop the charges? We leave, come back later and kick some fucking redneck ass. Isn't that better?"

"You're in training camp, right?"

"Yeah, Julio's fight is in two and a half weeks. It's a contender fight, too. It's my goddamn fault you're even down here, the biker asshole was supposed to be my responsibility, and—"

"Taking care of that racist pedophile fuck was a pure pleasure. It's not your fault, man. This kind of shit could happen to anyone, anywhere. I don't blame you for it."

"So let's vogue, partner. Go home, get healed up. I'll take Julio to his fight and we come back here in a couple months and drop some motherfuckers then."

Slick shook his head.

"I don't get it," Thumper said. "Why do you wanna stay in this shithole?"

"It's just … they tossed me my shoes and said, get out of town, you know?" Slick pushed his plate away. "Nobody throws me my shoes and tells me to beat it, nobody."

Thumper got that, right away, down deep where it counted. It was but one of many reasons that they had been friends for so long.

"Okay, let me make some calls, get things in Chicago situated—"

"Nah man, it's cool, you go on back, I know you got big things on your plate."

"I can't leave you alone here with hostiles, bro."

"I can handle it, you know that. I've been in tighter situations."

"Let me call someone, at least. What about your boy, the crazy shaved head monk dude you talk about—"

"Bodhi. He's in Thailand for a few months."

"What about Chuck and Lou?"

"In Canada. Listen, it'll be all right. I'll be careful and I'm not planning to do anything radical, really. Just want to fuck with them."

"Fuck with them how?"

Slick grinned at him, mimed his phone.

"No. You recorded it?"

"Whole thing. They kept the phone, so they suspect it, but—"

"Wait, if they kept your phone, how the hell—"

"Cloud-saved, dude."

"I don't even know what that means."

"It means it was saved instantaneously on a separate drive. In the cloud."

"You don't gotta plug the phone into something or—"

"Nope. Happens automatically. Dude, you got to get with the times. There is email, Internet. There's a whole world out there. Catch up. We have email."

"I hire people to do that for me. Damn. So what are you gonna do, show that shit to the ADA, make it public?"

"I don't know. I don't really want it out there. It gets on YouTube and my face is everywhere getting night-sticked by a cop, that ain't good business for us. But they don't know that. Right now it's leverage and I want to put the squeeze on this asshole and put the fear of karmic retribution into his soul."

Thumper thought about that for a minute then grinned.

"You're a piece of work, Slick, gotta say. What can I do?"

"I need a new phone, a burner if you got it."

Thumper pulled out a phone, handed it over. "It's a pre-paid. What else, you cool for money, got some dollars?"

"Yeah, I got my cards and the Stutz cash. I owe you your share."

"Fuck that, keep it. You sure about backup? I can call Skinny for a referral."

"No, don't. This isn't business down here. It's personal."

The restaurant door jingled and a man walked in, talking loud and cheerful on his cell phone to someone about a mortgage plan. He waved to the waiters and manager, taking a seat at a table by the door as he finished his call. He looked familiar, but Slick couldn't place him at first. A banker or an insurance broker, from the look of his expensive suit and shoes, and he carried with him the air of someone who believed he could get along with everyone. The man glanced over, a natural smile on his face, and did a double take when he noticed Slick.

The smile faded, and he stood back up and walked over to them. Thumper tensed; instantly ready to brain someone with a chair. Anger had built up in the smaller man ever since his friend hadn't checked in, and he was about to burst. Slick waved him off with a private signal of theirs. He remembered where he knew the man from, finally.

"Hey, sorry to bother you, you may not remember me, but…" he said.

"I remember you. You were in the diner the day I was allegedly arrested," Slick said. "You spoke up on my behalf, told the sheriff to give me a break because I was a tourist and tourists are good for business."

"Yes, that was me. I'm real sorry about what happened to you, I just wanted to come over and apologize on behalf of … well … the town I know and grew up with, the one I love. Del Martin," he held out his hand. Slick considered it for a moment then shook the man's hand.

"Jon Elder. This is my friend Tommy Olson."

"Pleased to meet you, really. Would it be intruding if…"

Slick waved and allowed the man to sit at the table with them. Thumper stayed silent, didn't shake hands, didn't speak, just caught Slick's eye and let him know this was Slick's show. Slick nodded and clocked their guest.

He was in his late forties, well fed and groomed, sporting an expensive pinky ring and watch. Hair slicked back in a style preferred by Pat Riley a couple decades previous, and probably colored to keep the dark strands from going gray. Slick knew the type from poker tables, a salesman, but a good one, the kind who could sell ice to Eskimos. Fast with a smile or joke, keeping a quick patter going while he took your money away from you, chip-by-chip, dollar by dollar.

"Listen, it was an ugly situation, what happened at the diner yesterday, and I … I can't tell you how bad I feel about it. Lots of people do."

"I imagine. The psychological damage of having to watch me get Rodney King'd must have really taken its toll on the good people of Bendijo."

"It's not how we are, the majority of us, we're not racists."

"Enough of a majority to elect a sheriff who is to represent you."

Del sighed. "I'm not going to try to excuse his behavior,

because it is terrible. Just want to put things in context for you. We've had a series of violent crimes the past few years, scary stuff, murders and drugs ... life around here has changed in many ways, and people are scared.

"There was a violent murder the night before, the murder of a beloved member of our community. It was, well, shocking. We're all shocked by it. Ted knew him, had known him all his life, in fact. They were in high school together. That's why he was there, to arrest the man responsible. So ... he wasn't himself, yesterday. Maybe not even today. But he's not really a bad guy. He cares about the community, all his men do, all of them are local, like us."

Hah, Slick thought. Del might think differently had he found himself in that interrogation room having his kidneys pummeled by a steroid freak of a deputy.

"We just want to raise our kids, know that they'll be able to get good grades and into good schools and do so without getting murdered by gangs of criminals. Ted, for all his faults, and he does have them, is relentless when it comes to confronting criminal activity. He gets things done. Does he get carried away? Sure. But who doesn't?"

Slick and Thumper just stared at Del, letting his last question hang there in the air. Del's smile faded and he sighed, put his hands on the table.

"I want to help. I know the mayor, I know Ted, I can make some phone calls..."

"You want to go on record as a witness?"

"That's tricky. I live here, my livelihood is very much dependent on—"

"In other words, you'll do what you can as long as it's

no risk to you."

"I wouldn't say it in such a bald way, but yes. Going on the record would be sticky for me. I can make some calls, and get other folks to make some phone calls, get you cut loose of whatever they charged you with."

"I already turned that offer down."

"You did?"

"Hell yes. I don't want the charges dropped. I want the sheriff's ass on a plate, and his deputies, too. You get Ted and his boys to resign, I'll leave town one happy camper. Otherwise no. I'm staying, I'm going to trial and I'm looking forward to it."

"Ted resign? That won't happen. There's no way."

"Great. Then I plan to see the sights and hang around."

Slick stood, as did Thumper, who pulled out a roll of bills. Del waved that off.

"No, please. Lunch is on me. I insist. I understand how you feel, I do. I'll make some calls, see what I can do to help you anyway. I just wanted to come over and apologize on behalf of the people of Bendijo. I am truly sorry for what happened to you. Here's my card, if I can be of assistance just call."

Slick took Del's card, nodded and he and Thumper walked out of the restaurant and into the blinding heat of the afternoon sun.

9

THUMPER COULDN'T WAIT to get into the car and get the air-conditioning going full blast. He started the engine and drove off down the street.

"What do you think? I have Sheriff Ted all wrong, he's really a cuddly bear on the inside who's all torn up by the murder of a friend?" Slick asked.

"Fuck that noise. Maybe THAT guy genuinely believes it, I'd buy that, but I know a racist fuckhole cop when I see one, I used to be one back in the day, for crissakes. Ted and his boys? That there is whole gaggle of racist gangrene-smelling fuckholes."

"Yeah, this whole thing smells, and not just the racist angle, I mean I can run into that shit anywhere. No doubt it's there, but ... something else about this bugs me, I just don't know what it is."

"What, the bigoted cop or the Mexican killer, which part?"

"All of it. Murder? That dude sitting next to me at the diner? I just don't see it."

"Hey, you never know. I knew this one old lady, back when I was in the job in Mississippi, her name was Celia, she was sweetest thing, silver hair, gloves and hat, very proper, went to church three times a week, never said a bad word about anyone, first to volunteer in the community fundraisers, shit like that. I mean, Celia was like the old lady who owned Tweety Bird, you know, the classic Warner Brothers cartoon?

"Hells yeah. Tweety and Sylvester the cat."

"Yeah, she was like that lady, only even sweeter, I shit you not. I used to see her every day on patrol, she'd be going for a walk with her hat and parasol, she always said good morning with a big smile. I even helped her carry groceries home once. Nice and polite as pie. Then she got busted for multiple murders."

"Serious? Who?"

"She was killing her boyfriends off, one at a time. She'd pick an old guy, date him awhile and then knock him off when she got bored. Made it look all natural, too, I mean they were all real old, her boyfriends, so nobody really thought twice about it. She'd slip 'em something in their tea, sometimes she'd push them down the stairs and they'd end up breaking their neck, she varied her method, she was smart about it, which was what made it interesting.

"Celia got caught when one old fella survived a couple of attempts on his life and called the cops on her. He claimed she once tried to drown him in the tub but he fought her off. She told him she was only playing around, but he didn't buy it. Later she did something to the basement stairs, set it up so they were broke then asked him to go get something from down there for her.

"When he went down, he crashed through, fell about ten feet and broke his hip. Swore she set him up. She claimed he was senile and that she never asked him to go to the basement in the first place. Cops believed her, hell, I believed her, I mean the old fucker claimed that she tried to drown him the week before, so why the hell did he stick around after that?"

"Yeah, what was that about?"

"I asked him about that later, he said he just couldn't bring himself to leave her because she was a fucking tiger in the sack, completely unbelievable in bed. Best he ever had— he'd had a lot of it over the years, or so he said. And he supplied plenty of graphic details, too. Leather, whips, ice cream, the works."

"Ah man, now I'm sorry I asked."

"Hey man, older women, beautiful lovers, et cetera, et cetera. Anyway, most of the department thought it was all a joke, we all knew Celia and loved her, I mean she was literally the nicest lady ever, but we had this homicide guy, Danny, smart bastard, he smelled something wrong with it, I don't know why, he just didn't like her.

"Danny did some research and it turned out that thirteen men, all senior citizens, had died soon after meeting and dating Celia. All in the past eight years. All the deaths seemed natural or accidental, but it turned out they weren't. Danny got permission from family members, dug up a couple of the corpses, had some tests done and found that at least one had been poisoned, another smothered with a pillow."

"Holy shit."

"Holy shit is right. Danny got a warrant, went through her house and found three more bodies buried in the basement, not really bodies but bones. Never identified who they were. And when she was arrested and confronted with all the evidence, she just looked at us, smiled and said, 'Yeah, so?'"

"Whoa. She ever say anything else?"

"Danny asked her, when he had her in the box, if she thought she was putting them out of their misery, as an act of mercy. He was actually trying to help set up an insanity defense for her, he thought she was crazy and, well, we all did. We were all shocked by it. He asked her that and she said no. So Danny asked her why she did it. She said, 'No reason, really.' And that's all she ever said."

"Fuck man. What happened to her?"

"Died before trial. In her sleep, in jail. Completely natural. Heard tell she had a smile on her face when she went. The old guy, the one with the broken pelvis who called the cops, he wept like a baby when she died, too."

"No reason, huh."

"No reason. That's what I'm telling you, I know you're damn good at seeing people's insides and motivations, but some folks, you just never know what makes 'em tick, and you're never gonna. Sometimes there's fucking nothing in there."

"There's always a reason, bro. Whether it's a good reason or a selfish, egotistical one, that's the question."

"Christ, don't get all metaphysical on me now, I prefer she had no reason for it, I'm a simple guy like that. And, hey, in Celia's house, know what else we found? Sex toys. Closets full, dude. Nasty ones, too. Huge, black dildos, velvet handcuffs, nipple clamps, anal beads, she had it all."

"I'm glad you told me that after lunch. Hey. Behind us.

You see them, right?"

Slick had been watching the rear view.

"Hells yeah. I'm no fucking amateur, I made them the minute we pulled out. Blue pickup, couple cars back. There's another one, too, rusty brown Chevy. They're alternating on us, but they ain't doing it like cops. Some local rednecks, I'd say."

Thumper glanced over at Slick. "So whatta wanna do?"

Slick dug around in the glove compartment, found a state map, opened and studied it for a bit. He found what he was looking for.

"I may need another favor or two."

"Anything, bro, you name it, you got it, but can I ask, will there be bolos thrown?"

"I'd say heavy bolos are in the forecast."

"Then that's a favor more for me than for you, dude."

10

ORVILLE AND JAY followed Slick and Thumper for the rest of the afternoon, alternating different eyes on him throughout the day so they wouldn't notice someone was on their ass, watching. They stayed in touch via their cell phones. They found out what hotel Slick had checked into, a cheap fleabag on the edge of town. Just got one room, with one bed. Orville, watching from his truck, shook his head when he heard that.

After checking in, Slick and his little buddy drove around the city awhile longer, then parked at a meter along the business strip of town and did some shopping, bought clothes and shit. Orville wondered if they'd hold hands and model thongs for each other when they got back to the motel.

Orville thought having shifts watching the nig probably wasn't necessary, he figured white people probably all looked the same to the big black bastard, just like niggers all looked the same to him, but it was good surveillance procedure and maintaining good training mattered, especially these days. He pulled his pickup in at a meter and watched as Slick walked along the sidewalk with his little buddy, who was supposed to be a boxer or some shit like that, and supposedly killed a guy some years back with his bare hands. He even did time for it, it was said.

Orville had trouble buying that. He was fucking tiny, that guy. And that made him the bitch of the pair, of course. Had to be, he was the black bastard's bitch. Don't care how much boxing the little bitch knew, size matters in a fight, always has and always will. A big dude will fuck up a little dude every time. Orville himself weighed two-fifty, could bench his weight and then some. He'd pick that fucking munchkin up and roll him into a human shitball with his bare hands.

Orville liked to fight, and, even better, he liked to fight guys who were smaller than he was. He thought about what he'd do to the little guy for staining his white heritage by being that black fucker's prison bitch, maybe he'd turn the little dude out himself, if he had the chance, though he wasn't that way. He wasn't gay and would beat the high holy fuck out of anyone who'd dare suggest that he might be, but he knew prison was different, even though he'd never done hard time himself.

He'd been in county lockup for drunk driving and fighting, of course, but Orville knew that wasn't real prison and didn't count. Orville knew real prison, or he thought he did. He loved watching OZ, he owned the whole series on DVD, it was his all-time favorite fucking show and he'd been devastated when it finally ended.

He always fantasized about it, doing hard time, what he'd do and who he'd turn out. Beat the shit out of fuckers, put them on their knees and tell 'em to make him happy or die. Orville liked that, and it wasn't gay, either. It was fucking prison; it's what you had to do to survive. You had to turn punks out and make 'em your bitches to earn respect. Nothing gay about it.

He amused himself with those thoughts as Slick and Thumper went into Radioshack and bought some stuff, he couldn't see what, exactly, but it didn't matter. You could buy guns in most stores in Arizona, but Radioshack wasn't one of them.

They came out and walked to their rental car, stopped and talked for a while. Shook hands, came in for a man-hug, a tight one, too. *Shit,* Orville thought, *they might even kiss right there on the street, fuck.* He was gonna like busting this nigger up.

After serious man-love hugs, the little guy got into the car and drove off. Orville picked up his cell, called in.

"Yo Jay."

"What's up?"

"They're separating, the short bitch is getting into the car and driving off without his husband. Just went down Beltran Avenue."

"What about the jig?"

"He's on foot, pimp-strutting down the street like he fucking owns it."

"I'm on the little bitch. Same car, right? The sedan?"

"Yeah. The way they hugged seemed like the bitch was leaving town."

"Faggots. I'm on him, no worries."

Slick kept walking down the street, bags in hand, and went into a car rental office, Hertz, the O.J. Simpson rental place. *That figures, just fucking figures,* Orville thought. Orville would like to put some hurts on that black fucker's ass, and soon.

When Slick pulled out of Hertz in a convertible, top down for all the world to see, Orville put his truck into gear and followed him. He drove all around town, taking in the sights, for at least two fucking hours, if not longer. Orville was getting hungry, and the hungrier he got, the more pissed he got at having to follow this asshole.

Slick found the mall, parked the convertible in the lot and went inside. After thinking about it, Orville also parked and went inside. He wandered around until he spotted Slick shopping at a bookstore. Bookstore! Probably checking out the latest issue of *Cosmopolitan*, shit like that. Orville picked up a paper from the newsstand and pretended to read it. Slick left the bookstore without buying anything, going right past the food court without stopping to eat there—it fucking tortured Orville, it really did. Would it kill the black bastard to stop for a burger and fries or something? Then Orville could eat, too. He could smell the beef tacos and his stomach growled.

Then Slick went into a café and ordered tea, for crissakes, tea! Orville could tell it was tea because he dipped the tea bag into the cup just like a proper lady would. Orville shook his head and waited. And waited. He hated waiting, he really did. Especially while hungry. The fucking coon just sat there and sipped his tea. Christ Almighty. Orville's cell rang. He saw it was Jay and answered.

"What up?"

"The little dude left, he's gone, man. I followed him all the way to Carver City, he's in the airport now. Just turned his rental car in, too. He's flying out, looks like."

"Fuck, I wanted a piece of that little bitch, damn," Orville said.

"What do you want me to do? I can't get into the airport, not without a boarding pass, anyway. Should I wait, or what?"

"Nah. Head on back home. Call up the boys. I'll stay on the nig, and when the sun goes down, it's party time, border-style."

"Yee-haw!"

Orville hung up and wondered if he could chance a run at the food court before it was too late. Probably not, looked like the coon was done with tea. He got up and left. Orville followed him out of the mall, cursing the entire way out.

11

ORVILLE STAYED ON Slick's ass for the next two hours, his mood going from bad to terrible to fucking-nuclear-meltdown levels as he watched the other man just drive around town aimlessly, without a destination or purpose. Not only was Orville hungry as hell, this was burning serious gasoline. He'd started with a full tank and most of it was gone already, his truck inhaled premium like it was mother's milk.

That shit was up to four bucks a gallon, which meant it cost Orville plenty to fill this monster up. And he doubted he'd be getting reimbursed for it either.

Orville hoped, hoped and prayed with every fiber of his being, that he'd be able to put a boot up this coon's ass for the mental anguish he'd caused Orville, he just needed the nig to at some point pull over and get out of the car and in a dark, secluded area. It looked promising when Slick took a sudden turn and got on the highway, heading out of town. Orville picked up his phone.

"Jay, yo. He's hightailing it, driving out on the five."

"He spot you and decided to run for it?"

"Nah, he didn't see shit, and he still ain't in no hurry, not that I can tell. Still looks like he's sightseeing. Where you at, can you pick him up? My truck's down to fumes."

"Yeah, I can swing around, I ain't far away. By the time you hit the Shell Station, I should be on his ass. We still gonna do this, right?"

"Hells yeah, try to fucking stop me, I wanna stomp this nigger so bad I can taste it. He's gotta stop soon. He pulls over outside city limits that's even better for us, in fact, we get him far enough out of town, we'll run him off the road and fucking tap dance on his skull. Call Hartzler, tell him to meet me at the station. And Freddie, too."

"Got ya, I already picked up Vaughn, he's in the truck with me. That gonna be enough? This fucking spear-chucker is supposed to be a black belt in karate."

"Five guys is too many for anyone, don't care what they know. And fuck him and his black belt, I used to beat the shit out of those fucking college boy black belts back in the day every time we went out to the bars. I'll make him eat that shit, watch me. Nothing I like better than hearing that some fuckhole's got a black belt right before I break his fucking leg. This is gonna be sweet, Jay."

"We ain't supposed to kill him, remember—"

"I know that, asshole, I know what I'm doin'. He's gonna be one hurtful nigger when I'm through, I'm gonna turn his ass out."

12

AFTER FUELING HIS pickup at the Shell Station, Orville met up with Jay and the boys about an hour outside of town, this roadhouse called Missy's that he'd been to once or twice, decent beer on tap, okay food, usually had a band on the weekends and so on. It was a weeknight, though, so only the serious drinkers would be there and they'd only be interested in what was in their glass.

Orville climbed out of his pickup, nodded to Hartzler and Jay and Freddie sitting on the tailgate of Jay's truck. He unwrapped another candy bar; he'd been chowing down on the chocolate since the gas station.

"He in there?"

"Yeah," Jay grinned. He was missing a couple front teeth and never got around to having them replaced. "He's in there at the bar, eating a goddamn salad. Vaughn's inside, keeping an eye on him, but he ain't going nowhere."

"And after?"

"Luke Paulson owns this place," Hartzler said. "I know him, he's good folks. He'll pass the word around, story will be nobody saw nothing, and if they did, the coon started it. Said just to make sure we keep it outside, that's all."

Orville nodded, his bad mood lifting at the thought of what he was gonna do to this black fucker. He cracked his knuckles and stared at his buddies, who were dressed as he was—jeans and boots, trucker caps and flannel shirts with the sleeves torn off. Orville was bigger than any of them and the most fearsome brawler. He wanted this.

"All right, I'll go in and get this party started."

"I dunno, Orville, he might not want nothin' to do with you," Freddie said. "Even a big bastard like him might have second thoughts about stepping outside with someone your size. Vaughn's the smallest one, maybe we should just have him—"

Orville finished his candy bar and spit on the ground.

"Hell no, I'm sick of waiting for this fuckhole. I'm goin' in, I'll get him out here if I have to drag him by his big ass lips. You fellas, you don't do nothin' when it starts, you wait until I'm done before you wade in, got me?"

They all nodded, nobody wanted to be on Orville's bad side, and plus there was nothing they loved better than watching Orville kick some fucking ass. Jay leaned into his truck cab, pulled out a pistol and checked the rounds.

"You ain't gonna need that," Orville said and went on inside.

13

ORVILLE PAUSED ONCE inside Missy's, waiting for his eyes to adjust to the gloom of the bar. A few dedicated drinkers dotted the tables here and there, but the bar was nearly deserted and it wasn't hard to see why. The black bastard sat there, the remains of a salad on a plate in front of him, fiddling with his phone. Stupid fucker.

Orville saw Vaughn at the other end of the bar, caught his eye and grinned. Orville jerked his chin and Vaughn finished up his beer and scurried on out of there, smirking the whole way. Orville hitched up his pants, walked over to the bar and sat down heavily next to Slick, signaled for a beer from the tap. Better to quench his thirst before letting the beast out of the cage.

Orville took a deep drink, belched, licked his lips and turned to Slick. Orville had the perfect opening line, too, he knew just was he was gonna say to this spade. Before he could open his mouth, though, the big black bastard turned and spoke to him.

"You must be Orville."

Orville was struck dumb by that and couldn't speak, just stared at Slick.

"What you do walk around at, two-fifty, two sixty, right? Big, mean and with a lot of obvious white space between the ears. That makes you Orville."

All the righteous and clever insults Orville had considered lobbing at Slick for the past two hours fled him at that moment. He stayed silent, mind working fast as it could, but that wasn't fast enough. He was frozen, couldn't even take another drink of beer.

"Dumb, man, real dumb. You gonna follow someone, you might consider NOT using your own vehicle or, at the very least, change the license plate. Too easy."

Slick drained his beer, set the mug down. He dug out some cash, tossed it on the bar to pay the bill then stood up and stared at Orville.

"Well? We gonna do this inside or out?"

Orville finally found his voice, anger flooding his body anew. "Outside."

Slick nodded, turned and headed for the door. Orville followed, his rage growing with every step. He'd been pissed before, but now he was absolutely fucking furious. So the jungle bunny made him, so what? He was still gonna stomp his ass but good.

14

SLICK STEPPED OUT of the bar, sliding carefully to the side so that Orville wasn't standing behind him, getting the wall of the bar to his back. He glanced at the four men waiting for him and Orville. Slick pointed his finger at each one, checking them off.

"Dumb. Dumber. Special needs. Tea bagger—" Slick turned to Orville "—and you, you are the missing link that confirms Darwin's Theory of Evolution. Who taught you to walk upright without dragging your knuckles? Whoever it was, they should have taught you to wipe your mouth after eating a candy bar."

He could feel Orville's fury cresting.

"You fucking nigger, I'm gonna KILL you—"

"Racial epitaphs, now that's fucking offensive," Thumper said, stepping out from the shadows. "I am shocked, shocked at this kind of behavior from a white man, I have to tell you, every time I turn on Fox News they claim this racism shit is over and done."

"That's what they say right before they dump on a black president," Slick said.

Orville and his guys swiveled around at Thumper's appearance, startled. Orville recovered and glared at Jay. "You said he got on the goddamned plane!"

"I did get on a plane," Thumper said. "Then I got right back off it again. Not that Slick here needs the help, but because I get jealous when he gets to have all the fun for himself. And, besides, somebody here needs to be a positive white role model for the kids and it sure as hell ain't gonna be any of you backward-ass fuckholes."

The boys got their confidence back fast, figuring that it was still five against two, plus Thumper was small. He may be a boxer, so they were told, but he wasn't big, and size matters in a fight, damn it, that's why they had weight classes. And while Slick was a big man, Orville was even bigger. Plus, Jay had his gun.

"We'll see who the fuckholes are real quick, bitch," Orville said. "After I get done with the jig, I'm gonna turn your ass out."

Thumper glowered. "Slick, I want this fat bastard first, lemme have him."

"Hey man, be my guest, they all look and smell the same to me anyway, but he might have other ideas. What about it, Orville? You wanna dance with my friend here first, one on one? I'll wait, I'm not going anywhere, I promise."

"You got that right, boy, you ain't goin' nowhere. Jay, watch his black ass, hear me? Don't none of you let the coon run. After I beat his bitch into the ground, he's next."

"He's not anybody's bitch, Orville," Slick said, "but you're about to be his. Go on ahead, though. Like I said, I'm not going anywhere."

Orville laughed and stepped into the middle of the circle formed by the group, swinging his arms as a warm up, his eyes hard on Thumper. A full foot taller and at least a hundred pounds heavier, he didn't fear the smaller man in the slightest.

Thumper grinned, took off his smart phone, which was attached to his belt, and set it on the hood of a nearby car. He removed the headphones, pressed play and classic rap, Run-DMC, played over its speaker. Thumper loved to fight to music.

"Figures you'd be into nigger music," Orville sneered.

Slick gave Thumper a look, his special one that read, 'No casualties.' Thumper held up his hand as if to say, 'I got this,' and walked into the middle of the circle, squaring off with Orville, his hands down at his sides. Just waiting. Orville grinned and ambled close, taking his time with it, wanting to milk the moment.

He swiped a big meaty paw out at Thumper, who slipped it with ease, just turning his hips slightly but not moving his feet. Orville threw out two more punches, neither of which touched Thumper who kept rooted to his spot, bobbing and weaving.

"That's it, that's the best you got?" Thumper smirked.

Orville gritted his teeth, embarrassed now, and threw a big roundhouse haymaker that Thumper saw coming from miles away. Thumper stepped under it, sliding behind Orville. He gave the bigger man a slight push, putting him off balance enough to fall to his hands and knees. The other four men watching straightened up, they'd never seen Orville get knocked down ever, much less by a small push from behind.

Thumper glanced at Slick. "Now?"

"Not yet."

Orville roared in anger as he got to his feet and barreled at Thumper. He grabbed hold of the smaller man by the shirt, tried pummeling with him. Thumper twisted from his grip, slipping from one side to the other without running away, keeping close without letting the larger man get a bead on him. Orville roared again and tried to kick Thumper in the groin, missed and fell right down on his ass.

Thumper casually walked a few steps away, squared off again. Orville, panting now, took his time to get to his feet. Took a deep breath, let it out as he sized Thumper up. The others stirred, nervous.

Jay brandished the pistol. "Orville, you want me to—"

"Shut up and stay out of it until I give you the word, I got this." He turned to Thumper. "You can't run from me forever, bitch."

"Way you're wheezing, I don't need to run forever, just longer than you," Thumper said. "But nobody's running, shitbird. Come get some."

Thumper glanced at Slick, "Now?"

"Now."

Orville, more careful now, stepped close to Thumper, determined to tag him good, waiting for his moment. Thumper waited before him, arms still at his sides. Orville licked his lips, his fists raised. Feinted a left jab that Thumper didn't respond to. Feinted again and then followed that with a hard, straight right punch that would have taken Thumper's head off, had it landed on its target.

It didn't, however, as Thumper again slipped it, stepped inside and landed a hellacious left hook right to Orville's liver that stopped him cold and left him unable to speak or move, his face whiter than a Klan member's Sunday sheets.

"Who's the bitch now, redneck?" Thumper said and bounced three more blindingly fast hooks off the big man's side, breaking his ribs this time. Orville gasped and looked to his friends, desperate for help. Vaughn and Freddie rushed to his aid.

Thumper spun on a dime to meet both men, his fists up and ready and before they could stop their momentum. Vaughn and Freddy ran straight into a couple of hard punches to the chin that rattled their teeth and caused their eyes to roll back in their heads. Both men toppled straight down to the ground, unconscious.

Jay shouted and tried to bring his pistol up. He was shocked to discover that he couldn't as Slick had skipped over to where he stood and grabbed the wrist that held the pistol, gripping it tight as a vise.

"Uh-uh." Slick wagged a finger at him. "Let's keep this firearm free, shall we?"

Slick twisted Jay's wrist into an impossible angle, forcing him to drop the pistol. It clattered to the pavement and Slick kicked it under a nearby truck. Hartzler jumped on Slick from behind, going for a rear naked choke. Slick reached up with his free hand, grabbed Hartzler's little pinky, cranked it until it broke and the man released him, screaming in pain.

Slick dipped under Hartzler without releasing his hold on either man and guided Jay right into Hartzler. Their skulls collided with a sickening thud and both men went down hard. Slick glanced back in Thumper's direction, where his friend stood before a frozen Orville, who just stood there hunched over, his arms wrapped tight around his body, his abdomen in too much pain for him to move.

"What you got to say now, shitkicker?" Thumper asked. "You still gonna turn me out? Still think I'm a bitch? C'mon man, let's hear it."

Slick grinned as Orville could only gasp, trying to get his breath back. Slick reached under the truck and retrieved the pistol.

"I ain't even hit you with my best shot yet," Thumper said. "I was saving it, didn't want to blow my wad too early, you know? I'm ready for it now, though, you ready?"

Orville shook his head, in near tears and still unable to speak. Slick checked on the other four men, they'd need a visit to the ER and some plaster, but other than that, they'd live. He joined Thumper, chambered a round in the pistol.

"So, Orville, before my bud here finishes the fight, maybe you could share with us who hired you to run me off."

Orville gasped, "My ribs ... I think they're broke..."

"They damned well better be broke, hard as I hit 'em," Thumper said. "Otherwise I'm gonna be seriously ashamed of myself. Now answer Slick's question."

"No one ... we were just ... fucking around and thought we'd—"

"Orville, please. Do I look like I'm gullible enough to believe that? You were following me around all day and night. Someone put you on me. Who?"

Orville blinked, still unable to stand up straight, his eyes on the pistol in Slick's hand, hanging down by his side.

"I were you, I wouldn't worry about this gun," Slick said. "I'd worry about what my buddy here would like to do to you. He's not lying, he can hit a lot harder, I've seen it. You think you're hurting now but you have no idea how much pain he can visit upon your person, trust me. So ... who hired you?"

Orville swallowed, closed his eyes. "One of the deputies, I went to school with him. His name is Collins. He gave me and Jay a call, asked us to run you off."

"Collins. The steroid freak," Slick said.

"Yeah, he's into the juice. We weren't supposed to do nothin' but rough you up, get you to scat, we weren't supposed to kill you or nothin', honest."

"How very considerate of him. Did he tell you why?"

"What?"

"Did he tell you WHY he wanted me roughed up and run off?"

"Uh-uh ... just that he wanted it done and outside of county lines if possible. He didn't say shit 'bout nothin' else, honest."

Slick stared at him for a moment, assessing the truth in that. The other four men on the ground moaned, regaining consciousness. Thumper kept glaring at Orville, his eyes glittering. Slick glanced at Thumper, nodded.

"Okay, we're done here. Let's vogue, brother," Slick said.

"Hold on a sec, Slick, I wanna have more fun with this Klan wannabe first."

"We got a time issue, bro ... someone inside's gonna see that this didn't go as planned and call the local police."

"Listen," Orville said, "I'm done, honest. You beat me, fair and square."

"Since when have you EVER been in a fair fight, shitkicker? I know your type, you like to pick on little brown people, don't ya? Talk some shit, get 'em outside and beat the hell outta 'em in front of your friends?"

"You won. I'm done with this, my word—"

"Your word don't mean SHIT to me, son. But folks who know me know my word is good, and I'm gonna give you my word on something right now. If anything bad happens to my friend Slick while he's in Arizona, I'm gonna come back to this pisshole and kill you, your friends, and your friends' friends. I hate racists like you with a passion, and if I have to, I will come back here and kill you all in your own kitchens. Understand me?"

"I understand, you won't get no more problems from me, I swear," Orville pleaded, his arms wrapped around his sides, still unable to posture up straight.

"He's done, bro, let's full tilt boogie on out of here." Slick touched Thumper's arm. Thumper nodded and turned away. Orville breathed a sigh of relief as best he could.

"Almost forgot. One last thing," Thumper said.

He whirled and caught Orville on the chin with a vicious hook, one that snapped the large man's head back with a crack and spun his entire body around until he toppled unconscious to the ground, his jaw broken.

"That's for calling my best friend a nigger and a jig."

15

S LICK SLEPT WELL, considering. He'd gotten some bath salts and soaked his aching body in the tub for a long time. Collins knew where to hit him, that was for sure. The motel room wasn't bad, functional for what it needed to be and he was on the quiet side of the building, far away from the front office. He preferred it isolated so no one could see him coming or going.

Before he left, Thumper had gone in and booked the room for him under the name of John Bender, Judd Nelson's character from The Breakfast Club. As far as anyone knew, there was a short white guy named Bender staying in this room. Slick had rented another room himself at a different motel on the opposite end of town, under his own name, but he had no intention of staying there.

He bathed, did some light yoga to get his muscles breathing and crashed in the king sized bed. He slept a good ten hours. His body had evidently needed it, being unconscious doesn't have nearly the same recuperative value as deep sleep. He woke up refreshed and glad to be alive. There were a couple text messages on his prepaid cell, one from Thumper, who'd landed back home in Chicago safe and sound, and the other from Melvin the lawyer, who wanted to meet as soon as possible, for breakfast if he was up for it.

He sent a text back, agreeing, and then flipped open his netbook and checked his email.

He had an email from Camilla Leon. It read, "Call me," followed by a cell number. Very interesting. He smiled, for some reason just seeing her name made him smile. It was his semi-public email address, so she'd done some work to dig it up. He wrote her number down and tucked it into his wallet.

He showered and left to meet Melvin.

"FIRST THINGS FIRST. They're dropping the charges," Melvin said.

"All of them?"

"Every single one. No explanation, no apology, just that the entire list of charges against you has been dismissed. She called me at the ass-crack of dawn to tell me."

"It's not surprising. She say anything else?"

"She asked for your number. Wouldn't say why. I told her I'd have to check with you before passing it on. Since you're no longer a defendant there's no reason not to talk to her, if you wish, but no real reason that you have to, either. I'm presuming she wants to know if we plan to file a civil suit against Sheriff Ted and the department. Are we?"

"I don't know yet," Slick said, though he did know the answer to that, he just didn't want Melvin to know. He sipped some orange juice and thought about her, again. Melvin cleared his throat before continuing.

"I checked, as of today there are already three civil suits pending against the department here, all for false arrest and use of unnecessary force. There've been others, multiple suits, but they've either been dismissed or settled out of court. Most have been dismissed, but if you do have, shall we say, a pair of aces under your hat, as you mentioned previously, then she may be sniffing around to find out if they need to prepare to fork over a large settlement to keep us, or rather you, quiet."

Melvin was the one sniffing around, Slick saw, practically licking his chops at the thought of a large cash civil suit settled at the Bendijo taxpayer's expense.

"I'll check in with her and let you know when and what I decide. I want to think about it. What about the other guys?"

"The charges against Manual Rodriguez and Luiz Carrera have also been dropped, which wasn't at all surprising, the police department literally had nothing on them by way of evidence, the two men simply just had the misfortune to have had breakfast with Pedro Garcia that morning. They worked together, though they say they don't know him all that well. They're free and clear of the charges, but they're in this country illegally, so they now face deportation back to Mexico."

"And Pedro?"

"More complicated. He's in a coma, still, which means he can't even be officially indicted. The law here gets tricky as the accused has to be able to offer up a defense and, as it stands, he can't even agree to let me represent him. He has no family, at least none here in Arizona. He's also an illegal.

"So right now I'm trying to work out something with his public defender, who is more than happy to hand everything over to me if at all possible. Currently, we're waiting for a judge to decide how we can do that or if Pedro can even stand trial in his current state, which seems unlikely due to the statutes on the matter. It's a mess."

"How's the case against him? You get a look at it?"

"Yes, his public defender handed everything over, unofficially as of yet, of course, but he doesn't want to touch it and hopes the judge lets me take over. It's a good case for the prosecution. Not so good for Pedro."

"And?"

"And technically I shouldn't discuss details of his case with you."

"Technically you're not even Pedro's lawyer yet."

"True. But—"

"Just lay out the broad strokes, you won't have to violate privilege for that. If he wants you to keep everything to yourself when he wakes up, that's his right. I don't have any issue with it, I just want to know what I'm buying."

"And that's 'if' Pedro even wakes up, his doctors think there's a good chance he'll never come out of that coma. Okay, well, he's charged with the murder of a man by the name of Roger Carlson, he's a farmer, one of the big ones in the area, he hires a lot of vegetable pickers during harvest season, and one of the men he's hired in the past was Pedro, though it seems that Pedro hasn't worked for him for a couple seasons.

"His body was found outside one of his work sheds, early on the same morning as Pedro's arrest. Medical examiner puts time of death around midnight the night before. Cause of death was blunt force trauma to the head and torso."

"Beaten to death?"

"Yes, with a shovel. It wasn't a pretty sight, I've seen the photos. The bad news? They have the shovel, it was left on scene. And the shovel has Pedro's prints on it. No one can really account for his whereabouts at the time of the murder, either. His buddies thought he was home in bed. No one knows for sure."

"That's not good."

"As I said, good for the prosecution, not so good for Pedro."

"Motive?"

"That's murkier. It could be anything. He was once employed by the man, after all, and is no longer. Carlson employs illegal workers pretty regularly, and employers like that have been known to take advantage of their workers, but so far there's nothing to suggest that's the situation with Carlson. According to the report, Carlson had a few out of the norm political beliefs but was well liked in the community. I won't know for certain until I get deeper into the case. At the moment, it reads to me like they have nothing for motive and aren't too worried about it.

"They have the murder weapon with his prints, Pedro has no alibi, at least not that I've been able to find thus far, and add to that he's an illegal—the police figure they have a slam dunk with what they have. And between you and me they do. If Pedro wakes up and provides an alibi, a verifiable one, we're good. But if he just went home and went to bed by himself, like most every normal person would do, he's officially fucked."

"Love it when you lawyers toss the legal jargon around."

"If he wakes up, I'll bust my ass for him, with or without

an alibi. I'm good at this, Jon. You and I don't know each other but I'm one of the best defense attorneys in the state, that's why Thumper called me. But I'm no miracle worker, in the end it comes down to a jury, and I don't have to tell you what a jury will think when confronted with the evidence the police have now. An upstanding local farmer murdered by one of his illegal workers? My advice would be to go for a plea and cut a deal if there's one to be had. The headlines on the trial alone will doom Pedro."

"Yeah, it's a helluva story, isn't it?" Slick thought about that.

"It may be all moot. My gut tells me that the judge will say that they can't try him if he doesn't wake up. It's likely that he may not."

"What time was the farmer's body found?"

"Uh, let me see…" Melvin checked his notes. "A few minutes before six."

"Had Pedro ever been arrested before?"

"Not in this country. I'll check with Mexican authorities to see about a criminal record there, but it seems unlikely. According to his co-workers, the two I've spoken to, he was quiet and law-abiding, shy even. Devout Catholic, single, went to church every Friday night, Saturday and Sunday. He'd been here for five years and, like many illegals, he tried hard to stay out of trouble."

"Carlson's body was found at six in the morning, right? More or less. And Pedro was arrested in the diner sometime after eight?"

"Eight-twenty."

"That's pretty fast police work, ain't it?"

Melvin thought about that and nodded. "Real fast."

"Too fast. How'd they identify him so quick? If he'd never been arrested before, his prints weren't in the system. Yet in two hours they knew who he was and where he was. Two fucking hours. You think the cops here are that good?"

"I don't know of cops anywhere who are that good. Nothing in the arrest report, either. It's pretty sparse, in fact. I'll double-check, but it could be an opening. Good catch. You could be a good lawyer."

"I make more money at cards than you do at law. But thanks anyway."

Melvin was less than amused by that comment but ignored it. "So are you going back to … where is it you live?"

"New York City. No. I'm not going back, not just yet."

"Really?" Melvin raised an eyebrow. "You're staying here?"

Slick could see that Melvin thought this boded well for his potential civil suit against the department. "A little while, anyway. I'm not ready to go just yet."

"You mentioned yesterday that you might have … what was your phrase for it, for the aces in the hole?"

"Bullets."

"Bullets, yes. You mentioned you might have something to that effect with regard to your encounter with Sheriff Ted?"

"I might. I might not."

"You can tell me, you know. I am your lawyer, after all."

"Not anymore. I don't need a lawyer now, right? But if I do, I'll give you a call. You have my numbers, I have yours, and if things change I'll be in touch."

Slick stood and walked out, leaving a perturbed Melvin to deal with the check. It wouldn't be much, at least from his end. There hadn't been much for him to eat there.

16

SLICK PULLED INTO the long drive leading to the Carlson ranch. He wasn't sure what type of reception he'd get there, but thought it might be worth at least seeing where it happened and if anyone would possibly talk to him. Except for the work barns and a modest but well-maintained ranch house, there was nothing but lettuce fields as far as the eye could see.

He parked and climbed out of the car. No one around, no workers, no dogs, it was very quiet. He sensed movement in the house, a flutter of a window shade. He shut the car door and made his way up the front walk. The front door opened before he got close and a woman in her fifties stepped out, one foot and hand inside.

"You a reporter?" she asked.

"No, ma'am," Slick said.

"You ain't a salesman either."

"No, ma'am, definitely not."

She stared at him a moment and he at her. She wore jeans and a t-shirt, her hair up in a bun, a well-preserved woman but just as obviously barely holding it together. She finally nodded and opened the door all the way.

"Thirsty?"

"I surely am."

"Come on inside then, too hot out here."

Slick followed into the air-conditioned coolness of her house and noticed, once inside, that she held a shotgun in her free hand, the one she kept inside the house, partially hidden. She leaned the weapon against a counter once she got to the kitchen.

"For reporters?" he asked.

"And salesmen. You like iced tea?"

"Love iced tea."

She took out a pitcher of tea from the refrigerator, poured them both a glass.

"You want sugar with that?"

"No, thank you."

"You ain't from the south, then. But neither am I and that's also the way I like it, too. Straight up, with a slice of lemon and really cold."

"Me too."

She handed him his glass and they both took a deep drink. She leaned against the counter, staring at him. "I'm Doris Carlson, but you probably know that, since you drove all the way out here to my house."

"I did know that. My name is Jon Elder. I'm very sorry for your loss."

She cocked her head at his name. "You're the fella, one of them that was arrested the day they arrested Pedro for murdering my Roger."

"Yes, ma'am."

"Ted thought you might have something to do with what happened to Roger, but then they found out that you were just in the wrong place at the wrong time, right?"

"Pretty much, yep."

"If I recall, Ted also told me you hired some fancy lawyer for Pedro, too."

"I did, though it seems as though he might not live long enough to need a lawyer."

"I heard that, too." She sighed and took another drink.

Slick looked around. A picture of Roger, Doris and a young man stood on the mantle. Next to it was another picture of the same young man, older and much more serious in a Marine's uniform. Doris caught his look and nodded to it.

"Our son, Jim."

"Fine looking young man."

"Yeah. He was." She took another drink of tea. "He died in Iraq, nine years ago. Roadside bomb. Died protecting our country from Iraqi weapons of mass destruction that turned out not to exist. Now, of course, those who got us into that particular war say that it was never about that, but that's a load of shit, ain't it?"

"It surely is."

"Roger was really proud when Jim enlisted, so proud, he'd served, too, and he talked to our son all the time about his service, and it had its affect. Jim idolized his father and wanted to be like him, that's why he signed up. It changed Roger when Jim died. He was never into politics before that, other than maybe making conversation over the newspaper. But our son dying in a war that we were fighting for no real apparent reason, that changed him. I think it's why he took all these other young fellas, our workers, under his wing, gave them jobs, advice, money. He blamed himself and was trying to make up for what happened to Jim. He went way over the bend."

"How so?"

She regarded him for a moment then took a few steps over to a nearby door and opened it. What was once a pantry had been converted into a small office. "Take a look for yourself."

There was a small desk, covered in notebooks, Post-it notes and old coffee cups. Multiple clippings were taped over all the walls. Slick glanced at a few of the headlines from the printouts. Much of it was anti-war and conspiracy theories regarding nine-eleven. There were also a few pictures of the World Trade Center falling, along with arrows designating suspicious points of interest. Behind the door hung a big poster of George W. Bush on the wall, covered with darts.

"Ever seen anything like that before?" she asked.

"A couple times. I live in New York City. The tragedy affected people in a lot of different ways."

"That it did," she said. "Some got rich off it, some didn't and a few lost everything. That's what Roger used to say. But he didn't really pay attention to the details until we lost Jim. After that, I think he got lost in them."

She took another drink. "So what brings you out here, Mr. Elder?"

"Call me Jon. I'm here because I want to know what happened."

"With my husband? Why?"

"Some sheriff nearly caved in my skull and I'm of a mind to find out if there was a worthy reason behind it."

"Ted cracking your skull, or my husband's murder? Them's two separate things, and no worthy reason behind either, in my opinion. First one is just a result of Ted's ignorance, the second, well, I honestly can't make sense of it, not at all."

"Pedro murdering your husband, that doesn't make sense?"

"Not at all. Of all the boys Roger took under his wing, he was the nicest. Fact is, I can't imagine none of the boys we had working for us ever doing something like that, but Pedro? He was with us for three summers and we knew him well. Very polite, very religious, never got angry and worked hard. Prayed before every meal, heard he sent the majority of his pay home to his mother in Mexico.

"He'd still be working here, we would've kept him on, but he got hired in some construction work that was full time year round for more money, so he moved on. No hard feelings about it, we really liked him, and he liked us. Kept sending us Christmas cards at the holidays, too. Never had a bad word between us. That's why it don't make sense that he did this."

"Ted say what he thought the motive was?"

"Ted's full of hot air. He said something that maybe Pedro was trying to steal something from the farm, some equipment or some such, and when Roger caught him at it, Pedro killed him, but that's another crock. Pedro wouldn't steal a glance, much less anything else, and if he needed money Roger would have given him a job in a second and money even faster. Roger was a soft touch and everyone knew it. I told Ted so but doubt he heard me. Listening ain't his strong suit."

"If it wasn't Pedro, can you think of anyone else who might have had a grievance with your husband?"

"No, I honestly can't. Roger was pretty popular, much more than me. He grew up here. Folks thought he was eccentric due to his politics, he was way to the left of most people in this area, but even those who disagreed with Roger on nearly everything had to admit he was probably the nicest guy they ever met. Because, well, he was. He was kind and sweet and he cared about the whole world and all the people in it. He was the best, a whole sight better'n me, that's for sure."

She sighed, set her glass down. "I found him, you know. He usually came to bed real late, did so ever since we lost Jim, but he always came to bed eventually. I woke up before six because he wasn't there, went to look for him and … found him."

She turned away, her voice hitching. She took a deep breath and let it out.

"His funeral's this afternoon. I ain't gonna go, I don't care what the people will say. I can't bear to watch another one of my men put into the ground, I just can't."

Slick nodded at that and gave her some time and space to collect herself. She wiped her eyes and turned back around.

"Hard to be here, too, I see both of 'em everywhere I turn—in the kitchen, in the yard. Been going on nine years and I still swear I hear my son Jim knocking around in the rec room like he used to do. Roger felt the same way, though he'd never admit it to me.

"It's only been three days and I keep expecting Roger to bang on into the kitchen without wiping his boots, just like always. I don't think I'll be able to handle living here alone, not with the both of 'em doing this to me, it's too much. I guess I'll end up selling this place after all."

She nearly lost her emotions again but caught herself and looked Slick in the eye. "You want to get Pedro off, is that it?"

"No, ma'am. I just want to know if he did it. I don't think he did, but I want to know for sure. If he did do it, I'll let the wheels of justice turn however they do. If I find out that he didn't do it then I'll find out who did."

"Why would you do that?"

Slick didn't answer right away. "It's just how I'm wired."

She stared for a moment and then nodded. "I believe you. I don't think Pedro killed my Roger, either, but I don't know what else I can tell you. You should talk to his priest, though, at Saint Mary's. If anyone knew Pedro well, it'd be Father Jose."

"I will do that, thank you. And thank you for the iced tea and for the hospitality," Slick said. He gave her the empty glass. She held on to it, briefly.

"Do you think I'm a terrible person, for not going to the funeral?"

"No. You have the right to mourn however you see fit."

She nearly went again, caught it and nodded. "Thank you."

17

SLICK CAUGHT THE flashing lights in his rear view just as he pulled into city limits. He pulled over, rolled his window down and stuck both of his hands out of it so they could be seen. He watched in the mirror as Brower and Collins climbed out of a patrol car and took their time approaching him, Brower on his side, Collins on the other.

"Is there a problem, deputy?" Slick asked when they got close enough.

"License and registration, please," Brower said.

Slick eyed Collins on the other side, the big man was clearly seething, his hand on his pistol.

"I'm happy to do that, Deputy, but before I reach into the glove box for my rental agreement, I'd like to point something out to you."

"And what would that be, sir?"

"This, right here. This is a web camera." Slick pointed to a small device placed up on his visor. "There are more I've put in different spots in the interior, so everything that happens inside and outside this car is digitally recorded and instantly sent to a dedicated server in New York City where my lawyer can get at it. Should something unfortunate happen to me, he'll know exactly what, why and who. That includes our conversations, too. I share that because, well, I wouldn't want there to be some misunderstanding while I'm reaching for my car rental agreement and suddenly find myself shot because of something that LOOKS like a firearm but isn't, you know?"

Slick grinned. "You can get some good equipment these days."

Brower glanced involuntarily at Collins. "That's great, license and registration."

"Absolutely, Deputy." Slick slowly and carefully got the car rental registration out of the glove box, pulled his license from his wallet and handed them to Brower. Brower glanced at them and stepped back. "Step out of the car, please."

Slick opened his car door with great care and got out in the hot sun. Collins circled around the front of the car, eyeballing him behind mirrored shades.

"Just for the record, I have cameras aimed outside the car, too," Slick said. "So are you going to tell me what this is about, or not?"

"I pulled you over because you were driving ten miles above the speed limit." Brower pulled out his ticket book and started writing.

"I'm sure I wasn't."

"You can tell it to the judge."

"I'll do more than that, I'll give him or her the digital recording of my speedometer, which will show that I was driving exactly at the speed limit. I'll do that after I put it up on YouTube."

Brower flushed red but that didn't stop him from writing the ticket. "I'm sure the judge will enjoy the show."

"Yeah, now that you mention it, there are a few things I

could put up on YouTube that some folks might find illuminating and interesting. I'll have to think about that."

"Home movies of you in the shower, shit like that?" Brower ripped off the ticket and handed it to Slick.

"Yeah, shit like that, little movies of my adventures in redneck Valhalla. You never know what's gonna catch the public eye, you know. Can I go now?"

Brower just looked at him for a moment. "Just for the record, can you account for your whereabouts last night, around nine or so?"

"I sure can."

Brower waited a moment for Slick to elaborate, but he didn't. A muscle in his cheek clenched. "So where were you last night?"

"I was well outside your jurisdiction," Slick said. "Having dinner with a friend."

"Can you give me the name of your friend?"

"I can but I won't. As I said, it was outside your jurisdiction, ergo not any of your damned business. You want to know more, call my lawyer Melvin." Slick casually leaned back against his car. "But rest assured, I made certain my whereabouts were officially accounted for last night and, I have to tell ya, I'm sure glad I did.

"Because I heard a story this morning, another friend was telling me about these redneck country fuckholes who tried to start some shit with a random black man in some bar somewhere outside county lines. I guess they felt someone of his color didn't belong there and asked him to step outside, maybe thinking to themselves, *Hey, five on one, this is a piece of cake,* and this brother just … fucked their shit up, I mean, fucked them up but good. I'm sure glad I have an alibi, because I doubt that dumb assholes like them could even tell one black man from another in a lineup, especially in the dark like that."

Slick winked at Collins. "But thankfully I don't have to worry about them mistaking me for some whole other body, now do I?"

Brower glanced at Collins, who was nearly purple with rage and stepping close, hand on his weapon. Brower stepped in between them, cutting the big man off.

"Yeah, that's a helluva story, all right," Brower said. "Can I take it, from the direction you drove in from, you were out at Roger Carlson's place, right?"

"I was, in fact, out at Roger Carlson's place, speaking with his wife Doris."

"What about?"

"Offering my condolences. She's a nice lady who's suffered two terrible losses."

"A word of advice…" Brower leaned in close, his voice a whisper. "Stay away from Doris, stay away from the Carlson place. You got lucky, got all your charges dropped, you're a free man, why don't you quit while you're ahead and move on?"

"Yeah, why don't I do that? That's a good question. I'll have to think about it." Slick opened his car door and slid in, glad for the air conditioning. "Okay, I thought about it. I'll move on when I'm damned good and ready to move on, Deputy."

Brower really didn't like that. He leaned down into Slick's window.

"Seems to me that you're the type of person who likes to play with fire. And you know what they say about those who play with fire?" Brower said.

"Yeah. They shit thunder and piss lightning."

Slick rolled the window up, put the car into gear and drove away.

18

S LICK HAD TO go back to the Indian restaurant, eventually. They had a decent vegetarian menu, better than
anywhere else in Bendijo, and he was tired of eating fruit in
his car. He went there for lunch, after sending a text
message or two, and savored a meal indoors in the dark,
humming cool of air conditioning.

It was seriously hot outside and, while Slick would happily identify his cultural heritage as African, he was no fan
of Africa-style heat. Arizona got fucking hot, for real. He'd
never been to Africa, at least not yet, but had no doubt the
Arizona desert gave the Africa a run for its money when it
came to stifling heat.

The door jangled and Camilla walked in and sat down
without saying hello.

"What do you have?" she asked.

"Vegetable delight." Slick gestured to his plate. "Would
you like to try it?"

"That's not what I meant and you know it. I meant what
do you have on the sheriff? I know you have something."

"How do you know that?"

Slick's prepaid cell buzzed. He checked it. Melvin calling. He silenced it and went back to his guest. She wasn't
sweating. Somehow, even in this heat she managed to look

cool, dressed in a business skirt and suit jacket with a dark blue silk shirt. Slick felt positively bohemian in his t-shirt and jeans, recently purchased from the mall, and he was already experiencing major pitting underneath his arms. Not her, she was cool as grape juice. At least on the exterior. He wondered if the cool held the deeper you got.

"Because my boss informed me first thing this morning that we were dropping all charges against you. George was in the office this morning. Early. He's never there before ten, but today he was there before I was, and I'm always the first one at the office. He was there specifically to tell me that we weren't indicting you."

"I heard, Melvin told me at breakfast that you guys were cutting me loose."

"So what is it, what do you have?"

"Who says I have anything?"

"Come on, I don't have time for this shit, I really don't. There's no way he'd give me a direct order like that without pressure from somewhere. And it wasn't your pricey lawyer, either. You have something, you have leverage. I want it."

"If I did have something like that, why would I just hand it over?"

Slick's phone buzzed once more. Melvin again. He silenced it, but wondered what it was. It had to be important.

She took a moment, sizing him up. Slick never seemed to tire of that.

"Because Pedro Garcia is dead. He never woke from his coma, just died."

Now Slick knew why Melvin kept calling, likely with the same news.

"That's too bad," Slick said.

"It is. And you have a digital video of his arrest, if I'm not mistaken. That's why you're being cut loose. You recorded it on your phone and it got cloud-saved before they could destroy it. Am I right?"

"That appears to be what some folks think. Got an email from a friend of mine this morning, seems someone hired a hacker to break into my cloud files and erase everything. But I have friends who are serious real computer ninjas who guard my online gates, so whoever it was had no luck."

"I want it, I want the video, give it to me."

"For the sake of argument, let's say I DO have a digital video like that, hypothetically, and I gave it to you, what would you do with it?"

"I'd bring charges against Ted."

"What sort of charges?"

"Manslaughter, for one, for what he did to Pedro—"

"Who was considered a murderer, at least that's what folks around here believe. You think your boss or the population at large is gonna be outraged that Sheriff Ted killed the murderer of a local farmer? Excess force, sure, but it's doubtful that you'll get much traction on it. You'll be lucky if he gets a slap on the wrist."

"I can charge him with assault and battery for what he did to you."

"Yeah, and I'd appreciate that, but let me remind you of something. Rodney King. A video of a gang of white cops beating the shit out of a black man, on the ground, and what happened to them? Nothing. No jail time, nothing. Sure, some folks were outraged, riots ensued, but it still was not enough to make a difference. Those cops never went to jail, nothing happened to them. If anything, the riots made white folks feel the cops were justified in what they did."

"And that was twenty-some years ago—"

"Just a few years ago, there was video of a policeman shooting some poor black kid in a subway station in Oakland, he had the kid handcuffed, knees on his back, and he shot him. Said he was reaching for his Taser. That's what he SAID. Nobody thought to ask him, 'Hey, you got the kid handcuffed, why do you need the Taser?' If they did, I never heard it. And is he in jail, that cop? Nah.

"Hell, just earlier this year, in Brooklyn, cops rolled up on some black kids and shot one of them to death. Five shots in the front, four in his back. They said he was reaching for a weapon. There was a pistol on the scene. Funny, though, that witnesses on the scene not only claim the kid wasn't reaching for a weapon, but that he never had one. Yet after he was shot dead, one of the cops conveniently FOUND a gun. No prints on it."

"This isn't Brooklyn or Oakland—"

"It's not, it's the American Southwest, isn't it? You're telling me it's better in the South? There's a large portion of this country who, when they see a white sheriff nightstick-ing a black man, believes that THAT is the proper way of the world. So yeah, we could put the video up on YouTube and I could get a civil settlement at taxpayers' expense and maybe some sort of bullshit public apology, but the reality is him cracking my skull will also make him more popular than ever around here, really. They'll say, 'You go, Ted, show that uppity negro what for.'

"I'm sure Ted doesn't want the video to get out, no doubt about that, but if it does, so what? He was doing what he was elected to do, which is protect his community."

She sat there, steaming. "So what are you still doing here, then? If this is such a terribly racist place, why hang around?"

"Let me ask you a question. If it was known, with certainty, that Pedro Garcia DIDN'T murder Roger Carlson and we have our good sheriff on video killing Pedro, that WOULD be bad for his career, would it not?"

She thought about that for only an instant. "That would be bad. On digital video, killing an innocent man, very bad. I could get definite manslaughter charges against him, no matter what my boss says. I'll go federal if I have to. But I took a look at the case against Pedro, it's good, they have his prints on the murder weapon—"

"Doris Carlson doesn't think Pedro killed her husband. Nor do I. I don't think he had it in him. We clear Pedro's name and then we can let the good citizens of Bendijo know what their sheriff has done with his authority."

She looked at him, fully engaged, as if she were trying to peer into his soul. "If WE can prove Pedro's innocent, of course, but that's the tricky part, isn't it? He's dead, he can't defend himself or his innocence. How do WE do that?"

Slick liked how she said WE just then. And he thought she kind of liked it, too.

"Doris told me that Father Jose at Saint Mary's knows Pedro better than anybody, so that's one place we can start. Are you in?"

She took a moment before she answered. "I'm an officer

of the court, you understand that, right? I know you play cards for a living, maybe you think this is some kind of game or something. I'm not playing games, I'm not here for kicks and giggles, I live here and I'm interested in justice."

"Me, too. Justice for Pedro and anyone else who had their skull and kidneys caved in by an asshole in uniform just because they were the wrong color in the wrong town."

She stared at him again, and Slick basked in it. She grabbed her bag and stood.

"Okay then, let's go," she said.

Slick grinned, threw down some money and followed her out.

19

"I DON'T KNOW if I can tell you anything that I haven't already told the police," Father Jose said. He was a small, elderly man with a look of perpetual mournfulness upon his face. "It is unimaginable to me that Pedro did this. Pedro never even said a foul word, as far as I know, did not drink except to take communion and was here three, four times a week. I saw him the night before he was arrested, he came for confession."

They stood in the foyer of a small Catholic church, where it was dark and cool. Slick never cared for churches as a rule, but this one was simpler and more modest than most. A few older women saw them standing there and, at the sight of Camilla, made the sign of the cross. Slick wondered at that.

"Do you know where he went, after he left here?" Camilla asked.

"He went home, to my knowledge. Pedro rarely went out like some do. He lived in a boarding house, as I'm sure you probably know, one that caters to undocumented workers such as himself, and probably went straight home after seeing me. After he was arrested, I asked some of his roommates, men who might not talk to the police but will speak with me, and no one else was home when he got there, they'd gone out drinking and no one can confirm that he was there. He usually went to bed early, before they even came home, so it wasn't unusual. No one can verify that he was there."

"When you saw him that night, was there anything unusual about his behavior?" Slick asked.

"I'm sorry, remind me who you are and how you're involved again?"

"Jon Elder."

"I know that name. You're the man who arranged for Pedro's lawyer—"

"Yes."

"We are in your debt for that," Father Jose said, glancing at Camilla and Slick, obviously trying to figure out why the two of them were there together.

"So, Pedro's behavior that night, was it…"

"Nothing out of the ordinary. He was always smiling, always pleasant. Pedro could and should have been a priest, I think. In many ways he humbled me with his devotion."

"Why didn't he become a priest, if he was that devout?" Slick asked.

"Because he had to take care of his mother. Taking a vow of poverty would likely be fine for him, but he needed to make money to take care of her, she's elderly and sick and requires constant care back in the old country. Pedro originally came here for work because he couldn't make enough of a living in Mexico. Nearly every penny he made he sent back home for her. I don't know what's to come of her now. This is all so very tragic.

"Pedro stayed out of trouble, he was very aware of how

undocumented workers were viewed in Arizona, but there was simply more work here than anywhere else. We have fields lying fallow because no one is there to pick the vegetables, farmers selling their land because they can't harvest the crop and it lies there, rotting under the sun while people in other parts of the world go hungry.

"The undocumented workers who come here simply want the same thing everyone else wants—to put food on their table and provide for their families. Work is here and they want work. No one else wants to do this work, so they do it. They are not evil, Ms. Leon."

"I'm well aware of that, Father."

"Are you? Because that's not what I see and hear every time your boss is quoted in the paper or gives a speech. He thinks that Mexicans are 'stealing jobs' from Americans. I don't see any white people lined up to pick lettuce, do you?"

"Father, I understand—"

"I have many undocumented families in my parish, some who have been here for decades, their children were born here, others came when they were little, they know no other life or home. They can't go back, either because of what they've left behind or what they've already built here. And what they hear every day is that they are criminals, fiends who only want to sell real citizens drugs, steal from them and chop off their heads. It's all a vicious lie. That's not who they are."

Slick watched Camilla take this from the priest, obviously not happy but bearing it anyway. She nodded and moved on like a pro.

"Okay. So how can I help?"

"Help with what? Pedro is dead and your office and the papers all call him a murderer. What more do you want to do to him?"

"If he's innocent, clear his name."

"Yes, of course, I'm SURE that is what you're here for."

Slick was pretty sure that was sarcasm from the holy man. Father Jose snorted and turned away, heading up the center aisle of the church. Slick and Camilla followed him.

"Father, I assure you that is EXACTLY why I am here."

"You are here, Ms. Leon, to do what you usually do ... make your boss look like he is fair to Latinos. So he can point to you and say, 'See, it's not about skin color,' when we all know that's exactly what it is about. You are here for show."

Slick could see that Camilla was steaming and about to blow a gasket, so he interjected. "She's not here on behalf of her office or her boss, Father."

The priest stopped, turned to her. "Is this true?"

She nodded. "George doesn't know I'm here. I'm doing this on my own."

He thought about that, eyes on her. "I see. So that's why you are with Mr. Elder. I know that Pedro did not murder Roger Carlson. He spoke highly of Roger, looked up to him and thought the world of him and his wife. I cannot prove that Pedro did not do this, but I would bet my soul on it."

"Did he have any friends that we can talk to?" Camilla asked.

"He volunteered here for everything, but Pedro was very shy, did not make friends easily. I will ask around and see what I can find out, but these days my church regulars are mostly older people, not young like Pedro was. You should try where he worked, too. Some of the people he lived with worked with him."

"We don't know where that is, all we know is that he was a day laborer, but we haven't yet found out where he worked or for whom," Camilla said. "No one who hires undocumented workers will talk to us."

"He worked for Banning Construction, they are building a new Walmart by the freeway. He didn't like working for them, my impression was that he took a lot of abuse, but the money was too good for him to pass up. That is all I can tell you."

Camilla just waited. Father Jose came to an internal decision.

"I do know of one man who Pedro worked with there, his name is Sergio, you can tell him that I vouched for you. He may speak to you or he may not, I don't know. He is also undocumented and will be reluctant to expose himself. That is everything that I can tell you."

"Thank you, Father. If you think of anything else, please call me directly. Here's my cell phone number," Camilla handed him her card.

He studied it, glanced back up at her. "Are you Catholic?"

"Weren't we all, once upon a time?" she replied.

20

"THE BOARDING HOUSE Pedro lived in is now empty," Camilla said as she drove down the street. "That's the first place that was hit, all his roommates basically fled the moment word got around of his arrest."

"They didn't leave town, though, right? Just moved somewhere else."

"Yes. We don't have the names of anyone who lived there, at least, not officially. I could ask around, but I'm not the most popular person in the Latino community here, as you may have noticed."

"I did observe that, yes."

"Relations have never been great between our office and the Latino community, but the past five or six years it's been terrible. I understand why they're upset, I do. But if I quit my job, that changes nothing. I stick with it long enough, I could possibly make some real changes."

"So what happens when your boss finds out what you're snooping around the Pedro case?"

"He'll give me a verbal spanking, but that's it. He won't fire me, it'll be too embarrassing for his office. I'm the only female and Hispanic on staff."

"You knew where Pedro worked, when you asked him, you just wanted to see if the padre would tell you."

"I wanted a name. He gave us one." She made a turn, heading outside of town.

"He knows more than he's telling us."

"Probably he knows something from confession but cannot say, that's why I wanted a name. He knows somebody who knows something who won't be bound by the confessional. And now we know who that somebody is."

"Nice," Slick said, and then sat and simply enjoyed the silence between them. This should have felt awkward, she worked for the District Attorney's office, after all, she was John Q. Law personified. It shouldn't be this easy, joining up with her on this venture, but somehow it came so natural, and for her, too. He caught her glancing at him out of the corner of her eye and that pleased him. He grinned.

"What?" she finally asked.

"You're pretty smart ... for a COP," he said, but with a smile.

"A cop AND a lawyer, so I got the double hex on me."

"Yeah, how the hell did that happen?"

She didn't answer right away, just drove.

"I'm the brown daughter of Mexican born immigrants," she finally said. "My whole life, people have been telling me what I couldn't do, simply because I'm female, my last name is Leon and my skin is dark. And whenever someone tells me I CAN'T do something..."

"It makes you want to do it even more."

She glanced over, nodded. "I'm built that way. Tell me I'm never gonna be smart enough to graduate college? I'll earn a four year degree in just three. Tell me I'm too fragile for law school? I'll get into to the toughest one and graduate number one in my class. And as for why I work where I work? Because of the words 'and justice for all'. I believe in justice like Father Jose believes in God. It's not perfect, our system, but if I don't do my part to make it better, who will?"

Slick liked that, liked that a lot. Camilla pulled up to a massive construction project and parked in the lot. Workers toiled in the hot sun, laying bricks and mixing cement.

"Why do you do what you do?" she asked.

"Same reason you do."

"That's why you play cards professionally?"

"No. I play cards for fun and I do other things for money. I do what I do because I believe in karma and justice. Something ain't right here and it bothers me enough to do something about it. Like you said, if we don't, who will?"

She looked at him for a moment and then smiled before she turned the engine off.

"Who, indeed?" she said.

Slick liked that smile very much and was thankful once again for his dark cultural heritage because it hid the fact that blood was rushing to his face and he was blushing.

21

THEY APPROACHED A group of Mexican laborers sweating under the hot sun. Camilla showed a man her ID and asked him, in Spanish, if he could tell her which one of the workers was Sergio. He shook his head, put down his wheelbarrow and walked away.

The rest of the workers also put down their tools and slid away, all refusing her questions and wanting nothing to do with her. Before they all disappeared, Slick touched one of the men on the arm.

"*We're here as friends of Pedro,*" Slick said in slow Spanish. "*You recognize me? You know who I am? We're here to help him.*"

"*Pedro's dead,*" the man replied simply.

"*But he's no murderer. We want to prove that. That's why we want to talk to his friend Sergio. Please, just tell him we only want to help Pedro.*"

The man hesitated at that, as did some of his coworkers. Before the man could speak further, however, a profane bellow echoed out over the site.

"What the fuck is going on over here? What's all this standing around shit?" A construction foreman barreled over. Camilla stepped forward, her ID out.

"Camilla Leon, District Attorney's office. We're here to

talk to one of your workers on an official matter."

"Well, he's not here and you shouldn't be either. Get off my site!"

The foreman was a burly guy in his fifties with a substantial gut and sideburns. He pushed forward but Camilla stood her ground.

"You don't even know WHO we want to talk to, so how do you know he's not here?" she asked him.

"It doesn't matter who it is, he ain't here. You ain't talking to nobody on my crew," he said. He turned to the workers. "Anybody says word one to this bitch, you're done and never working for me ever again, understand?"

"Bitch?" Camilla's eyes narrowed. "I could shut this whole site down and have you arrested for obstruction."

"Go ahead, doll, do it. I'll be out by the afternoon and the charges dismissed. Shut the site down, it'll be going again by morning. Arrest this whole bunch and send 'em back to Mexico where they came from and I'll have another crew in their place faster than you can say wetback. I know who you are. I have friends who are a lot more important than you. Now, either you take your tamale-eating ass off my site or I'll have you escorted off. Randy! Tommy! Move these two out of here!"

Two big white men stepped out from behind the foreman, grinning. Camilla reached for her cell phone, furious. Slick put a hand on her arm.

"No need to call the police. The man we're looking for isn't here and it's obvious none of the men even know who he is," he told her. "Just let it go."

"Yeah, listen to your buddy Kunta Kinte and scram,"

the foreman said.

"Oh, we're not leaving yet," Slick said. "I think I want to know what goes into building a department store, so I've decided to hang around for a while, take some pictures of you all at work, do the tourist thing, you know. I bet I can catch some good images on my camera of this construction process, maybe even post it on Facebook. Of course, if you're cutting corners or breaking OSHA regulations, that'll get out, but—"

"You ain't taking pictures of nothing and you ain't spending one minute more here."

"Oh, I'm pretty sure I am," Slick said. "Free country and all that jazz."

"People get hurt at worksites like this all the time, boy. You hang around here, you're gonna get hurt," the foreman said.

"I'll take my chances, friend."

The foreman glanced at Randy and Tommy and nodded. The two men stepped forward, rolling their shoulders. Slick shot a look at the Mexican laborers, who stopped dispersing and drifted back for the show.

"This isn't necessary," Camilla said. "We can go."

"Sure we'll go," Slick said. "But when we're damn good and ready to go and not one second sooner."

Slick clocked the two white men, both of whom had meaty forearms, barrel chests and obviously spent most of their time working outdoors and lifting heavy objects. Tommy had his own name tattooed across his chest, a handlebar mustache and a shaved head. Slick would bet good money that he'd driven to work on a Harley.

Randy had long hair pulled back into a ponytail and a beard, but what Slick was most concerned about was the clip on his belt that held a work knife. If Randy pulled that knife out, this could possibly get a lot uglier than it needed to be.

"You guys get good benefits through this gig, health insurance, workman's comp?" Slick asked as they circled him. "Because if either one of you puts a hand on me, I guarantee you're going to need both."

Tommy just grinned, reached forward and grabbed Slick by the arm to drag him away. Slick reversed it, snatched Tommy's hand, stepped inside and twisted it up in a very neat jiu-jitsu move, putting Tommy on his knees and making him yelp in pain.

Randy leaped in to help his buddy, and as he did, Slick met him with a head butt right on the larger man's nose, breaking it. Randy howled and went to his knees, holding his nose in pain.

Tommy tried to punch up with his free hand. Slick responded with a kick to Tommy's groin. The air went out of the bigger man and Slick followed that up with an elbow to the back of Tommy's head that put him down and out for good.

"Okay, that's enough," Camilla said. "Stop this!"

By then Randy had come back to his senses, roared in anger and charged. He dove for a leg and attempted a tackle, but Slick stuffed it without a problem by sprawling. He reached over Randy's back, grabbed the man's belt and, with his leg hooked on the inside of the white man's knee, sat back on his ass and rolled, tossing the bigger man over his head, putting him on his back and Slick in full mount on top.

Slick punched Randy in the nose again, but before he could follow it up with more combinations, the fat foreman jumped on his back and wrenched him off. Slick twisted out of the large man's grip and, in the same motion, hooked a punch into the foreman's ample gut. Two more blows followed in quick succession, to the man's belly and jaw, knocking him down to the ground on his ass.

"I said THAT'S ENOUGH!" Camilla said. "I'm leaving."

Slick took a breath, let it out and wiped his brow. "That's okay. We're done."

Randy and Tommy were out cold. The fat foreman tried unsuccessfully to get to his feet, wobbly and wheezy.

"I'm gonna … call the cops on you…" he said, gasping.

Camilla spun on him. "And tell them WHAT? Who do you think I am? Who do you think I work for? Go ahead, call Ted and his buddies, TRY to press charges. I'm an ADA, I'll go to the judge and get it all on record as a witness! Your men attacked us, that's exactly what I'll tell the judge and jury. You think the color of your skin will get you past ME once I testify? I'm an officer of the court! I am the law! Who do you think they'll believe in the end?"

She let that hang in the air for a moment. "Maybe your friends aren't as important as you think they are, or you to them. I'm going back to my office to think about whether or not I want to toss your fat butt in jail. I'll make a decision when I'm finished being furious, which may take quite a while, but if my office gets any frivolous bullshit calls from you while I'm mulling it over, that will be the tipping point and you'll go to jail for obstruction, assault and as many other reasons as I can think of. And if they DO let you out, I'll be back again the next day, and the day after that, and the day after that and you'll find out just how big of a BITCH I can be. Do you understand me?"

Camilla waited until the man finally nodded then she turned and stalked away. Slick kneeled down next to the fat foreman, stared at him for a moment.

"And my name," Slick said, "ain't Kunte Kinte."

22

SLICK HAD TO jog a bit to catch up to Camilla as she stalked off the work site.

"Nice speech. Remind me not to get you mad at me," he said once he got close enough.

"You're too late. I'm just as angry at you as I am at them."

"Me? What for?"

She stopped and wheeled around. "Are you PROUD of the show you put on? Who do you think you were impressing with that tough guy act? Did you think that beating those men up would make me swoon? I hate that male macho bullshit!"

Slick smiled and walked on past her, toward her car.

"Two things. One, I am proud, yes. And two, it wasn't for you."

"What do you mean it wasn't for me?"

"The show, it wasn't for you. It was for them. The workers. I wanted to demonstrate we were most definitely not on the side of management. I wanted to earn their trust. And look at this, it seems to have worked."

There was a tiny slip of paper tucked under the windshield wiper of her car. Slick snatched it quick and palmed it.

"Give me that—"

"Not here. In the car, once we're out and away from prying eyes."

She didn't say anything else, just unlocked the car and climbed in. Slick smiled and followed suit. He could sense she was still steaming but working hard to readjust and adapt. He kept talking as she started the engine and pulled out of the lot.

"You got to figure that these workers have even less reason to trust you than the priest did, right? And me, while it's known that I paid for the lawyer, I'm still considered an outsider. So I wanted to make it clear, in no uncertain terms, where we stood in terms of Pedro. I did that, and so did you at the end. You tore that fat boy a new asshole, and you can bet even the workers who didn't speak English understood exactly what you were doing in no uncertain terms. It played well, and it got us something."

He held up the slip of paper and opened it. She snatched it out of his hand before he could read it. He held his tongue, letting her read it as she drove. She folded it back up and tucked it away.

"Well?"

"It says to be at Barrios, which is a Mexican bar downtown, well off the beaten track, tonight at nine."

"And that's it?"

"I try to tell you that's all it says and you'll look at me and tell me I'm lying, right? No, that's not all, it says only the black man should be there, not the *puerco*."

"Pork? Pig, ah, I get it, they still view you as a cop."

"Barrios is a rough place. I know of it, there've been

people killed there and it's been shut down three times and it always finds a way to open again. You shouldn't go there alone."

"Note says it has to be just me that shows up, right? If that's what it says, that's what we have to do to find Sergio."

"It'll be dangerous."

Slick just grinned at her. She shook her head. "Did you miss the part where I said I hate male macho bullshit?"

"Did you miss the fact that I am, at my essence, the walking personification of a bullshit macho male?"

"No, you're not, because if you were ..." she trailed off.

"If I were, what?"

"Nothing."

She nearly smiled in spite of herself and then bit it back. Slick smiled, too. He knew the last half of what she nearly said was that, if he were that, then she wouldn't like him as much as she did, and that made him very glad.

"I can't allow you to do this alone, you're a civilian. If something happens to you—"

"It won't. Or rather, if something does, it won't be from Sergio and his friends. They know something, I can feel it. They're not the problem. The biggest threat is Ted and his friends, they are probably none-too-happy that I'm poking around."

"All the more reason you need me with you—"

"It has to be me, alone. I'll call you right afterward and tell you what I found out."

"No, that's not the deal. We're in this together. You take me with you or I'll go there by myself. I have to prove to this community that I'm worth trusting at some point."

"We could lose the lead—"

"We won't. Whatever it is this Sergio knows, he wants to tell us. He just needs a reason to trust us. No one at Barrios is going to be scared off by me. They don't like me, but no one is afraid of me, anymore than that fat foreman was. To them, I'm just an empty suit, I'm window dressing and nothing more. I'm going to show them what I really stand for and in order to do that, I have to be there."

Slick thought about that and had to finally nod in agreement.

"Well, I guess that's the play, then. There's something else, and I'm ashamed to admit that I didn't even think of it until this morning," he said.

"What's that?"

"If Pedro didn't kill Roger Carlson, and nobody I know with any sense believes that he did, then the question is who did and why?"

Camilla thought about that. "He was pretty well liked in the community. I've met him many times, both he and his wife. Roger was very active in local politics and the community. His politics weren't popular, to say the least, but there isn't a man or a woman who'd spent any time with him who didn't like him, he was very genial and good-natured, could get along with anyone."

"Yet someone disliked him enough to kill him with Pedro's shovel."

"And Pedro, according to everything we've heard thus far, was basically a saint who didn't drink, swear or even spit on the sidewalk."

"He wasn't a killer, but no one's a saint."

"No one?"

"Not even saints are saints. That's my credo, I stand by it."

"Not even you?"

"Especially not me."

"Yet here you are, risking life and limb for an undocumented Mexican you just happened to sit next to at a diner and did not know."

"I'm not doing that because I'm a saint. I'm doing that because it's hard for me to let stupid racist shit go. And I'm a big believer in karma."

"Karma? Wasn't the Buddha a saint?"

"He didn't think so. He considered himself to be just a teacher and, according to a Zen Buddhist buddy of mine, often said, 'If you ever meet a man who CLAIMS to be a Buddha, kill him, because he's NOT the Buddha.' The idea being that anyone egotistical enough to make that claim is obviously disillusioned or dishonest and therefore can't be."

She smiled at that, smiled for first time since she'd gotten back into the car, and that made Slick feel all warm inside. Evidently he was forgiven.

"So why Roger Carlson, why kill him, if he was so beloved?" he asked.

"I don't know. And what's also very curious," she said, "is that if you wanted to kill Roger Carlson and get away with it, there are probably far better suspects than Pedro to pin the murder on. I know there are. Why pick a choir boy?"

"Because he's the one Mexican that they'd know would be home by himself at midnight on a Friday night?"

"They didn't know for certain he'd be home alone. A lot of them work on Saturday mornings, didn't Pedro? Wasn't he at that diner to have breakfast before work?"

"Good point. And also, how did whoever it was had to know that Roger would be roaming outside on his grounds at midnight?"

"Maybe he heard something and went out to investigate."

"Without his shotgun? Doris had one in her hand when I visited her, during the day, I can't see Roger stepping out into the night without it to see what was making noise. Standard rancher procedure when one hears a noise, ain't it?"

"I'll have his messages checked. And a conversation with Doris, I think."

"Don't have someone else check his messages, do it yourself," Slick said. "If someone did frame Pedro, they'd have to get his shovel."

"Yes. Now I am very interested to hear what this Sergio has to say." Camilla's phone buzzed a message. She checked it and sighed. "I have to get back to work. I will pick you up tonight at eight-thirty. Where are you staying?"

She pulled in and parked in front of the Indian restaurant where Slick had left his rental car.

"I'll meet you right here, this same spot, at eight-thirty sharp."

"Don't you dare try to ditch me, I will make you pay if you do."

For some reason the way she said that sent a tiny thrill through Slick's body. He grinned at her. "Wouldn't dream of it."

A thought hit him as he climbed out of her car. He stopped and leaned back inside. "Just remembered something."

"What?"

"When I visited Doris Carlson earlier today, she said, 'Maybe I'll end up selling this place after all.' I didn't think anything of it at the time, but…"

"'After all,' she said. Like it'd been under discussion before."

"Exactly. I'd thought at the time that maybe it was something she'd been thinking about since her husband's death, but the way she phrased it, it sounds like—"

"Someone had been trying to buy their land from before that and they'd turned them down. I can check that out. See you tonight."

"Can't wait."

"Jon."

She said his name. He liked that, he liked that quite a lot. "Yeah?"

"Be careful when you're … driving around town on your own. Try not to get pulled over. Stay in public areas and … just be careful. Okay?"

"You have my word on that, counselor."

"You can call me Camilla."

He smiled. "Camilla. See you tonight, Camilla."

He shut the door, not trusting himself to say anything more. He felt like a damn school kid and was fairly certain that his grin was giving his bubbling emotions away to the whole wide world. But the other thing he was pretty certain of was that, when he'd said her name out loud to her, Camilla had blushed from head to toe.

He thought about that as he went back to his car, the image of her whole body blushing lodged in his mind, and for the first time he didn't even notice the stifling Arizona heat.

23

SLICK HAD PLANNED to get into his car and go back to his room, but he spotted a familiar face inside the restaurant and stepped inside.

"How do," Navajo Joe said, his lanky frame nearly overwhelming the small table and chair he sat at. He nibbled at some bread. "Figured I'd find you here."

"Food's good, ain't it?"

"It's still hard to overcome the irony of finding myself dining at an 'Indian' restaurant, but once a fella gets past that, yeah. Have a seat. Hungry?"

"I can always eat."

Slick joined him, picked up the menu.

"Heard they dropped all the charges, letting you go. But that you ain't going."

"Yep."

"Also heard five local rednecks got tuned up pretty good outside at a roadhouse outside county lines. Every one of those rubes is gonna spend some time in hospital and sport plaster for a while. Musta been fun times. Your work?"

"Ask me no questions and I will tell you no lies."

"I know those boys, pretty sure they likely had it coming, so no complaints from me, excepting that I wish I'd been there to dish some of that out to them myself."

Slick just smiled. The waiter came and he ordered food.

"So what's your plan?" Navajo Joe asked after the waiter disappeared. "Just hang around and be a boil on Ted's ass?"

"Is that a bad thing? No, wait, I'm pretty sure that is a bad thing, probably on the very bottom of karmic totem pole. A man commits grievous sins against mankind and finds himself reborn as a boil on Ted's ass."

"Heh. You said totem pole, heh-heh."

"Feel free to reference basketball, rap music or watermelon if you want."

"Maybe later. But in the interests of your personal safety, I am keen to know what your exact plan is."

"Find out who killed Roger Carlson and why."

The food came and, as he ate, Slick recounted what he and Camilla had deduced thus far, but left out the upcoming meeting of Sergio at Barrio's later that night. Slick figured that was best kept between him and Camilla. Navajo Joe just listened as the other man ran it down for him, deep in thought.

"I knew Roger, everyone did around here," the trooper said after some consideration. "Have the same response, he had some kooky political ideas, way out there kinda stuff, but I don't know a soul who disliked him. Always had his checkbook ready, too, to donate to good causes. Same can't be said for many others. Haven't heard any whispers that someone wanted to buy his place, but even if they did, why would that be worth killing a man over? It's a fine spread, surely, one of the largest in these parts, but it's not like there's a shortage of lettuce farms."

"Or undocumented workers. He hired a bunch, didn't

he? Maybe that inflamed some of the local hate groups."

"I don't see it. You gonna kill everyone who hired un-documented workers, that's a mighty long list with many a fine upstanding citizen on it, including some in office. The powers-that-be like to demonize the undocumented and call 'em illegals, but they ain't never gonna to go so far as to criminalize those who hire them.

"They're needed for the local economy, unless we want Arizona to get out of the farming industry as a whole. Lots of unemployed white boys around here wouldn't be caught dead picking lettuce. Same ones who turn their nose up at those collecting welfare and yet collect unemployment and workman's comp for themselves."

"And jump on black and brown folks in roadhouse parking lots."

Navajo Joe laughed at that. "I have to tell ya, I've had a run-in or two with Orville, he was the really big dumb one of that group. He liked to call me Tonto, and I've often thought about doing a thunder dance on his ass a few times myself, with the badge off. Wish I coulda been there."

"Thunder dance, that's good. I'd like to see that, too."

Navajo Joe sighed and slid back in his chair. "Thing is, though, Orville and his boys, they're amateurs, you know? Just big, stupid, racist idiots looking for trouble with more time than brains on their hands."

"I noticed that about them."

"They ain't the problem. At least, they're not the biggest problem. There're others in this state who share the same viewpoint and violent tendencies as Orville who ain't amateurs, who take this race war shit serious, who are preparing for it, who are arming and training and even praying to their white god for it. Some of those fellows even work in law enforcement, I'm sad to say. Those are the ones I worry about, should they take an interest in your presence here."

"Yeah, I've heard of groups like that. Have even run into a member or two during my travels."

"They're for-certain-sure bad news." Navajo Joe stood up and stretched. "Watch your back and if you feel the need, give me a call. I don't have as much swing in these parts as I'd like, but what little I do have I'm happy to share."

"Will do and thanks."

Navajo Joe nodded and stepped away then turned back.

"Always interesting, the pictures these white folks have of their churches showing Jesus as blonde and blue-eyed, isn't it?"

"Surely is."

Navajo Joe grinned and walked out.

24

WHEN CAMILLA PULLED up to the restaurant at eight-thirty sharp, Slick was waiting outside in the shade. Even at this hour, the setting sun was still harsh. She honked at him. Slick had changed into a nice button down short sleeve shirt and khaki pants, recently purchased. He told himself he'd sweated out the other clothes, but he knew the real reason was that he wanted to look good for her.

He waited until she rolled down the window and could hear him.

"Lock it up and follow me."

She did as instructed and followed him inside the restaurant. He kept walking through the dining area and into the back, through the kitchen. The waiters and cooks all nodded and smiled at him as they passed through and out the back door.

"I think I'm their best customer," Slick said. "Certainly their most dedicated."

In the back lot an elderly Indian waiter waited with an old car, a Chevy Nova. Slick palmed a fifty into the man's hand and climbed into the driver's seat. Started it up.

Camilla just stared at the creaky old beater, eyebrow raised.

"Is this really necessary?"

"Incognito," he said.

"That's one word for it. I can think of others."

"Tell me on the way."

She sighed and climbed into the passenger seat, moving some old papers and fast food containers out of the way.

"Ghetto rental, sorry about that," Slick said. "I didn't have time to be picky."

"How is it that a waiter at a vegetarian restaurant eats at McDonalds?"

"It's a mystery to me. You'd have to put a gun to my head, and even then I might choose a bullet over a big Mac."

Slick put the car into gear and pulled out into the street, zipping fast and watching behind him in the rear view mirror.

"Doris Carlson isn't answering my calls, I left a message but if I don't hear from her, I'll drive out there tomorrow afternoon and speak with her in person," Camilla said. "I read through the police report and Doris did tell the first responders that it was pretty common for Roger to go out walking on the ranch late nearly every night. It was a habit of his ever since the loss of his son."

"So anyone watching him on a regular basis would know he'd be out to walk his grounds at some point in the evening and would only have to wait for him."

"Pretty much. I also have a friend who might know if someone was looking to buy the Carlson ranch, Del's in real estate and he knows pretty much every deal going on in town. I'll call him tomorrow, too."

"Did you say Del? That's his name? Del Martin? I met him."

"You did?"

"Yeah. He was in the diner the morning I got my head dented by Brower and Ted. He found me later on to apologize for what happened to me on behalf of the town's citizens, though he didn't feel bad enough to go officially on record on my behalf."

"Yeah, that would be Del. He's all about gestures. But he'll know if anyone's trying to buy any property. And according to the file, they checked Roger's phone for text messages, there was nothing from anyone for the last few days."

"No messages at all?"

"Yeah, I know. It's suspicious. But he and his wife lived and worked at home together, there was no reason to text each other."

"I dunno. I know a guy who would text his wife when she was in the next room."

"I'll have to ask Doris when we talk. Recent calls were few, too, and that's suspicious, Roger was definitely very social and you'd expect a lot of calls. His phone was found on him at the scene, so whoever it was took the time to erase messages, maybe?"

"And why would Pedro do that? You should still be able to track that, the deletions."

"Yes. But it's tricky because it's not my case and I have to be, well, circumspect about it. I wouldn't like it if someone else snooped on one of my cases, which is what I'm basically doing to George, so I have to be careful. But I have a very good friend who can help me with the phone without anyone knowing. I called him today and left a message. I should hear back from him soon. He always calls me back in less than twenty-four hours, no matter where he is."

"A very good friend?"

"A very good friend."

"I see. You trust him to keep his mouth shut?"

"Absolutely. He and I go way back."

"So just how far back do you and he go?"

"We grew up together."

"And he can help you retrieve deleted messages without your office elders knowing what you're doing … ah, I get it."

"You get what?"

"He works in law enforcement, but not local and probably not state. Federal, ATF, NSA, FBI, Homeland Security or…"

"FBI. How do you DO that?"

"You wouldn't go to a hacker, that ain't your style, you don't bend laws, much less break them. If it was a statie solution, you could ask Joe Stormcloud just as easily, but staties also face certain privacy issues. Feds don't, they can access phone records quick as pressing a button and it's legal, plus your guy, he's a very good friend, but he ain't around too much, ergo, he's a fed of some kind."

"Yes. FBI, based in Phoenix, but he travels a lot. And if we prove Pedro is innocent and Ted guilty of manslaughter, having Javier in on this will help at some point. Ted is sheriff, after all. None of Ted's deputies or cronies are going to help us put him in jail, and we won't be able to try him here. George can't do it, he's a friend of Ted's and there's a conflict of interest. We'll need Javier to make this work."

Slick glanced at her, computing something in his head.

"So how long?"

"How long what?"

"How long did the two of you go out? You and Javier."

"Damn your poker eyes, is nothing secret from you?"

"It's not like I can turn it on or off, it just happens."

"It was quite some time ago and it wasn't for very long, but it was long enough that I trust him. We stayed friends."

"How come?"

"How come we stayed friends?"

"Yes."

"He's a very good guy."

"If he was such a good guy, why didn't it last?"

"Is this really relevant?"

"Just of interest. Just wondering why, if he was such a good guy, you let him go."

"You're ASSUMING that I broke up with him. Maybe it was the other way around and he broke up with me."

"I'm not assuming anything, I KNOW you broke up with him. There's no way any sane straight man would break up with YOU on his own, no way, uh-uh."

She allowed herself a small smile at that.

"Okay, you're right, I broke up with him. Sometimes things don't work out. Javier is a very good guy and we had a lot in common, grew up on the same block, both children of immigrant parents from Mexico, both drawn to law. But he is very ambitious. Had I been willing to leave this city, or had he been willing to stay here, maybe it would have worked out. Maybe, maybe not, I don't know for sure. But he is all about his career. Nothing else matters to him but the job. I love my job, too, but I'm not in Javier's league in that regard. He won't even be happy being in Phoenix for much longer, he wants to go all the way to DC, be the first Hispanic Bureau Director, perhaps. I can't see myself working in Washington, or just being a DC housewife. I love my hometown, I want to stay here and I want to do what I do. So I broke it off. But we're still good friends."

They drove comfortably in silence for a few moments.

"I don't even know why I'm telling you all this," Camilla said. "If you meet him, you can't ever tell him I told you any of that. He has a lot of pride and he'd be very hurt."

"I'll bet. Mexican-American. Blue-flaming fibbie. I bet he's a fountain of that male macho bullshit you dearly love so much."

"You have no idea." Camilla shook her head and cursed affectionately in Spanish. "You and he have a lot in common. Neither of you seem able to walk away from a conflict, I mean, why do that when you can punch somebody, instead?"

"That is one of my flaws, true."

"But he is a good guy."

"Just not a GREAT one."

"He's a GREAT FBI agent."

"But not a great boyfriend."

"Well … much as it pains me to say it, yes."

Slick felt her eyes on him as he drove, and it pleased him.

"You deserve a great one," he said after a few moments.

She didn't respond at first, just stared out the window until Slick parked the old car in front of Barrios and turned the engine off.

"We all do," she said.

25

S LICK AND CAMILLA stepped inside the smoke-filled bar called Barrios, which was filled to the brim with Mexican workers, nearly all of them male, working class and drinking hard as marimba music blared loud from a jukebox.

Conversation halted when they were noticed and every eye in the establishment turned on them. The music cut off suddenly and the silence weighed on them nearly as heavily as the combined glare of hatred from the customers.

"Wow. They really DON'T like you in this town, do they?" Slick whispered to her out of the side of his mouth.

It seemed as if the entire group took a collective step in their direction then stopped when someone in the back barked out something indistinguishable in Spanish. Everyone turned and, without a word or sound, just flowed on out of the bar, through the back and through the front, gliding by Slick and Camilla without touching or looking at them. In a mere instant the bar was empty save for them, a bartender and a single solitary man sitting at a table in the back.

"So it seems that you completely disregarded my instructions, which were that you were to come alone, Mr. Elder," said the man. "No matter, I still welcome you.

Please, have a seat and join me. You also, Ms. Leon."

Slick and Camilla hesitated a moment then did as the man requested. Slick clocked him close as he sat down. Mexican, around fifty, well dressed in an expensive leisure suit with plenty of jewelry everywhere and a waxed mustache. His eyes twinkled.

"It is an unexpected pleasure to make your acquaintance, Ms. Leon. I have heard much about you."

"None of it good, I imagine."

"You'd be surprised. It is thought that, with the right positioning and advisement, you could be our first female Mexican-American District Attorney. You have brains, beauty and ambition, which is a very potent political cocktail once one learns how to mix the three together and use them properly. A nearly unstoppable combination, in fact."

Camilla was momentarily speechless, a condition she wasn't used to, Slick observed. A bartender brought over a bottle of tequila and three glasses, set them on the table and then quickly left the room. The man poured for them.

"Granted, those are the opinions from those of us in the Hispanic community who have the position and patience to take the longer view. There are those who harbor anger against you for what they think you represent in the short term. What is it, your unfortunate nickname? Dubya Dee? Short for window dressing, yes?"

"Yes."

"You are much more than that, but now that I've finally met you, I can understand how one might make such a mistake. You are a stunning woman."

"You're Sergio?" Camilla asked.

"No," said Slick. "He's not Sergio. I don't know who he is, but he's not Sergio."

"Mr. Elder is correct, I am not Sergio, but I am here on his behalf. My name is Angel and this is my establishment. Sorry for the theatrics, but I'd anticipated meeting Mr. Elder alone, and since Ms. Leon is now here I fear it necessary for her reputation that we have some privacy."

"You're Sergio's friend?" she asked.

"I did not know Sergio, but he knew of me and reached out for assistance."

"Where is he?"

"I have heard that Sergio was picked up and taken away by two men in uniform early this morning. Sadly, I fear that he won't be back."

"He was arrested? He'll be in the system and I can get him out—"

"He wasn't arrested," Slick said. "Was he?"

"No. Your friend is correct, he was not arrested. Just picked up."

"But … if he wasn't arrested, where did they take him—"

"To some remote spot in the desert where, I imagine, they forced him to dig his own grave before shooting him. Likely they flipped a coin afterward and whoever lost had to bury the poor fellow once he was dead."

"How do you know this?"

"I don't know for certain, I can only speculate. But my speculation is based on what I've observed from the position I've held in my community for the past thirty years. There are many, many bodies buried in the deep of the desert."

Camilla didn't care for such speculation and it showed on her face. "You know because you've buried some of them there yourself," she said.

"No." Angel just smiled at that. "You have the wrong idea of me. I'm just a simple businessman."

"Every drug dealer and gang member ever prosecuted has made that very same claim. You're connected, somehow, and—"

"I am my own man, I assure you. I belong to no gang or cartel, nor do I traffic in drugs or women, I won't have it. I prefer ordinary sins myself, wine, tequila ... understandable weaknesses of the flesh. I own a place such as this one in many a town in this state and the next, each with the same name, Barrios. That is where my income is derived, from the honest business of selling spirits to the poor souls in need of them. But you are correct in that this is not all that I do.

"And to explain further I must place myself in your confidence, Ms. Leon. If you are uncomfortable with this, I ask that you leave us so that we can continue without you."

"I'm staying right here and if you confess to a crime, any crime, then I'm sworn by my oath of office to—"

"He hasn't," Slick said. "At least, not one that you'd be concerned with. No drugs, no sex trafficking, no gang violence. That's not who he is."

"And how do you know, have you met him before?" she demanded.

"No, but I've met many a man like him before. He's basically a Bumpy."

"Bumpy?"

"Ah, Mr. Elder, you flatter me," Angel laughed. "Though to be precise, Bumpy Johnson, while a hero of Harlem of the twenties, was eventually convicted of drug dealing multiple times later in his life. I have little patience for drugs myself, especially since I am Mexican. I am a legal resident of Arizona and a naturalized citizen of this country, of course, but in my heart and soul I am Mexican and hate with every fiber of my being what drugs have done to my culture."

Camilla thought about that for a moment then nodded. "Okay, fine. Go on."

Angel took a drink. "Very well, Ms. Leon. As you are of no doubt well aware, there are significant numbers of undocumented Mexicans throughout the southwest. Many have been here for decades and are good members of society, they work hard. However, while they contribute, they are not afforded the protections of society.

"A man's house is robbed, and he thinks he may even know who did it. But he has no papers, what is he to do about it? An undocumented maid is raped, who can she go to for help? The police? Who can any of them go to for justice, since they are denied it from the country in which they work and pour their money and sweat and blood into? Who can they go to for help when they need it?"

"You," Slick said.

"Yes. Me. Sometimes I mediate between parties with grievances, sometimes I do more and sometimes there is nothing that I can do. But I am the man these people come to in times of injustice. I do what I can, which inside the community of the undocumented can be considerable, but outside the community, not so much. I am, after all, still considered an immigrant in the eyes of the, ah … *natives* … of this land. It was not my ambition, this small role I play, but when destiny rings, only the foolish ignore the call."

Angel poured another drink into his glass. "Which brings us to Pedro Garcia and his good friend Sergio."

"You knew Pedro?"

"No, Pedro was not the kind of man to be found in one of my establishments. I know of him only because of the crime he is accused of committing. I have no idea who killed Roger Carlson. I do not spend much time in this county, my interests span this state and the next, after all. Sergio knows of my reputation and reached out to me, we spoke briefly on the phone. He was scared, with what happened to his friend, and for other reasons. It was well known he was Pedro's only confidant, next to the priest. Very well known.

"Did you know that Sergio was supposed to be at the diner with Pedro when he was arrested? He overslept and just missed being arrested himself. Once he heard, he hid out for as long as he could, trying to arrange for passage back to Mexico. Sadly, I was too late to help him with that."

Slick thought about that, thought about how Ted had just ordered the arrest of the two men with Pedro in the diner without hesitation.

"What did Sergio say?"

"Two very important things. Firstly, Roger Carlson was murdered at midnight on Friday night, with Pedro's work shovel, which was left on the scene, yes?"

"Yes. And Pedro was home alone, with no one who could verify—"

"Except that he wasn't, Ms. Leon."

"I'm sorry."

"He wasn't home, that's what Sergio told me. Pedro was not at home."

"But that doesn't get him off, in fact, that means he had the opportunity—"

"Where was he?" Slick asked. "Why wasn't he home?"

"Why is any man … not at home … on a Friday night?" Angel asked.

Camilla glanced at Slick, confused. Slick got it and nodded.

"A woman."

"Yes, of course."

Camilla sat up straighter. "But Pedro was religious, he didn't drink, didn't fool around—"

"All true," Angel said. "But even the pious are not immune to falling in love. Even priests have been known to do so. Sometimes even with a woman."

"Pedro was in love and meeting with her that night," Slick said. "Which means we have someone who can vouch for his whereabouts. Do you know who she is?"

"I have no idea, nor did Sergio. He just knew his friend was in love, deeply in love for the first time in his life, and that's why Sergio was sick to his soul for what had happened and the role that he played in it."

"Role? What role?" Camilla asked.

"Oh no. He didn't," Slick said.

"Yes, I'm afraid he did."

"What are you two talking about?"

Slick stared at Angel, working it out in his mind. "Sergio

snagged Pedro's shovel for whoever it was that killed Roger. It had always bothered me, if someone set him up, they had to get his shovel to use and plant at the scene. Sergio supplied the shovel. That's what he told you."

"Is this true?" Camilla asked. "Sergio told you this?"

Angel just smiled. "The pious go to the priest when they need to unburden their souls. The rest go to their bartender. Yes. He needed money and someone offered him a few quick dollars just to procure his roommate's shovel. He didn't ask why and he was devastated when he found out what had been done with it."

"And whoever it was had planned for him to be arrested at the same time as Pedro," Slick said. "He wouldn't have been in any position to say anything once he was in jail."

"True, if he even survived his arrest."

"Who paid him to get the shovel?" Camilla asked.

"He did not say, nor do I have a clue as to who it was. He was sobbing when we spoke on the phone. We were to meet today, when I arrived back in town, and I'd hoped to find out more as I arranged to get him back to Mexico. But it was not to be, I am sorry to say. Policemen found him and you know how that ended up."

"Hold on, that's the second time you've made that claim and I want to know more. How do you know it was two men in uniform who picked him up?" Camilla asked.

"I know it the way I know anything, through my network."

"Did someone SEE them take Sergio, are they willing to go on record—"

"Go on record, my people? No, no." Angel laughed.

"Testify against the police, in this town? I think not."

"Do they have the names of these officers?"

"No, no names. I am sorry."

"But that's proof of nothing, it's simply hearsay at best, Sergio could have just easily gone back to Mexico, he could have—"

"And I wish that he had. You don't understand, even if Sergio was still alive, which I assure you he is not, he wouldn't testify as to what he'd done or knew. No."

"You're telling me he was murdered by two policemen, but offer no proof—"

"I'm not here to offer proof, only information. I was asked to pass it along, and I honored that request. You can judge the veracity of the information for yourselves. But I'm certain that Mr. Elder has no problem believing the tale."

"No," Slick said. "I do not."

"But if Sergio was murdered and we don't have his body, how can we—"

"Sergio is not the issue, Pedro is," Slick said. "The girl is. We prove Pedro is innocent, not only do we fuck Ted over, we then force them to reopen Roger's case, too, which will result in justice for Roger and for Sergio. We focus on the girl."

Camilla seethed for a moment, stifled by the enormity of what she'd heard. Slick watched her as she stuffed it all back inside and put her game face back on. "Do you have any idea who the girl is?"

"None," Angel said. "I will make some inquiries, of course. If I find out anything, I will contact you right away. Now, if you don't mind, in light of Sergio's sudden demise, I am leaving the area tonight, without delay."

Angel stood up.

"You are? Why?" Camilla asked.

"Because I can be detained and taken out to the desert to dig a hole just as easily as anyone. I may be a naturalized citizen, but I'm still a brown person. And to be honest, I'm a facilitator, not a fighter. I leave those battles to others, which is the only reason I've lived as long as I have.

"I especially avoid conflict with white people whenever I can. In most circumstances I would have stayed out of this, but in addition to Sergio's request, I have found myself in Mr. Elder's debt, and it's my belief that all debts must be paid."

"Debt? You said you didn't know him," Camilla asked Slick.

"I don't, I've never met him before," he replied.

"We haven't, but we do have a mutual friend," Angel said. "His name is Esteban and he has a younger sister who was recently the victim of violence. You were of considerable assistance in their circumstances and for that you have my gratitude."

Slick sat up straight as he got that. Angel was the man who arranged for the disposal of Stutz, evidently he'd interceded with the broker and thus was the sole reason for Slick's presence in Arizona.

"What is he talking about?" Camilla asked. "I thought you were a professional poker player?"

Slick didn't answer right away, taken aback. Thankfully Angel spoke up.

"We are, none of us, only just what we get paid for, but

also for what we do. I make my living pouring drinks, but I do much more than that, sometimes for money, sometimes for more complicated reasons. You make your living as a lawyer and an officer of the court, Ms. Leon, but I've heard there is much more to you than meets the eye, however pleasing on the eyes you may be.

"And as for Mr. Elder, while it's true that he makes his money at the card table, he has other, even more apprecia-ble, talents."

Slick felt her gaze on him and didn't look back.

Angel held out his hand to Slick. They shook.

"Mr. Elder, I hope this information was of assistance to you. If you decide to stay in town, which is seems you have, please use caution. Extreme caution, yes?"

"I will. And, please, my friends call me Slick."

"Then it will be my honor to call you such. Ms. Leon, I imagine this will be our only meeting in person and I want you to know it was a distinct pleasure."

"Thank you, but I still don't trust you," she said as she shook his hand.

"What was it a wise man once said?" Angel asked. "Trust, then verify."

26

SLICK FELT CAMILLA'S anger as a palatable presence as he guided the old Nova away from the bar. He wasn't quite sure what she was angry about, but the anger was heavy in the air between them. He just kept quiet and drove. Finally she spoke.

"What did he mean, he OWED you? What did you do for him?"

"For him? Nothing. But it seems I once helped out a friend of his."

"What did you do?"

"A favor."

"For this … Esteban and his little sister, who was a victim of violence? What happened to her? And you helped them? How? What did you do?"

"Like I said, it was a favor, the nature of which is just between me and them."

She snorted. "Uh-huh. You think you're a priest now?"

"Uh, hell no."

"And you're not a lawyer, there's no privilege to violate. So answer the question."

"Just some kids in trouble. I can't really say any more than that. Kids in a jam and I helped them out. I do that from time to time, get involved in small local dramas. I'm weak like that." He smiled at her but it didn't really thaw her out. "As I said, sometimes it's hard for me to let certain things go. That's my fatal flaw."

"What are these other 'appreciable talents' of yours?"

"I play a mean game of Scrabble."

"I don't appreciate your jokes right now."

"That's one of my other appreciable talents."

"I'm being serious."

"Me, too."

She whipped her eyes front and steamed, cursing under her breath in Spanish.

"What are you so pissed off about? Do we or don't we know a LOT more than we did this morning?" Slick asked.

"It's all hearsay and conjecture."

"Like every case you work doesn't start off exactly like that. Conjecture is a tool of your trade and so is hearsay."

"Don't tell me what my job is."

"So what's your beef? And not the one you have with me. What's your beef with Angel's story, what are you bumping up against?"

She didn't answer right away, just sat and burned. Finally she turned to him.

"I just cannot believe that two of our uniformed officers picked up a man, drove him out to the desert and murdered him, I can't believe that."

"Why is that so hard to believe?"

"They're officers of the law, not murderers!"

"Officers of the law, deputies, who told me when I was in custody that they were gonna beat me to death if I didn't confess to a crime I did not commit."

"That's what they SAID. That doesn't mean they would have followed through."

"Oh, COME ON!"

"I believe you were abused, I have no trouble with that, but they were simply trying to intimidate you into—"

"No trouble believing they were beating my ass but not gonna go all the way and kill my ass, that's what you're saying?"

"I can believe that Ted and his cronies bend the law, lean on suspects, tailor testimony to fit what they think they know and can prove, yes. That happens in every police department in every major city. I don't condone it, but it happens, in ours especially. I believe that they have a significant racial bias, absolutely, and use that accordingly against non-whites and illegals. I believe that they've committed police brutality as a result of that bias.

"What I don't believe is that there is some murderous conspiracy afoot and they're taking people out to the desert and executing them. Ted is bigoted and dumb, but that's it. He's not some criminal mastermind. He's guilty of manslaughter and terminal stupidity. But I don't for a second think any of this was premeditated by him or his department. I work with these people! They're far from perfect but I don't ... I can't ... buy this premise. I can't. I think this 'Angel' character is telling us stories for his own purposes and I don't trust him."

"You've had suspects die in custody?"

"Sure, but—"

"And you don't think it was ever intentional?"

"No, violent offenders get arrested and sometimes when

they resist... I'm not condoning, it's wrong but happens, happens in every city in America—"

"I'm talking about THIS city, this department, this sheriff. You believe he'll beat suspects, force confessions from innocent people, fabricate evidence—"

"I believe he's CAPABLE of that, I don't have solid proof that he's actually done any of that. If I did, I'd be all over him in a second—"

"You believe he's capable of THAT, but not outright murder?"

"No. No, I just ... I can't imagine it."

"Yet what other explanation is there? Why would Angel lie about this, what does he have to gain from this? All he's done is expose himself for no real reason and invite heat upon himself for talking to you or me about it. Why would he do that?"

"I don't know. And that's what makes me suspicious."

Slick shook his head and cooked up a real beauty of a retort in his head, but before he could let it loose upon her a black SUV appeared out of nowhere and sideswiped the Nova, nearly putting it into a storefront.

Camilla screamed and Slick wrestled with the steering wheel as the SUV rammed the old car again, nearly pushing it into a truck parked nearby.

Slick slammed on the brakes. The SUV shot past them on the deserted city street. It braked hard and spun around three hundred and sixty degrees to a stop, facing them. The windows were tinted so they couldn't see inside. The license plates had been removed, too. The SUV raced its engine and jolted forward at them.

"Buckle up," Slick said and stomped on the accelerator. The Nova jolted forward and Slick cranked on the steering wheel, turning down a side street. The SUV slid around the turn close behind, ramming the rear bumper. Camilla screamed again.

Slick grappled with the wheel, struggling to keep the old car on the road as the SUV rammed them again and again. It was clear that whoever was driving it was trying to put them into a wall. Slick had the pedal all the way to the floor but the old car was pushed to its very limit as it was.

He reached the end of the block and cranked another turn, SUV right behind him. A big crash as the larger vehicle rammed their rear wheel. They wouldn't be able to take many of those. Slick looked around quick as they roared down the street. It was an old business district, dying and dark, many of the shops closed for the night or simply closed for good. Sooner or later the SUV was going to total the Nova and likely them as well, once it started ramming it wouldn't stop until there was nothing left but a stain.

Slick had an idea. "Hang on!"

The SUV zoomed up parallel to them and bashed the right front wheel. Slick reached down and yanked up the emergency brake, putting the old car into an extended spin. Camilla braced her arms on the dash as they spun around twice and the SUV again shot past them. It skidded to a stop, turned around and roared back.

Slick threw the Nova into reverse and backed away as fast as he could get the car to go. The SUV bore down on them, a head-on collision imminent. As the last moment, Slick spun the steering wheel and drove the Nova backwards into a narrow alley between two old buildings. Sparks flew as the sides of the old car scraped the alley walls.

The SUV stopped at the alley entrance, too wide and large to enter the narrow space between the buildings. Slick kept going until the exited out the other side of the alley, spun the wheel again and sped off down the road, away from the SUV and danger.

Now that they were away and clear, Slick chuckled.

"What's so funny?" Camilla demanded.

"It looks like I just bought a shitty beat up car from a waiter."

Camilla let out a deep breath, her hands shaking.

"You okay?" he asked.

"No! Someone just tried to kill us!"

"You sure they weren't just trying to intimidate our ass, they actually INTENDED to kill us?"

"That's not funny!"

Camilla pulled absently at her hair, her whole body shaking now. Slick softened.

"It's okay, we got distance on them now. We're all right."

"We are NOT all right, someone tried to kill us! How can you be so calm?"

Slick shrugged. "I guess I'm just used to it."

27

SLICK PARKED ON a dark street a few blocks away from the organic restaurant where Camilla had left her car. He didn't know if they'd been followed from when they left in the Nova or they'd just had Barrios staked out, but either way it was best to be cautious. He left the old junker where it was and slipped into the shadows of a nearby storefront. Camilla started to get out but stopped when Slick held up his hand and clocked the nearby streets carefully. Finally he nodded and she joined him on the sidewalk.

They huddled close to the restaurant and Slick stopped them again at a corner, leaning around it to see what there was to see. He took in everything, her car, and the restaurant, which was just closing up, it all seemed normal, a slow, quiet and dark weeknight.

"Let me have your car keys," he said.

"Why?"

"I want to check it out."

"Is this really necessary?"

"You asked me that before, remember?"

She handed him the keys without a word. Slick glided over to the car, unlocked it and, with his pocket flashlight, checked the entire vehicle, inside and out, engine and underneath. He stood up and dusted his hands off, beckoning her over. She went, holding her purse tight against her body. Slick noticed her hands still shook and she was barely holding it together.

"All clear. You okay?"

"I'm fine."

"You sure? You don't look fine."

She swallowed and shook her head, flipping her hair back out of her eyes in a manner that momentarily distracted Slick from the purpose at hand. He focused.

"We're okay now. I promise you," he said. "And it's normal to be scared."

"I notice that you're not."

"That's just practice."

"You've had practice with someone trying to run you off the road?"

"In a fashion, yeah."

"You're not really a card player, are you?"

"Well, I also play cards."

"I was screaming like a girl."

"You are, in fact, female. I told you, it's normal. And men will do that, too, under the same circumstances."

"You didn't."

"I have in the past. No one is a saint."

She didn't say anything more, not wanting to get in her car and leave him, just stood there, rubbing her arms as if she were cold. Slick wanted to hold her but knew instinctively that would be a big mistake on his part. He waited for her to get her polarity back. She took a deep breath, let it out slowly and nodded.

"You got somewhere you can stay?" he asked.

"Stay? You mean other than my own home?"

"Yeah, that's exactly what I mean."

"But why would ... you can't be serious."

"We're fine now, but we're not out of the woods yet. Whoever is behind this is serious."

"I ... I need to call my boss, George."

"You really think that's a good idea?"

"Yes. I've worked with him for ten years. I know him. He's part of the old boy political network, yes, but he'll help me." She dug into her purse for her phone. She felt his weighted stare just as she got her hand on it.

"What?" she asked.

"There was no one on my tail, I wasn't followed here and we weren't followed after we left here together. Yet they were there. I think they're tracking you somehow."

"Tracking me? How?"

"There are lots of ways. Your phone for one."

"I didn't bring my work phone. This is my personal—"

"It can be tracked. Takes less than a minute to do that to your phone. That's how they knew where we were."

"This is ridiculous. My phone? I don't believe it. Whoever this is, they can't be that sophisticated. This is all just—"

"Which means whoever it is could show up here at any moment. Give it to me."

"No, I'm not giving you my phone!"

"You'll get it back, fork it over."

She did so, reluctantly. He checked out the apps. It was a smart phone, so he couldn't just flip it open. He powered it off.

"Until I can get this checked, consider it bugged. Depending on what they used, even powered off they can track it. I'll reach out to a friend tomorrow, and—"

Slick stopped when he realized what he just said.

"What is it?"

"Friend. Remember what Angel said? When they need to confess, the pious go to their priests, everyone else goes to their bartender."

"And?"

"And Sergio wasn't Pedro's ONLY confidant."

She blinked as it hit her. "Father Jose, we'd better—"

"We'll take your car. Let me drive. And leave your phone at the restaurant."

28

S LICK DROVE FAST and furiously for the church, which was on the other side of town. Camilla didn't say anything, just held on, feeling vulnerable without her phone.

"He knows, he definitely knows who she is. That's why he directed us to Sergio. Because he knew Sergio would tell us that Pedro was involved with a girl."

"If it came out in confession, he's bound against sharing any of that—"

"Right, but he can point us in the right direction without violating his vow. He was hinting at that, remember? He definitely knows who she is, which makes both Father Jose and she a threat to Ted and his buddies. She goes on record, testifies that she was with Pedro the night of Roger's murder and…"

"Ted is guilty of manslaughter."

"Boom! More, if he set it up that way."

"I still don't buy that … but … we still don't know WHY, why Roger was murdered, why HIM, why Pedro was set up for it, why… I need my phone! Do you have a phone?"

Slick pulled a smart phone out of his pocket, tossed it to her. "It's prepaid."

She turned it on. "She's probably undocumented like Pedro, which means it'll be difficult to get her to testify—"

"And even more difficult to get a jury of citizens to take her word over Ted's. But one step at a time. We have to find her first, and I bet she's still around, the way the priest was acting."

Camilla tapped away at the phone. "It still doesn't make sense, to me. Roger, Pedro … Ted. Someone set Pedro up, we know that, but that's definitely not Ted's style, too much thought involved. I can see him framing the wrong guy out of pure bigoted laziness, and when it looked bad for him, covering it up, but paying Sergio beforehand for the shovel in order to… Why do that? It's crazy."

"Who are you texting?"

"My friend Javier. And sooner or later, I have to talk to George. If there IS some sort of a murderous conspiracy that involves Ted's deputies, which I'm still not certain of, we'll need George and Javier both. I can't handle it on my own."

"Wait until we talk to Father Jose before you call your boss."

"I'm telling you, George was also friends with Roger."

Slick pulled up to the church and parked quickly. "Wait here."

"No. Don't even think of leaving me behind, we are in this together."

She hopped out after him and he decided not to argue.

"His living quarters are behind the church," she said.

They cut around behind the church toward the lit front door of the living quarters. Slick pounded on the door. No answer at first and he pounded again. A light came on inside and steps approached.

"Father, it's me, Camilla Leon, please let us in!"

Father Jose cracked the door open, eyes wide. "What is the meaning of this?"

Slick pushed past him and on inside as Camilla explained how their night had gone thus far. The priest's eyes only got wider upon hearing about Angel and the SUV attack. Slick shut the door and turned off the outside lights. Father Jose lived in a small, humble attached house with well-used furniture.

Slick took a spot by a window, staring outside into the night. When she finished, Father Jose lowered his head, crossed himself and muttered a prayer.

"Pedro met with someone the night before he was arrested. He was in love. You knew this. You know who she is," Slick asked.

"Yes."

"Who is she?"

"I am sorry, but I cannot say—"

"Bullshit."

"I cannot break the sanctity of the confessional, it's a mortal sin. That's why I sent you to Sergio, so he could tell you—"

"Sergio's dead, Father."

"What? How did … what—"

"Turn the lights out, now," Slick said, holding a finger up. Father Jose did as he was told and turned everything off. They stood there in the shadows, silent.

"What is it?" Camilla whispered.

"Vehicle just pulled up front. SUV. Tinted windows."

"Let me go out and see who it is," Father Jose said.

"The only other person who knew what you know about Pedro is dead, Father. So, no, I don't think that's a good idea."

Slick parted a curtain and checked the yard. He saw men dressed in black approach the living quarters. It was too dark to see who they were, but they walked without fear or hesitation.

"Do you have a back door?"

"No, we have to go through the church—"

"Then let's do it. And leave the lights off."

Father Jose led them through a far door that took them into the back passages of the humble church, shuffling quietly in the darkness. Someone hammered on the door of Father Jose's attached house. They heard the front door being kicked open.

Inside the church, Slick took point position and quietly guided them toward the front. Just as they reached the doors of the church, however, the handles turned, slowly.

Slick waved everyone back toward the sides, where the curtains hung. He quickly realized that they needed a better place to hide and motioned everyone to follow him. The three of them hit the floor on all fours and crawled under the pews, one person per pew. They stayed there, holding their breath.

Someone stepped through the front door of the church. They heard his boots as they clicked on the floor of the center aisle. Slick watched the boots as they moved carefully and methodically. Camilla's car was parked outside, so whoever it was knew they were there. Slick heard dishes breaking and other crashing noises coming from the attached home. Someone was trashing Father Jose's place while this man searched in here. This was going to get ugly quick, Slick thought, but he didn't have any ideas about how to improve their situation. He was unarmed.

The black boots stopped in the center of the aisle. Turned and walked down a row of pews, taking his time. Got to the end, turned, and walked down the next row of pews. Followed that slowly until he came to the end then turned.

The next row of pews was where Camilla was hiding, under the bench. She watched, her eyes wide, as the boots clicked closer and closer. They stopped right next to her and waited. Camilla put her hands to her mouth, not daring to breathe.

Radio static blared fast and furious, shattering the silence like cheap glass. The man in the boots turned it off quickly, but it seemed to decide something for him. He turned and walked fast up the row, made a turn and headed out the front door of the church. Slick, Father Jose and Camilla watched the boots go.

Slick caught her eye and she nodded.

Those were standard deputy boots the man had been wearing. In New York City, where Slick lived, cops wore thick black shoes but here in the southwest, they all wore boots. Those were cop boots. And the static noise they'd heard had come from a police radio, calling the man and his friends away somewhere else.

29

"**Y**OU'RE SURE YOU'RE okay?" Javier asked Camilla after he hugged her again.

He'd asked that same question at least five times upon entering, not even paying attention to anyone else in the diner. Not that Slick could blame him for that. Camilla drew most men's attention without effort, even after a night without sleep. "I want to hear everything, but I gotta know that you're all right," Javier said.

"I'm fine, honest. It was scary but I'm okay."

He finally turned his attention to everyone else.

"Joe Stormcloud, good to see you again," he said to the big trooper.

"And you, too, Javier. Phoenix keeping you busy?"

"Oh yeah. You have no idea. You must be Father Jose," Javier said and switched to Spanish, chatting with the priest too fast for Slick's sleep-deprived brain to translate.

The fibbie was about an inch or so under six foot, but a weightlifter so he came off a lot bigger, arms and shoulders stretched tight against his suit jacket, which looked like it was sprayed on. He probably accidentally ripped the pits out on his jackets at least once every other month, even if he got them specially fitted. He was intense, too, looked everyone in the eye a bit longer than was the norm, but it was in keeping with the other feds Slick had met and known over the years. They stared everyone in the eye as if they were interrogating them. Javier finished chatting with the priest and turned to him.

"Special Agent Javier Rivera, pleased to meet you."

"Jon Elder."

Slick shook hands with him and immediately regretted it. Javier was one of those who liked to try to break you with his handshake, something Slick was never fond of but unavoidable among ambitious types, especially in law enforcement. Card players didn't often shake hands, just tapped the table felt as a sign of mutual respect. In Asia everyone bowed. Slick preferred both to offering his fingers up for sacrifice.

"You're the poker pro, right?" Javier said when he finally took pity on Slick's hand and released it.

"Yep. Do you know Special Agent Matthew Louden? He's a friend of mine."

"Never heard of him. Where was he based?"

"Jersey, he retired ten years ago. Former interrogator."

"Before my time and the wrong coast."

Javier clocked him up and down, not missing much at all. Slick could tell that this fed was smart, stubborn as a bull and driven with a big capital 'D'.

The night before, after the intruders had left, they'd waited under the pews for a long time until finally Slick crawled out and assessed the situation. Either the men searching for them had come to the conclusion that Slick and company had left on foot beforehand, or they'd been called away to another scene, most likely the latter, given the radio call. Regardless, Slick had an opening and took advantage, slipping his charges out of the church and into Camilla's car.

He then called Navajo Joe, who met them at an all night diner around two in the morning and sat with them until Camilla's FBI friend Javier showed up four hours later. He'd driven half the night but looked none the worse for it, eyes wide open and nostrils flaring for a fight. And it was clear from his posture and how he looked at her that he still had a thing for Camilla. This was something that Slick could readily empathize with. It had to be hard to remain emotionally removed from her once one got involved.

"Now that Javier's here, if you folks don't mind, I'd best be on my way," Navajo Joe said. "I'm on duty in less than an hour."

"Appreciate you rolling out of bed in the middle of the night to lend a hand, Joe," Slick said. "I owe you."

"Hell, it weren't like I was doing anything important in there all by my lonesome. Can I expect that you're leaving town now?"

Slick just shrugged and Navajo Joe nodded. "Thought as much. Call if you need me, and watch your back. Thumper'll be pissed at me if misfortune finds you."

"Will do."

"Joe." Camilla gave him a hug. "Thank you."

"Easy now, my people aren't comfortable with physical expressions of affection, as you know. We don't even like shaking hands."

Navajo Joe tipped his hat to everyone and strolled out. Javier slid into the diner booth, which was a corner table with enough distance from the other customers to give them a modicum of privacy. The agent ordered scrambled eggs, grits, pancakes and a pot of coffee from the waitress. After she left, he fixed his eye on everyone else at the table.

"All right, I know the ESPN highlights but I want you to tell me the whole story, everything, from beginning to end, leave nothing out. Camilla, you first."

Camilla ran the whole thing down in order, Roger's murder, Pedro's arrest, Slick's involvement, Father Jose and the meeting with Angel, pausing only when the waitress brought food. Javier followed closely as he dug into his food, interrupting only to ask short clarifying questions. Slick had to look away when Javier ate the sausage, the smell alone was hard enough on him, let alone watching it go down.

When she reached the end of her version, Javier leaned back and, to his credit, thought hard about what he'd just heard. He turned his attention to the priest.

"Anything to add, Father?"

"No, that seems to be everything."

"It's true that Pedro was involved with a woman?"

Father Jose nodded.

"Who is she?"

"I cannot say, I'm sorry. It was revealed to me in confession. I cannot reveal it."

"Did you know Pedro was seeing her that night?"

"I did not, I was under the impression he was going straight home," Father Jose hesitated. He wanted to say more, Slick could tell. He knew something important. Javier sensed it, too, and pushed.

"But if you know something that clears him, or you

know of a crime, you—"

"I can't break my vow, I am so sorry."

"So you know who she is but you can't identify her for us, nor can you confirm Pedro was with her that night?"

Father Jose nodded. Javier rolled his eyes and sighed. He glanced at Slick. "Anything to add to that?"

"Nope."

"You have a digital video of Pedro's arrest and your assault, yes or no?"

"Yes."

"Can I see it?"

"I can send it to you, if need be."

"Oh yeah, mark that down as a definite need-be." Javier poured himself more coffee. "Okay, we got problems. Item one, unless you can prove definitively that Pedro did not murder Roger Carlson, you're absolutely right in that there's not much you can do. I'll have to watch the video, we can talk to the AG about civil rights violation, but Carlson was murdered with Pedro's fucking shovel, I don't have to tell you how that looks. Lots of judges and juries don't really have an issue with law enforcement braining a murderer. And in the eyes of most folks, that's who Pedro is.

"There's a girl who may or may not give Pedro an alibi for that night, but you don't know who she is and the priest can't tell us. Another friend of Pedro's, this ... Sergio ... he knew Pedro was with her that night, but he's gone and, according to a local gangster, Angel Martinez, was taken away by two cops and murdered. No proof that he didn't just run on his own or that Angel didn't do him himself. It could all be bullshit. I know who Angel is, by the way. I'd err on the side of bullshit where he's concerned."

"Except that—"

"I know, I know, except that someone tried to run your car off the road. But that could have just as easily been someone working for Angel. Then you go to Father Jose's place and while you're there somebody busts in and wrecks the place. And, though you didn't get a good look at anything but their shoes, you're sure that they were cops."

"We're sure," Slick said. "Cop boots."

Javier glanced at Camilla, who nodded.

"Okay, well. Here's what we know, here's what we don't know and here's what we can prove," Javier said. "We know somebody killed Roger Carlson with Pedro's shovel. We know someone's trying to hassle you, tried to run you off the road. What we don't know is who or why. And what we can prove? Nothing. Zero. Zippity do-dah. And I don't see it getting any better, even if you DO find this girl. Because, well, it seems pretty damn clear to me that Pedro did kill Roger Carlson."

Camilla started to speak but Javier held up his hand. "Hold on, babe, this is the agent talking, it's the suit here, it's not me. Personally, the fact that someone tried to hurt YOU makes me freakin' homicidal, but that is my professional assessment, as I see it. You think it's deputies behind all of this, but you didn't really see who it was and, other than Ted being his usual asshole self, you can't really prove for certain sure he's sicced his dogs on you BECAUSE of Roger Carlson. I don't see a conspiracy here, at least not the one that you're talking about. There's another possibility, though."

"What do you mean?" Camilla asked.

"Him." Javier pointed at Slick.

"What do you mean 'him', how does—"

"He's got a video of Ted assaulting him and beating another man to death. That's a large civil suit just waiting to happen, and you gotta know that Ted knows that. Ted's stupid, but he ain't dumb. He's aiming for higher office. What's the common denominator in these threats and intimidations? Him." Javier turned to Slick. "You. They've only happened to YOU. Let me guess, even before last night there have already been a few attempts to scare you off, right? Probably a couple of unnecessary traffic stops, some local trash hassling you, all that jazz."

Slick didn't say anything, just raised an eyebrow.

"Yeah, that's what I figured. I did grow up here after all, I know how it works with these crazy white folks. They've hinted to you that it's a question of personal health for you to scat. But that didn't work, because you're a tough guy, clearly, and so next they send someone to bump you a bit, turn up the heat. That was last night. Has nothing to do with Carlson or Camilla. It's YOU they're after, my man."

"But they showed up at Father Jose's church—" Camilla began.

"Nobody showed up until HE did. Maybe they were following him."

"Nobody followed me," Slick said.

"Come on, sport, you think you're that good?"

"Yeah, I do, actually."

Javier just smiled. "Nobody's that good. Nobody."

"If it was Jon they were after, why wreck Father Jose's

church quarters, then?" Camilla asked.

"Why not? They're local asshole cops, they don't really know what they're doing. They're just protecting their boss and trashing some Latino's home means nothing to rednecks like them. Even a church. Look, let's not pretend these homegrown white boys don't shit on brown people every chance they get. And that's ME talking, not the agent, not the suit."

"And Angel—"

"Angel Martinez has been under indictment multiple times. Nothing's ever stuck, at least not yet, but make no mistake, he's no good guy here. He's lying for his own benefit, mainly to cause trouble for Ted, who's a pain in his ass. Think about it."

Slick watched Father Jose and Camilla consider it all.

"Listen," Javier said, "I've never liked Ted, he's a redneck racist and I'm sure watching the video of him nightsticking Pedro isn't going to do anything but make me want to kick his ass up and down the street. But I don't see him being complicit in the murder of Roger Carlson, I just don't.

"I see him trying to cover up his own foul-up for hitting Pedro too hard and beating the hell out of this man here for no reason other than the color of his skin. And that's a crime, no doubt. I'll talk with the state AG, after I see the video. He should go down for that. I can make that happen, if the video does what you say it does. He's got a bad history with minorities and this could be the thing that finally bites him on the ass."

Camilla nodded, finally, this theory being the most

comforting to her view of the world. Slick glanced at the priest, who struggled with it but didn't know how to begin. Slick just shook his head.

"What?" Javier asked.

"If it was all just about me, they could've nabbed me at any time and hauled me back to jail. In the restaurant, on the street, hell—"

"They don't want to do that, you've got friends like Joe Stormcloud and a pricey lawyer who they're afraid of, they just want you to go away and not sue them, so they're bumping you when they can get away with it. I'm not saying it's smart but it is logical from their point of view. And that's what you SHOULD do, go away, get the lawsuit going or whatever you're gonna do and let me handle things here."

"I can see your point, but for one thing."

"Which is what?"

"I believe Angel's story. I know what he is, but I believe he was telling the truth. Criminals sometimes do tell the truth, believe it or not. No one is a saint, but no one is Satan, either. I believe Sergio was murdered. I believe Pedro is innocent. And they now know, somehow, likely through Sergio, that Father Jose might be able to prove that. I think they went to his place for HIM, last night, not for me. I may be a pain in their ass, but I don't know anything. He does. He knows who the girl is. And he's in danger."

"Why would he be? He can't say anything without breaking his vow."

"They don't care about that, you don't plan for what a person WOULD do, but what they COULD do. He could possibly clear Pedro, and they don't want that, for whatever reason. There's something hinky about the Carlson murder."

"Hinky. I haven't heard that phrase since the nineties." Javier shook his head and looked to Father Jose. "Hinky. Well, what do you think, padre? You afraid for your life?"

"I cannot say for certain if my life is in danger or not, but I, too, believe Pedro is innocent. I know that he was. I cannot say why, even on pain of death I couldn't tell you, but I swear upon my soul that he did not commit murder. If I could think of a way to help prove his innocence without breaking my vow, I would do it in an instant. He did not kill Roger Carlson."

Javier sighed heavily. "Everyone thinks that about someone they know. I've seen it time and time again, a family member or close friend swears on stacks of bibles that a person they know and cared for isn't capable of murder, and they believe they're absolutely right in spite of the DNA evidence, in spite of the testimony and logic, right up until the suspect himself admits that he did it. I've seen this. You're too close, both of you."

"I'm not, actually. I didn't know Pedro, I don't know Ted, I don't know this town," Slick said. "I just know an innocent man when I see one."

Javier gave him one of his overlong intense stares, thoughtful. Camilla piped up.

"Since you know who the girl is, Father Jose, perhaps you can speak with her," Camilla said. "See if you can get her to come forward on her own."

"I don't know," Father Jose said after a moment. "Speak to her? I can try. It may be … difficult. Very difficult."

"Why is that?"

"I cannot say," the priest said. "Without disclosing information that I am bound to keep private. But I will do what I can. It may take some time, but I will try to speak with her."

"So you're convinced it's not just about you, sport?" Javier asked Slick.

"I'd bet good money on it. And I don't bet good money on anything unless I'm certain."

"Okay then, first things first," Javier said after a moment. "Just for the sake of argument, let's operate under the assumption that you are right and Father Jose IS in grave danger. I'm not yet convinced, but I wasn't there last night, you were. If it is true then we have to get him out of town until we get things settled. You have somewhere you can stay, Father?"

"Yes, a friend upstate, but my parish—"

"Will still be here when you get back. It'll just be for a few days until I can get a bead on things here. I'll drive you to wherever it is, we'll stop by the church, pick up some of your things, and then I'll take you out of town. No one will know where you are but me. Not even these two. Don't call, text or email anyone except me, okay?"

The priest nodded. Javier touched Camilla's arm.

"Look, babe, I'm pretty certain I'm right that our big man here was the target, not you, but just to be on the safe side, maybe you should also get out of town for a couple weeks, too. Call an audible, take some time off from work and go on a short vacation."

"Thanks, but no, I think you're right, too, so I'm staying. I'll be fine."

"You're sure? What about just a couple days in the country? I have a friend with a cabin in Sedona, I'll hook you up. You can go up in the mountains and relax. Just for a couple days, until I get a handle on things here."

"Thank you, Javier, but it's not necessary. I have work to do here. And I'll be careful, I promise."

"I'll call Navajo Joe, have him station a couple troopers at your house and at your office, just as a safeguard. He owes me a favor and I got some fed border money that needs to go somewhere, so overtime for troopers seems reasonable to me."

"You don't need to do that for me—"

"It's not for you, it's for ME, more than anything. I gotta know you're safe. Do me a favor, if you're that determined stay here, don't go anywhere else but work and home, okay? And I'd prefer it if you stayed home the whole time."

"I won't be a prisoner in my own home or my town."

"Just … be careful. Okay? You call me or Joe Storm-cloud if you think anything looks or feels even remotely off, understand? Call me ASAP." Javier turned to Slick. "And you, big man, go back home and by home I mean New York City, because that's where you're from, right?"

"It's not where I'm from but it is where I live most of the time, yeah. But I'm starting to dig the climate here, thinking of spending more time in this area."

Javier stared at Slick, not liking that at all. He finally stood, pulled out his wallet.

"I got this, don't worry about it." Slick grabbed the check.

"Appreciate that, but I got it. Uncle Sam is paying for breakfast." Javier snatched the check back again.

"Uncle Sam can get the next one, I got this."

"Yeah, uh, no, Uncle Sam has this one and the next one and the one after that. I appreciate the offer, but I can't have civilians buying me things, not even breakfast, it looks bad, you know? I go by the book, sport, so this one is on me. End of story."

Slick caught Camilla smiling at him in the corner of his eye and understood that this could go on all day. Javier was one of those guys who had to win at everything, which made them two peas in a pod.

Everyone climbed out of the diner booth and stretched. Father Jose excused himself to use the restroom and Camilla also followed suit for the ladies room, which left Javier and Slick alone. Slick waited for what he knew was coming and it didn't take long.

"Okay, we only got a couple minutes while they're in the head, so let's cut the bullshit," Javier said.

"Fine, let's do that."

"You're leaving town NOW, if not like fucking five minutes ago, I want you to get your ass out. Understand? You're a fucking magnet for trouble."

"Yeah, that's totally why Ted and his friends beat the shit out of me, I'm magnetic. They couldn't help themselves, clearly it was all my fault."

"No, it's not, they did that because they're bigoted fucking morons, but you're now making things worse by being a fucking pill about it. You got a legit complaint, no argument from me on that, so sue his fucking ass and take him to the cleaners, but stop fucking around in town here and getting innocent folks like the padre involved. I will take care of this situation, that is my job, that is what I do. You have my promise on that. But the last thing I need is you running around like a fucking cowboy pouring gasoline on a fire that me and mine have been trying to keep under control for years, understand?"

"A good fire can be cleansing, especially when one is burning trash."

"Let's cut to the chase, sport. You're leaving town."

"I am?"

"Yeah, you are. And if you don't, I'll have you picked up and detained for an undetermined amount of time. I'm not one of these local shitheads who can get scared off by an expensive lawyer. I'm federal, I can and will put you in a cell in Gitmo and you'll stay there until I say you can go and you'll be kissing my shoes when I finally do. And I hope you ARE recording this threat, because it won't make one damn bit of difference."

"And that's strictly by the book?"

"The book was rewritten in the fall of 2001, no one's changed it since and I'm not complaining. I checked up on you. You have a few friends who get federal attention. Hinky friends, if you prefer. One of them is your little boxing buddy, he hangs out in the kind of Chicago circles that get RICO attention. That's ONE step to you and a RICO charge. I don't need six degrees of separation of Kevin Bacon to bust your ass for anything, I got one degree and that's more than enough if I decide that's what I need to do. And I will absolutely do that, if you stick around."

Javier leaned close, intense. "Maybe you think I'm being an unreasonable asshole. I don't care. I care about three things and three things only—my country, my job and Camilla Leon. It's a short list and you're not on it. I don't care about you. I care about her. You brought her into harm's way last night and I have no patience at all for that. None. Zero. Ted and his friends, if they DID have something to do with last night, are about to find out exactly how big an asshole I can be. And so are you, if you don't take my advice and leave. Because, trust me, if you decide to stick around anyway and then something unfortunate DOES happen to Camilla because of shit you stirred up, I will be a nightmare in your world that you will never, ever wake up from. Is that absolutely fucking clear?"

Slick held his gaze, waiting a few moments before speaking.

"Seems pretty clear, Agent Rivera. It's your chicken farm, not mine."

Javier gave Slick his badass federal stare for a bit longer then relaxed.

"I know you like her. I don't blame you," the agent said. "There's a lot to like. But playing the hero isn't going to get you into bed with her any faster."

"I only met her the day before yesterday, Agent Rivera, and the only reason we've spent any time together since is because she has the same interest that I do, which is finding out who really killed Roger Carlson and clearing Pedro's name. That's it," Slick said, though he knew deep inside that it wasn't entirely true and he didn't know if he quite pulled that lie off. They spent time together because they liked each other. Javier had to have noticed how she looked at Slick, and he at her.

"Uh-huh. Sure. Look, she'll either let you into her life or she won't. Trust me, I know. Give it some time and distance and be cool. I can be an asshole, sure, but I'm not being an asshole about her personal life, I'm really not. She's a big girl. If she likes you, she likes you, I got no problem with that. She and I, that's ancient history. I just want her out of harm's way. She ends up hurt in any fashion, I'm going find the people responsible and hurt them big time. If you do like her at all, you'll understand that."

"I surely can."

Father Jose and Camilla exited their respective rest rooms and joined them. Javier switched off the tough guy act like a light switch, fussing over Camilla as they all walked together. It'd been a pretty professional piece of ass-chewing by the fed, Slick thought, no doubt Javier was a bull that no one in their right mind tangled with unless absolutely necessary. Something else was niggling at him, though, and Slick mentally shelved the angry fed problem for the time being, his mind on that other problem.

"Camilla, are you going home or to the office?" Javier asked.

"After I drop Jon off to his car, home first, for a shower, then to the office."

"I'll take care of these two, you go on home," Javier said. "Sleep in, take a day."

"No, I'll take Jon to his car, I have to pick up my phone at the restaurant where I left it and he's parked there, so it's on the way. Only makes sense."

Javier chewed his lip, clearly not liking that one bit. She gave him an affectionate push on the shoulder. "Javier, it'll be fine. It's broad daylight, no one is going to mess with an ADA in the light of day. I'll drop him off and go home."

"Okay, okay, text me later. Promise?"

"Yes, and thank you so much for dropping everything and coming out here in the middle of the night, for ... being here. For being you."

She held out her arms for a hug.

"For you, babe, anything." Javier enfolded her and squeezed hard, clearly not wanting to release her any time this century. They chattered at each other in Spanish.

Ancient history, Slick thought. Yeah, RIGHT. Not as far as you're concerned, sport. Father Jose held his hand out to Slick, who shook it.

"I want to thank you for what you've done and continue to do, Mr. Elder."

"My pleasure. Call me Slick. I do have a question, if you don't mind."

"Certainly."

"Other than work and the church, did Pedro have any outside activities or interests? What else did he do, besides send his money to Mexico? He did something besides go to church and work at least ONCE in a while, right?"

Father Jose stared at him, thinking hard. Suddenly he broke into a rare smile.

"He mentioned something once, after service," Father Jose said. "I just remembered. He couldn't stay after to help on that day, as he usually did, because he'd volunteered to help with the Rosewood Park clean up. This was three months ago."

The priest stared at Slick, intent. Slick got that.

"Thanks Father. I'll pass that on." Slick nodded.

Javier released Camilla from his bear hug finally, tapped the hood of his car. "Father, you ready?"

Camilla gave the priest a hug before walking to the driver's side of her car. Javier eyeballed Slick. "You got my card, sport. Let me know when you get back home and send me that video ASAP."

"Sure thing ... sport."

Camilla glanced back and forth between them as Slick and she climbed into her car. Javier honked his horn as they pulled out of the lot and drove their separate ways.

30

SLICK KEPT THINKING about what the priest had said as Camilla drove back toward the restaurant.

"Admit it, it makes sense." Camilla broke the silence.

"What does?"

"What Javier said."

"That this is all about me and my tiny home movie and has nothing to do with Roger Carlson?"

"Doesn't it?"

"It's neat and tidy, sure. Too neat, for me. Real life is pretty sloppy most of the time. Did you ever hear from Doris Carlson? Or your buddy Del the real estate guy?"

"Not yet, but it's not even seven in the morning. I haven't even called Del yet, his number's in my personal phone. I'm sure I'll hear from Doris today," she glanced over at him. "What are you thinking about?"

"I'm wondering why it would be difficult for Father Jose to talk to Pedro's girl. Difficult but not ... impossible. Difficult. Why?"

"He speaks to her, he risks breaking his vow."

"No, then he would have said it was impossible. He didn't say that. He doesn't break his vow. He just needs to say to her, 'I'm Pedro's friend, Father Jose,' and she'll know, right away. If the church was his life, Pedro was sure to have spoken of him. If she loves Pedro, she'll immediately fall into Father Jose's arms upon introduction, sobbing, right? So why is it difficult? Why does the priest wonder how to convince her to come forward?" Slick turned to her in the seat. "If she was Mexican, he wouldn't describe the process as 'difficult'."

"He would if she was undocumented, she wouldn't want to come forward. Expose her status and be arrested."

"That wasn't what he was referencing. It's been poking at me ever since he said it. Think about how he phrased it. 'Speak to her? I can try. That might be difficult. Very difficult.' That's what he said. He wasn't referring to getting her to come forward, but simply just the act of speaking to her. Right?"

Camilla thought about that. "Which means she's not a member of Pedro's church. If she were a member, he'd see her often. Speaking to her would not be a problem."

"And probably not Mexican. None of Pedro's work friends or crowd knew about her, he shared it with his priest and named her ONLY in confession. He told only ONE friend, Sergio, about her and even he didn't know who she was. If she were Mexican, Sergio would know who she is. If Pedro were in love, he'd want to shout it out at the top of his lungs from the rooftops. That's how love works. He didn't. For a reason. Why hide it, otherwise?"

"She wasn't Mexican. She was white."

"Exactly. Our Romeo fell in love with a Juliet from the other side of the tracks. That's why Pedro didn't tell any-body. Because he knew he'd catch a bunch of shit for dating outside his gene pool, and so would she—which means she's not just white, she's the rich kind of white. That's why Father Jose believed it'd be difficult to speak to her."

"Why hasn't she come forward then? Is she married or something?"

Camilla pulled into the Indian restaurant and looked around.

"That doesn't seem in keeping with Pedro's style," Slick said. "Nor did I get that impression from Father Jose. It doesn't read that way to me. And—"

"Where's your car? It was parked right there last night," she said. "What—"

"Hah. Ted had it towed, most likely."

"Damn him, I'm going to—"

"It's just a rental, don't worry about it. I'll cab it from here to my motel."

"No, I can take you, let me just—"

"Listen, I don't know why the woman involved with Pedro hasn't come forward. But the priest DID tell me something important that he'd just remembered, right before we got into the car. He said, with significance, that Pedro had told him once he couldn't stay after Sunday services because he had volunteered to help clean up Rosewood Park."

"What? He said that?"

"Yeah, and he said it like it was important. You know what that means?"

"That's where he met her."

"Yeah," Slick said.

"That was a few months ago. I was there that day."

"You were?"

"Yes, our entire office was, it was mandatory for the whole staff. It'd been part of a community outreach program. The park is placed right between … for lack of a better word, the good part of town and the poor part of town, which are known as the flats. The park was dark and dirty, the kind of place one didn't wander into after the sun went down. Hookers and junkies and other bad company hung out there and did business in the trees and bushes. Funds had been raised to clean it up by the community and we spent the whole weekend picking up garbage, cleaning and cutting grass and making it hospitable. Later new lights and playground equipment were installed, but that weekend was all about cleaning and, well, bringing everyone together."

"He was there and so were you. Did you see him?"

"If I did, I don't remember it at all. There were hundreds of people there. We had free food, a barbecue, for the volunteers, t-shirts, hats, there was a raffle and a band."

"That's sounds like a ripe environment where a rich white girl could meet and fall in love with a Mexican day laborer who she might never run into otherwise."

Camilla stared at Slick, her mind elsewhere for a brief moment. She put her car into gear and spun out of the parking spot, driving fast.

"Where are we going?" Slick asked.

"My place. I've got an idea."

"I like the sound of that."

She glanced at him, suddenly conscious of the possible double meaning in both of their comments, but she didn't say anything to correct it, she just smiled. That smile sent a small thrilling jolt of adrenaline through Slick's body.

31

S LICK QUITE LIKED Camilla's apartment, a newish condo on the third floor in a good neighborhood, seeing her personality reflected within it. She clearly got a condo because she was far too busy to be bothered with a house and the responsibilities that came with it, such as mowing a lawn, trimming hedges and whatnot.

She'd decorated it with taste and a touch of southwestern flair, a tacit acknowledgement of her heritage. A couch with a big screen television that was dusty, meaning it was rarely used. Sliding glass doors that led to a balcony where she likely ate an early breakfast, whenever she had a chance to eat at home in the morning, which, Slick thought, probably wasn't all that often.

After unlocking the front door and leading him inside, Camilla bustled into the kitchen and put water in a kettle and heated it up. She pulled out a box of tea bags, herbal, he noticed, and two cups. She didn't ask him if he wanted some, just presumed that he did. He liked that, too.

"Okay, I just need a quick minute to freshen up and then I'll explain," she said.

He nodded and she hurried into the bathroom, shut the door and turned on the shower. It then hit Slick like a ton of bricks. She was, at that moment, naked on the other side of the bathroom door. Once he started thinking about that, it crowded everything else out for a moment. He shook that off and examined her condo.

A small dining table, which meant she didn't often have guests or dinner here and if she entertained, she did it at restaurants. The kitchen had the essentials but not much else. It didn't feel like many other people spent much time in here at all. Nearly all the items were female and very specific to her. A mantel with many pictures, mostly of her with obvious family members, a few with what appeared to be local television personalities, some baseball players, none of whom he recognized.

The kettle whistled and he turned the heat off, poured hot water into the two cups, popped a bag in each and let them steep. He kept prowling around her apartment.

Two bedrooms, one converted into a home office with lots of books, files and clutter. The other, the bedroom, had wood carved dressers and a king sized bed with a canopy. The bed was made, the room pristine with no dirty laundry on the floor, nothing. Slick thought about that canopy, which brought him back to thinking about Camilla in the shower. He thought about both a lot, more than he wanted to, since he wanted to focus on the problem at hand. He was drawn toward the closed bathroom door.

The shower turned off and that helped ease the distraction. He walked back toward the open kitchen counter, picked up his tea and sipped it. It scalded his lip, which was a good thing because he needed to be snapped out of this hormonal stupor. The bathroom door opened and she came back in covered in a big fluffy robe, her hair wrapped in a towel. He held out her cup of tea and she took it with a big sigh.

"Thank you. Sorry to make you wait, but I can't seem to think straight in the morning until I've had a quick shower, I don't know why."

Slick thought that she must rarely wear makeup since, as she stood there before him now, she obviously had none on at the moment and he couldn't tell the difference between before and afterwards. Evidently she didn't need any. She sipped her cup and shot a quick smile at him.

"Most people around here are big coffee drinkers, but I've always been a tea person."

"Me, too. Herbal especially."

"I had you pegged as a coffee guy."

"Not usually. Only when I need to stay awake and there's nothing else."

"No Red Bull?"

"Uh-uh, not for me, too much of the evil version of sugar. I'll only do coffee if I need the jolt, and even then, if I can get green tea, the real stuff, not the bagged store bought version, I go that way. It's got more caffeine and it's healthier for you."

"I've heard that. I need to try some of that."

"It's good stuff."

They sipped their tea, a comfortable silence between them. Slick rarely felt self-conscious, but he was feeling that way now. He was very conscious of the fluffy robe she wore and nothing else. And he could smell her wet hair and the shampoo she used. Scented shampoo that smelled like mango. He had to think of something else, and quick, so he nodded at the pictures on the mantel.

"That's your mother and father?"

"Mommy and Poppy, yes. Still together after forty years."

"He looks like a tough egg. They both do. You have your father's eyes."

"Thank you. Here I am with my brothers and sisters, all of us together. This one, my older brother, Raphael, in Mexico last year, on vacation."

"What's he do down there?"

"He builds bridges and power plants. He's very smart."

"Who's this?" Slick pointed at a picture of her with an older white man, silver haired and in an expensive suit.

"That's my boss. That's George and his family."

Next to Camilla in the picture, an older white man stood with his arm possessively around his wife, middle-aged but well preserved with blonde, frosted hair. She had her three kids in front of her, two girls and a boy, the oldest barely in their teens, youngest about ten. Everyone in the picture grinned widely.

"That was taken ten years ago, the night of his election to District Attorney. He'd asked me to join his staff earlier in his campaign and this is the moment just after we got word that he'd won. I keep it because, well, it's the night I realized my dream. This job. I know a lot more now about the world than I did back then, that's the other reason I keep it up there—to constantly remind myself of why I chose this path. It's easy to forget sometimes. I look back to when I still had my ideals intact and unblemished, in order to remember."

"Your ideals don't strike me as blemished."

"You'd be surprised. But if I didn't work at it, they'd be much, much worse. Occupational hazard."

"Every field has them."

"That they do," she said after a moment. "So."

"So."

"So okay, here's my idea. This way."

She led him back toward her home office and sat at her desk, setting the cup down. She cleared some files off of a spare chair and slid it close so he could see as she fired up her laptop. The scene of mango shampoo filled his nostrils as he sat.

"As I said before, that park was a hot spot for all kinds of low level criminal activity, one reason we cleaned it up. But before the cleanup happened, we got some DEA money funneled our way and used it to set up a few cameras around town, including the park, which was done BEFORE the cleanup, to catch some criminal activity and jack up our prosecution numbers. George always thought like that."

"So you'll be able to go back and see Pedro at the cleanup on camera."

She turned and smiled at him. "I hope. We only have a few cameras in town, it was supposed to be a bigger project in terms of cameras when we got federal funding and it was going to cut down on crime everywhere, it certainly made my job easier, but some citizens of a certain political bent sued the city to halt the addition of any more. Ironically enough, the suit came from a couple of activist citizens who originally championed the cameras in the first place, only to change their mind once the scope of the project became apparent, that it would cover the entire city. They didn't want Big Brother catching them running a red light or driving drunk."

"So they were fine with pointing cameras in the flats at the poor brown people twenty-four hours a day, but not in the rich, white neighborhoods."

"Basically. So we don't have all that many cameras in town and only two in the park, but they're still operating. The footage is streamed into our main database and stored into a dedicated server, and everything should still be there since they were installed. I used this once before for a solicitation case and had the tech guys walk me through so I could do it at home from my laptop whenever I needed to."

She brought up the login screen, glanced at him and cleared her throat.

"Sorry," he said and looked away to give her privacy while she typed her password in.

"Okay. Here we go. There were a lot of people there that day, so it's going to be difficult. It was a two-day event, too. I'll start with Saturday first."

She typed a date into it and a duel camera screen popped up of a deserted park early in the morning. Camilla fast forwarded it and stopped it when people began to arrive. She hadn't been exaggerating, there were a lot of people. They gathered at the base of a statue of a woman holding a bible placed near the entrance of the park. The statue was covered in graffiti and people went to work immediately scrubbing and cleaning it. More people showed up to help.

"I told you it was crowded. This is going to be difficult."

"You can't zoom in?"

"Not from here, and not really. Back in the office we have someone who can do that, but it just blows the picture up, it doesn't zoom."

"Do you have the facial recognition program that we could plug this into?"

"Uh, no, this is still just a small township, after all, those programs are expensive. I could ask Javier to help us with that later on if we can't spot him ourselves."

"Okay. Let's see if we can do it. Fast forward, but not too fast. If we do regular speed, it'll take forever. I'll take this side, you take that side."

She did so and they both scanned the pictures. Images of people rushed by in a blur of unnatural movement.

"He might not have been there on Saturday either. Father Jose said Sunday."

"Okay, let's go to Sunday." She typed it in and new images came up. "There we go, Sunday."

She fast-forwarded it as slowly as she could as people arrived.

"Hey, I saw you!"

She put it on normal speed. "Where. Oh, yes. There I am. Ugh, I hate those red pants I'm wearing, I look like a tugboat. That's George and his family next to me."

"They're all dressed up for the part, too. Overalls?"

"Yes, it's all for show, at least on George and Matilda's part. They raked a few leaves, I think, had pictures taken and pretended to eat barbecue. They don't care to get dirty. Their kids were much more help, but kids often are."

They watched silently as the onscreen Camilla socialized

with everyone and helped clean. After a few moments she disappeared into the crowd of volunteers.

"Even more people were there on Sunday. That's when we scheduled the band and free food, so there was a good turnout."

She shook her head as they watched the footage.

"What is it?" Slick asked.

"Nothing, it's just … it's rare that you see a crowd of people this diverse working together toward a common goal. Around here, anyway. This was a weekend when we had people from every neighborhood, every economic stratosphere, pitching in to do something good. Both from the wealthy district and the flats, we all wanted the park cleaned up and safe. No one was fighting about anything, skin color, citizenship papers, nothing. Only focused on making the park a better place."

She sighed. "Everything should be like that."

"There's Ted."

"Yes. He just stood and watched with his deputies. Maybe made a few jokes about free labor, if I recall. God, I can't stand that man."

"I notice brown people avoiding him like the fucking plague."

"That's how he's viewed in that community. Wants everyone to show their papers like it's 1940s Germany. Of course, he only asks non-whites for papers. God forbid you leave them at home, because if you do, you're immediately detained. I've had so many arguments with him about that."

She scrolled through more images and eventually Ted disappeared from the scene.

"Stop," Slick said. "Go back."

She did as he asked.

"There he is. Pedro. Look." He pointed.

Onscreen, Pedro sat at the foot of the statue, eating a hot dog and watching the crowd. He was dirty, so evidently he'd been working somewhere in the park. He smiled widely at everyone near him. Onscreen, Camilla bustled right by him, talking and laughing with another volunteer and dragging some brush.

"I walked by him!" Camilla said. "Walked right by and didn't even look at him."

They watched as Pedro finished his hotdog, got up and put his trash into a nearby garbage can. He waved to someone unseen and slipped away into the crowd.

"Who did he wave to? Did you see?"

"I couldn't make it out, too many people," Slick said. "But yeah, he had someone there. He didn't eat lunch with them, but he knew someone."

They watched more footage scroll by, but couldn't make out anything else. Finally Camilla yawned widely.

"Oh, sorry about that."

"No worries, it's not like you've been up for twenty-four hours or anything."

"I know, right? I don't think I can look at this anymore, my vision is blurring from exhaustion. We should probably take a break. I haven't done an all-nighter since law school." She leaned back, stretched and yawned. Slick tried hard not to stare as she did so, but it was difficult, very difficult.

She picked up her cup of tea and smiled at him.

"So you know about my family, saw the pictures. What

are your parents like?"

"Didn't know my father. My mother, she was cool and tough. She told me … never take any shit from nobody. Never. I always remembered that. She died when I was fourteen or so."

"Oh, I'm so sorry."

"It's okay, it was a long time ago. I've made my peace with it."

"Were you a ward of the state?"

"For a while, yeah."

"That must have been difficult."

"It wasn't pleasant, that's for sure."

"And now you play cards?"

"For money, yeah."

"Are you good?"

"I am very good."

"Have you ever been on television? I see poker players on TV all the time."

"Not me, I avoid it. I mostly play cash games, specific games that are under the public radar, big ticket money events among those who want to play privately. The thing about TV is folks can study you, learn your tells and tactics. Gives your game away. I guess a lot of players make TV money from it, which is good, but I prefer card money myself. There are other players like me, great poker players you've never heard of. And I guess I just don't want to be famous. I prefer anonymity, to be able to go where I please and not be known or recognized. I like that. I like my life as it is, it's what I worked for and have no ambition beyond it."

"I didn't think there was anyone left in America who

didn't want to be on TV."

"Sure seems that way sometimes, don't it? People go on TV to lose weight, go through rehab or find a wife, it's nuts."

"So I guess you'll eventually move on from this town, sooner or later?" she said with a touch of forced casualness. Slick took a moment to consider that.

"Perhaps. I like to decide for myself on that, and as of now I'd prefer later, but it seems that it has to be sooner, lest your very good friend Javier will have me detained and thrown into a deep, dark hole in Gitmo where my lawyer won't be able to find me."

"What?"

"It's what he said, anyway. He let it be known that I need to be moving on ASAP, or he'll move me himself."

Slick could see that steamed her but she controlled it.

"It's okay, it happens," he said. "He's protecting you. I'm not offended by it."

"I am. He has no right. He shouldn't have said that."

"I understand his position, I do. He's simply worried about you. He blames me for you being in harm's way last night. It was an understandable reaction from him, even though I don't agree with it or like it."

"So ... you're leaving?"

"I'm thinking about it. I don't like anyone, no matter who they are, Ted, Javier, even the president, telling me I gotta hit the road when I don't wanna go. It's a thing of mine. I like that I can come and go when I want to. I really want to see the Pedro problem through to the end first. And there are ... other reasons I'd like to stick around."

"Other reasons?"

"One or two, yeah. So I'm mulling it over."

"Anything that I can say that might influence you one way or another?"

"I can think of many things you could say that would influence me."

Camilla smiled and sipped her tea, her eyes on him. "I wouldn't let Javier throw you in Gitmo. And even if he did, I'd find and rescue you."

"You'd do that for me?"

"I would."

They looked at each other for a full moment.

"You know what the nice thing is, about being our age?" she asked him. "And by our age I mean being much closer to forty than we are to thirty."

"What's that?"

"At our age, when it comes to certain matters of the heart, mind and body, we no longer see a need to fuck around. If we want to do something, we can simply just do it."

"There is that, yeah. And the other nice thing about being our age is that we generally have acquired, by now, the mileage and experience to also do it well."

"Very well."

"Extremely well."

"Hold that thought." She turned to her laptop, brought up her email and tapped out a quick message. "I need to send a quick email to my boss. I'm taking the day off after all. We can look at the rest of the park footage later, after we've both had some rest."

She hit send and then turned back to him.

"Sorry, but I had to do that now rather than later. Because if I waited until after I kissed you, I probably would have forgotten and never remembered to do it at all."

Slick didn't speak or comment. He couldn't.

She unwrapped the towel from her head, letting her wet hair fall to her shoulders. "Because once I start kissing you, I'm fairly certain I'm not going to want to stop for a long, long time."

She rose from her chair, went to him and kissed him. It was one of those epic kisses that started slow and built up momentum as it went on, seemingly never ending. She slid into his lap and put her hands around his head as they kissed and Slick lost himself in it. He put his left arm around her and pulled her tight.

He still had the cup of tea in his right hand and tried to set it on the desk. She took the cup from him and threw it out of the office. It shattered against the wall in the hallway but neither of them noticed.

He took her in both his arms and stood, cradling her as she kissed him on the way to the bedroom, tearing at his shirt hard enough that the buttons popped.

She opened her bathrobe as they reached her canopied bed and Slick lost himself completely in her body, in her lips and in her deep brown eyes.

32

SLICK WOKE UP in the bed hours later. He wasn't sure of the time, but it had to be late afternoon or early evening. Camilla lay in his arms, naked. They'd explored each other hungrily again and again until neither could stay awake a moment longer. He ran a finger up her hip, enjoying the curve of her body until she shivered and smiled.

"You were right," she said without opening her eyes. "The mileage and the experience, it matters a great deal when it comes to doing something properly."

She ran her hands up his body, opened her eyes and kissed him. "I don't know what it is, physical chemistry or what, but I've wanted to do that since the first moment I laid eyes on you. I couldn't stop thinking about it. Or you."

"Even when you were mad at me?"

"Especially then. I'm a Latina, what do you think? That's like foreplay for my people!"

"I wanted you, too. From the instant that you walked into the interrogation room, all business and lawyer-y."

"Yeah, but all men want every woman they see, don't they?"

"Not every woman."

"Just most of them."

"Well, maybe half. The hot ones, anyway."

"I knew it!"

"But most of the time, when a man sees an attractive woman, that initial attraction-slash-impulse passes soon after they leave your sight. That didn't happen with you. I couldn't stop thinking about you, even when you weren't around."

She kissed him again, with even more fire this time. He came up for air.

"This isn't fair, you got to shower and clean up beforehand. I'm grubby and probably stink. Let me get cleaned up."

She swung her feet to the floor, got out of bed and beckoned him with a finger.

"We can shower and clean up together."

Which they did, again and again, until the hot water ran out.

"This really isn't like me," she said as she dried off.

"Showering? This is like your second shower in less than eight hours."

"Not the shower, jackass. This, me and you, you and me, what we did before and during said shower. Moving … well, moving this fast to that point. With a man, any man. It's out of character for me. It takes me forever just to agree to a lunch date, not to mention invite a man home into my condo for even the most innocent of reasons."

She wrapped the towel around herself and handed him one. He chuckled.

"You mean to say that that you had an actual innocent

reason behind inviting me here?"

"Well, initially to check the park video. I couldn't bring you to the office, but … I must confess, there was probably an ulterior motive behind bringing you here, too, and once I got you inside my home, I kind of knew where it was going."

"I'm glad one of us did. I had no real idea."

"Oh come on, YOU? With the x-ray vision? Please! I took a shower, what did you think was going to happen?"

"Hell, I was trying NOT to think about it. It was killing me."

"Yeah, right. You knew, Mister Poker Eyes."

"I hoped, but I didn't know for sure. I'm not omniscient. No one is infallible, least of all me."

"So it excited you when I jumped in the shower?"

"You have no idea. And being in your home, by myself, with the smell and feel of you all around, it was killing me, killing me. I was running images of dead puppies in my head to distract myself, doing anything and everything I could so as not to think about you naked in the shower. Didn't work."

"Ah, poor baby, all wound up and nowhere to go."

"If I'd had more time, maybe I could've rubbed one out, but that might have been a bit embarrassing if you came out of the shower too early. I mean, oops, sorry!"

She laughed, hard. "And it might have affected your performance later."

"I don't think so, not with you. We're five for five already and if you don't put some clothes on real quick, we might have to do another round."

She opened her towel and flashed him.

"That's it, batter up."

"Sorry, we have work to do, first. Park video to scroll. Work first, play later."

"You're so mean."

She giggled. "Have you ever been in love?"

"Sure." He dried off his legs. "You?"

"Yes. Well, maybe not, yes. Probably, no, now that I think about it. I thought it was love, at the time, but in hindsight, it wasn't quite … love. It was more that I was infatuated with the person I was involved with and the idea of love and after a while it … became clear that it wasn't about that person. Does that make sense?"

"Absolutely. The IDEA of being with someone is sometimes more attractive than the person you're actually with, sometimes. I think that happens often, with some people. Not with us."

"No, definitely not with us. This is clearly a case of pure animal lust."

"Clearly. We couldn't help ourselves."

She sat on the toilet seat and watched him finish drying off, drinking in the sight of him in her bathroom. She liked watching him. He liked when she watched him.

"What was it like, being in love, for you?" she asked.

"Well…" He stood. "The first time, I was very young and … you know how it is when you're young. Everything is important, every little thing, every little gesture."

"Everything matters."

"Fucking everything about you and her matters, every small thing means something and it's almost life or death important, too. You hang on to every little thing and it's weighted with meaning specialized only for the two of you."

"Like how?"

"The first girl that I was in love with, the very first one, she gave me a shirt, nothing unique or special, just a regular shirt that she thought I might look good in. She bought me a shirt, this was early in the relationship, of course, and I was, at the time, wow. A shirt. She BOUGHT me a shirt.

"I was blown away by that, no girl had ever done that for me, at least then, and to me it was everything. I wore that fucking shirt all the time like a goddamn badge of honor. The shirt, man, the shirt, it became something more than just fabric that you pulled over your head. It was everything about us. It was everything.

"And after she broke up with me, I hung on to that shirt for years afterward, even after it didn't fit me anymore. Couldn't let it go. I'd carry it with me like a talisman, sleep with it, it was representative of everything good about her, or at least everything good about her that was in my head. I tore it once and was just about in tears, it wrecked me. I hadn't seen the woman in two years by that time and the fact that I accidentally ripped the shirt still fucked me up, you know?"

"Did she love you?"

"I think she did."

"Why'd she break up with you?"

"She couldn't handle me. I was young, angry and stupid, like a lot of guys are at that age. Me, maybe more than most. Definitely more than most. I didn't appreciate until much later how hard it must have been on her, the breakup. It had to have hurt her as much if not more than it did me. I didn't get that then, of course, because I was young and stupid. I made the breakup a lot uglier than it needed to be, too, when it ended. Too often at that age and in love, it's all about ME, ME, ME, you know? At least for guys, anyway. And that's how I looked at it for a long time—she left ME, she did this to ME, how could she fuck ME over like that, etc."

"Now how do you look at it?"

"Now, hell, I got the mileage and experience now, so today the way I look at it is that was something that *I* fucked up, that was a mistake that *I* made, *I* drove her away, a woman who loved me and who I loved left because *I* was an immature goof and an asshole. I realized, far, far too late, that it didn't work because of ME, not her."

Camilla looked at Slick, more serious than before, and nodded.

"I'm sorry for that. But I'm glad I got the grown up version of you."

"Me, too."

"What happened to the shirt?"

"I leaned into the pain and let it go, finally. Gave it to Goodwill. And it was the best thing I could have done. It was an anchor that held me to the past."

She stared off into space, in thought.

"I remember the first boy I ever kissed, first real kiss, not the little girl stuff, but a real kiss with my first crush, and the song that played on the radio at the time. I'm not even telling you what song it was, because it's embarrassing, but it became everything about the two of us, just like you said.

But when it was over, the relationship, and he hurt me when he ended it, every time I heard that song on the radio, every single time, I'd cry my eyes out."

"Was it *Desperado*?"

"Do I LOOK like an old white man?"

"Has to be a Spice Girls song then."

"Now that's just insulting. Stop."

"*She-bangs*?"

"Keep it up and I will hurt you."

Slick smiled as he wrapped the towel around his waist and looked at her, deep in thought. Camilla recognized the look in his eye and brought a finger up to stop him.

"Don't even think about—"

"*She Talks To Angels*."

"You … you … you are so BAD," she stuttered. "You are a bad man. I can't believe you figured that out. Unbelievable! I am never playing cards with you, never."

"There goes strip poker."

"Exactly right. And you only have yourself to blame. If I can't hide anything from you, how will this even work out? We're going to have to stop seeing each other, I guess," she smiled. "That's the only solution."

"That sucks," Slick said. "And I didn't even get a shirt out of this one."

"And without a shirt, how will you ever remember me?"

"I'll think of you every time I find myself handcuffed in a shiny new police interrogation room, which was where we first—" Slick stopped suddenly, staring at her. It hit him and hit him hard. "Oh shit."

"What is it? I was joking, I don't really mean—"

"I know you were joking, that's not it, I just got an... Come on!" Slick hurried out of the bathroom and into her home office. Camilla joined him.

"What is it?"

"The cameras, the park cameras, bring them back up."

She sat down at her desk, feeling his urgency, and woke up her laptop. She didn't even wait for him to turn away when she logged in. "Okay, what is it?"

"Go to the day of Roger Carlson's murder. That night."

She typed it in and the image of the park at night came up.

"Forward it to... He was at Friday mass, right? And that gets over around ten or so, something like that?"

"Something like that, yes. You think—"

"You said it yourself, the park bridges the two neighborhoods. His and hers. And if they first met at the park during that community event—"

"That place would be special for them. Oh my God. Is that him? It's too dark to really see—"

"It's him. It's definitely him."

Pedro walked happily out of the park shadows and headed toward the statue. He sat down at the foot of it, kicking his feet, obviously waiting for someone.

"That's our boy Pedro. What time is that?" Slick said.

"Just before eleven. He could still, theoretically, make it out to Roger Carlson's ranch in time to—"

"He didn't. He met her there, at that spot. They first met there, at that corner, and I bet they both consider it THEIR spot. She'll show up."

They both waited and watched. Onscreen, Pedro sat

patiently. Checked his phone for messages. Sent a text. Finally he got up and paced around the statue, agitated.

"She's late."

"Most women are late."

"I think this is different. Most guys who are used to their ladies being late handle it better than this, not Pedro. I think this is unusual. He's worried about something."

Camilla fast-forwarded the video and images of Pedro pacing and waiting flew by. "She's really late. He's been there thirty-five minutes so far. He's going to leave."

"No, he won't leave. She'll show up. I can feel it."

They watched him pace more. Then he stopped and stared. Camilla exhaled.

"There she is," she said. "Our mystery girl."

A young woman in a dark hoodie, her arms folded tight around herself, emerged from the shadows of the street opposite the statue, walking in a direct line to Pedro. He ran to her, smiling at first. He dropped the smile when he got a look at her face.

"Something is wrong," Slick said. "This wasn't how the night was supposed to go. She's upset about something."

"Can't see her face at all from this angle."

"Body language. Holding herself tight like that, she didn't let him hug her right away. And look at him, he's worried now, too."

"It's too hard to see anything in this light, damn it. Is she breaking up with him? It looks like she might be dumping him."

"I don't think so, I don't get that read at all. They're not yelling at each other. Whatever it is, it's not ... they're not mad at each other, I don't think."

"Her shoulders are shaking, she's crying, but he hasn't taken her in his arms."

"I know, but it's something else. If she were breaking up with him, her body language would be more defensive than this. Plus…"

"Plus what?"

"Plus the guy I sat next to in the diner the morning after wasn't a guy who'd just been dumped by a woman he loved. He was cheerful, happy. So she didn't dump him."

They watched the couple on the screen a little longer. The girl's face was still covered by her hoodie, leaving her features completely shadowed.

"Damn it, I wish I could see her face. We won't be able to identify her like this."

"Camilla, you're forgetting something. We don't NEED her anymore. Look at the time stamp on this. It's nearly midnight. That means, even without knowing who the girl is, we've—"

"We've cleared Pedro of Roger Carlson's murder! There's no way he could have committed the crime, not when he's on camera in the park. We did it!" Camilla hugged Slick. "Between this and your video of Ted arresting Pedro, Ted is officially screwed. I'll push for manslaughter charges and I'll get them, especially with Javier's help. It'll be a long trial, but I will nail his fat butt this time."

"He won't go to trial, trust me, he won't want people seeing the video I have of him beating Pedro to death."

"Is it bad?"

"Yeah, it's bad. He'll plead out, trust me. Hold on,

wait..." Slick padded out of the office. He returned, his pants in hand. He rooted through the pockets and pulled out his pre-paid smart phone.

"Crap, that reminds me, my personal phone is still at the restaurant. Javier's probably going crazy," Camilla said. "I have to call him. Who are you calling?"

"Nobody, I just want to record this and get the date and time stamp on it. This way you have another backup."

"I can download and email a copy to you."

"Do that, but just in case, I'll have this." Slick aimed the phone at her laptop and recorded the recording. On the screen, Pedro gestured and spoke with his companion, making a clear case for something, but with no anger, no desperation.

"He's pleading with her. But about what?" Camilla asked.

After a moment, the girl leant forward onto Pedro's shoulder. He took her in his arms and hugged her tight, comforting her. She opened up and put her arms around him and embraced him just as intensely.

"Now it looks like they've made up," Camilla said. "So whatever it is—"

"Oh shit," Slick said. "Oh shit."

"What?"

"How long ago was that park event again? The cleanup, the one where they met?"

"Three months ago."

"Three months ago. Three … months. You know?"

Camilla's hands went to her mouth as she got it. "Three months. Oh no."

"Yeah. She's late in more ways than one."

"Oh my God. She's pregnant."

"Catholics and condoms do not mix, or so I'm told."

"Especially serious Catholics. Oh no. That explains everything, look at her. Three months? She probably only just found out herself."

"And she just told him tonight, and was likely expecting the worst, and instead he's basically tap-dancing with joy, look at him."

Onscreen, Pedro waltzed his lady around, definitely more upbeat than earlier.

"Now that's the guy I ate breakfast next to. That guy was happy. That guy was probably planning a wedding in his head."

"Look at her, she's happy now, too, a load is off her shoulders now that she's told him. And the father of her baby is now dead." Camilla stood, furious. "Ted is going to pay for this. This makes it so much worse for him. He killed an expectant father. That's going to really hurt him politically. You have no idea what that means in this community, oh this is very bad. I'm going to … I need my cell phone, damn it. Excuse me, I have to check my messages."

Camilla picked up her home phone and dialed as she rushed out of her home office. Slick kept watching the footage.

"And I have to send the footage to George," she said from the other room.

"I'd wait on that, if I were you."

"I can't, he HAS to know, and as soon as possible. This is unequivocal, there won't be anything he'll be able to do to stop it, in fact, he'll want to be out in front of it and use it to his advantage. He's a political animal, first and foremost. He'll use this as leverage in the Latino community, trust me, I know him. There's no way around delaying his involvement. Plus, I need to be able to say I sent it to him the moment I found it."

"Send it to Javier first, then, as insurance."

"I have about seven messages on my cell from Javier, he's worried about me."

"He's going to be even more pissed when he finds out about us."

"No, he won't. He puts on an act, but he—"

"—is not over you."

"It doesn't matter if he is or he isn't." She bustled back into her home office, dressing herself with one hand, home phone still to her ear. "He's a grown-up and a professional and he'll know exactly how big this is politically. This can only help his career, too, as a Mexican-American federal agent. This is huge."

"Big for you, too."

"For everyone. I have to call Javier." She started dialing, stopped, glanced at Slick. "Seriously though, what do you think? Should I tell him about you and I now, tell him that we—"

"I wouldn't."

"He'll ask about you, where you are now. I know him. He told you to leave and he's going to make sure you did. You think he'll figure it out if I don't say anything? I've never lied to him before. And now you've got me self-conscious about getting caught with your poker eyes, he's kinda like you that way, even over the phone he might sniff it out. What do I do?"

"Counselor, are you asking me to help you lie?"

"I'm asking you to help me NOT to lie, actually. I don't want to lie to him, if I can help it. Just want to put off telling him about us. Come on, help me, you're the expert at this, aren't you?"

"Okay, so the way to do this is to stay ahead of it and control the conversation as much as possible so it doesn't go there. Let me ask, do you speak Spanish or English with him, most of the time? What's the ratio?"

"Sixty-forty, English to Spanish. Maybe more like seventy-thirty, even. I know that sounds weird, but because of our jobs, it's sort of like a professional language—"

"I totally get it. And when you DO speak Spanish with him, it's always a more informal situation, right? You do it when you're very happy or excited or relaxed, yes?"

"Wow. Sometimes you really scare me."

"So when you call him, you start off right away in Spanish, don't mention me personally, just tell him what Father Jose said and that you decided to look it up and found Pedro and the girl on digital video at the time of the murder. Go right past me and into the explanation of what it means and, if he asks about me, and he will, tell him that you dropped me off at my motel because my rental got towed. That will be the truth, because when we leave here, that's exactly what you're going to do, you're going to drop me off at my motel. So you won't be lying to him, just omitting when you actually dropped me off. Gloss right over that and then launch right into the massive Ted shit storm you're about to unleash, tell him you're emailing him the video right now and that this is huge."

"Okay." She bit her lip. "I hate to do this to him, but it is for the best."

She went back to the phone and dialed.

"Don't look at me while you're doing this, either," Slick said. "Put me out of your mind, think that I'm away, at my motel."

She nodded and went into the living room. He heard her start off in Spanish and she did very well, her voice pitched high with excitement. She went too fast for him to keep up and translate, but it sounded authentic to his ear. Slick went to the bedroom, found his underwear and pulled them on, followed by his pants. He looked around for his shirt. He heard Camilla go into her home office and sit at her laptop, still chattering away to Javier. She was emailing him the video and talking about her boss.

Slick found his shirt and pulled it on. But as he tried to close it, he found that it was impossible because the buttons were gone. Camilla had ripped the shirt off his body so hard the buttons had popped off. He heard Camilla finish up her call and hang up. He stepped into the doorway of her home office, smiled and showed her his shirt, which flapped open and showed his chest and abdomen.

"That's a good look for you," she said.

"Very tropical."

"It went just like you said, Javier asked about you just like you said he would and didn't question it when I told him I dropped you off. I did tell him that I asked you to stay in town a couple more days because this is all going to happen very fast, regarding Ted, and we need you to go on record. After all, this isn't just about Ted, but the false reports his deputies gave and also the witnesses. They all perjured themselves and I'm going to take them all down and it helps if you're here. He didn't like that, but he understood. As I said, he knows what this will mean for Ted and for both of our careers. He's going to meet me at the office in an hour and we're both going to present it to George and box him in with it. I know Javier, this is a federal case now and he's going to be all over it. This is a major coup for him and he knows it."

"And for you."

"I don't care about me, really. I simply want things to be better for my community, and getting rid of Ted and his deputies will be a great start."

She glanced at her laptop and brought the footage back up, scrolling through it.

"The only other thing is that I'd really like to find out who this girl is."

"Why? You don't need her."

"I know, but ... she's going to have a baby, without the father, who she lost tragically. I just want to know who she is."

"Did you see which way they went?"

"Yes, they wandered out of the park, back toward her neighborhood. I never did get a clear look at her face."

Camilla turned, her eyes set, and finished dressing.

"Listen, I've been thinking about it. I know that I just told Javier I dropped you off at your motel and I meant it when I said that, but ... now ... I don't think I should do that, take you to your motel, I mean."

"You don't want to take me to my motel?"

"No. I don't think that you should go out at all. I'll be at the office for a few hours, and I think you should stay here."

"Why?"

"Because I do think Javier is right. I think Ted and his boys are after you because of the video you took of them and if you go out around town … you're a target, especially once it gets dark, there's no telling what might happen if they pull you over. Just stay here. It's nearly six o'clock now, I'll be back before ten—"

"But I have to get a new shirt."

She smiled. "I'll stop somewhere on the way home and buy you a new shirt."

"Buy me a shirt? You'd do that for me?"

"It would be my pleasure."

Slick smiled, enjoying the moment between them.

"Well. Since you put it that way, okay."

She stood up and took him in her arms, giving him a long, lingering kiss.

"You're getting a shirt out of this after all."

"Hopefully a lot more than that."

33

SLICK STAYED AT Camilla's condo, inside and out of the way. He watched from the window when she pulled out of her parking garage and noted that there was a state trooper parked across the street, keeping an eye on the place. The unit pulled out and followed her as she left, which made Slick feel better about letting her go.

Maybe the fed was right and Slick WAS the only target. He hoped that was the case, but his instinct told him otherwise, and Slick had learned a long time ago to listen to what his instinct told him.

He sat down at Camilla's laptop computer and signed into his cloud, accessing his files. He brought up the digital video he'd recorded of his arrest and emailed it to Camilla and Javier. He thought for a moment and then hit play to watch it again.

He watched the whole scene in the diner unfold, this time as a viewer rather than a participant. Pedro's beating was ugly, very ugly and the situation played out even colder after it was over, when his body was cuffed and callously dragged out of there. Slick had kept it subtle but he caught everything on his camera.

Slick watched Ted interrogate him in the diner after Pedro's arrest, his camera picture wobbly. A quick close up of Ted's face zoomed as he examined the phone. Slick listened to the ensuing conversation between himself and the sheriff, shaking his head not only at the violence he knew was to come, but also because he knew that he'd mishandled the situation himself and could hear it in his voice. Slick could have just as easily ended up dead like Pedro after all.

That wasn't the smart play, not the smart play at all. Slick got lucky. He listened to the recording as he went on his diatribe at Ted. *Fine speech,* Slick thought, *but not worth the beating.* The picture was of the floor of the diner, now that Ted held Slick's phone. He winced as he heard Brower's baton bounce off the back of his head. More thumps and kicks as Ted and Brower both beat him senseless. They finally stopped.

"Get him out of here," Ted said in the recording. Slick still couldn't see anything, Ted had the phone in his hand, pointing down.

"Ted, what the hell are you doing?" said an unknown voice.

"My job, what do you think I'm doing? He attacked me, you all saw it."

"Ted, goddamn it, he's clearly a tourist, now a potential witness, and you just put him in the hospital! This isn't the proper way of doing things."

Slick recognized the voice. It belonged to Camilla's friend Del Martin, the real estate king who had approached Slick and Thumper the next day at the restaurant.

"Don't you tell me how to do my job," Ted said. "I'm getting things done, just like I'm supposed to do. He attacked me, you all saw it. You all saw it. We can't have these types coming into our town. He came looking for trouble and that's what he found. He assaulted me. Anyone here have any problem with that? Anybody?"

No one in the diner spoke another word. Slick listened as the deputies dragged him out of the diner and Ted followed. He stuck Slick's phone in his pocket and the screen got very dark but the audio continued. He heard Ted wheeze as he eased his bulk into the squad car. The car doors slammed shut.

"Goddamn lippy nigger," Ted said. "When he wakes up, you take care of him."

"If he wakes up," Brower said.

"He'll wake up, niggers are hard-headed. That's what my daddy always told me, he was an MP in the army, he said you couldn't hurt niggers by hitting 'em in the head. You had to aim the baton for the shins." Ted coughed.

Slick chuckled. This was really going to play well, once it got out. He got the impression that Ted was one of those bigots who got all sensitive and offended whenever someone accused them of racism. There wasn't going to be any denying this shit.

"He's gonna have a headache, that's for damn sure," Brower said.

"I hit the beaner a helluva a lot harder. I've been doing this long enough, I know exactly how hard to hit someone. That's one done taco, done and done."

And that flushing sound you hear, Slick thought, *is the sound of Ted's life going straight down into a prison toilet.* This was a one-way express ticket to jail for the good Sheriff

Ted Rawlings, who just all but admitted that he killed Pedro on purpose and took this from manslaughter to murder two, at least. Go straight to jail, do not pass go, do not collect two hundred dollars. Boom!

And they said nothing more. His phone was tossed into a desk drawer and the screen went black and stayed quiet for a long time.

Slick finally clicked it off and thought about what he'd watched. He still didn't want this video getting out and going public if he could help it, but that might be too difficult. At the very least, they should protect his identity. He sent a copy of it to Melvin, along with an explanation of what was going on and his wishes to keep his identity in the video private, if possible. He knew Melvin would be doing somersaults of joy once he watched it anyway, as he was Pedro's lawyer, too.

Slick sat and thought about things for a long time. Something bothered him but he couldn't put his finger on it. He sat and mulled it for hours.

It was well after dark when Camilla came home, carrying takeout from his favorite restaurant. She set it on the counter and gave him a big kiss and a package.

"New shirt!" he said.

"Shirts, plural. I got you a couple, I hope you like pink."

"I've got no problem with pink, pink and black are Elvis colors, after all. I'm a big Elvis man. How'd it go?"

"Ted Rawlings is through," she announced. "He doesn't know it yet, but he is."

"So it went well?"

"Yes! Javier and I met with George and broke it down,

and he'll break the news to Ted first thing tomorrow morning. Ted's an elected official, of course, but this is a federal case now, Javier's got him in his sights and his goose is cooked. George knew it the minute he saw both videos. He went pale. It's going to be difficult for him, since he's friends with Ted. He'll have to step aside and let a federal prosecutor handle it, starting tomorrow, but he requested that he be the one to break the news to Ted and ask for his badge. Javier and someone from the state AG's office will also be there. That video from your phone is the nail in the coffin, especially what he said at the end about a done taco, oh my God. I had no idea it was that bad. Why didn't you show me this right away?"

"Because it wouldn't have really mattered until we cleared Pedro."

"What he said about you would have mattered, it would have."

"Not for most white people around here. Now it does, now he's cooked."

"More than cooked. Burned, more like. Ted is done."

"Done and done."

"You should have seen Javier, he was on fire. Oh, he's going to play this up and make the most out of it. He's never liked Ted and this will play well, a Latino federal officer involving himself in a civil suit concerning the unlawful death of an undocumented Mexican worker at the hands of bigoted law enforcement. This is his big ticket to Washington."

"Yeah, it's quite a story. What about you, do you get anything out of this?"

"I don't want anything out of it."

"Everybody wants something."

"I already got what I wanted." She smiled at him. "Don't read into that more than necessary. What I meant was, I wanted Ted gone and now he's gone."

"Not yet, maybe by morning."

"Oh, he's gone. I know Javier. And George. By the way, George wants you in his office tomorrow, to give an official statement, on the record, about your digital recording, the arrest and everything. And Javier wants your phone number, he needs it."

"Right. So he can have a government drone drop something on my head."

"He's not like that, really."

"Not yet."

Camilla pulled a bottle of wine out of a bag. "Okay, so what's wrong?"

"We still don't know who killed Roger Carlson or why."

"George is going to re-open that case, he promised me. It's still a county crime, so Javier can't officially involve himself, but he said he'd keep tabs on it and George gave me his word that he'd see it through himself. Roger was a friend of his, too. And I had a message on my phone from Doris Carlson, she left town to stay with friends, but said that she has to come into town for business and could meet me for breakfast tomorrow morning at City Diner at eight. Do you want to come with me?"

"Yes. She left town?"

"On her message, she said she couldn't spend another day in her house. I called her back, left her a message that

I'd meet her there."

"It doesn't add up."

"Which part?"

"All of it. Look, we got two things here that are connected, somehow..." Slick grabbed a fork and a spoon. He set them apart from each other on the counter. "Two things. One, the setting up of Pedro, and two, the murder of Roger Carlson. Related, but how? If you wanted to murder Roger Carlson, why use Pedro, someone who knew him?"

Camilla took down some plates and unwrapped the food. They both began to eat with an easy familiarity, as if they'd known each other for years rather than just days. Slick enjoyed it more than he'd enjoyed anything else in quite some time.

"Well, from an outside point of view, it looks like Roger was simply murdered by an undocumented Mexican. Hardly anyone knew Pedro, except Roger and his wife and Pedro's priest. And his friend Sergio," she said.

"He fit a profile. A loner and an illegal."

"Yes. It looks good on the outside. They had a shovel with his fingerprints, no alibi, you have it all. If we hadn't found the footage of Pedro at the park, nobody would believe that he DIDN'T murder Roger. Even Javier didn't want to believe it, remember?"

"Maybe. Had I not sat next to him, maybe I wouldn't have believed it, either."

"Exactly. Citizens always want to believe the worst about others, especially brown people. It doesn't matter how devout they are, how often they go to church or how much they love their mother. In a way, that makes it worse, because we're sure that someone like that is going to snap and kill somebody. What was it you said?"

"No one is a saint. So if the goal is to murder Roger Carlson, Pedro seemed like a good bet from an outside point of view because he knew the man, didn't have many friends and was usually home on a Friday night. And HAD he been home, it would have worked. Except…"

"Except that he wasn't."

"He wasn't home and he wasn't a virginal saint. I don't think he WAS a perfect suspect, actually. I keep feeling like there was some other reason he was involved. But for the life of me, I can't put my thumb on what it is or why."

Slick sighed as he dug into tofu. "And besides, the goal wasn't to kill Roger Carlson. Or to set up Pedro. There was some other goal that both of those events served. And that's the other thing I can't figure out. Why kill him, what purpose did that serve?"

"Someone wanted his farm. Oh, shit, I forgot to call Del and ask about that."

"Why is that worth murder? There are a lot of lettuce farms after all, right? What's one more? What's the purpose behind it? Why murder a man over that?"

"Why does anyone murder anyone?" Camilla poured them both a glass of wine.

"In my experience, usually for two reasons."

"And they are?"

"Love or money."

"Just those two?"

"There are more, but those are the two big ones. Someone wants to buy Roger's farm, he says no, so they have him murdered so they can buy it from his widow. But if she says no they still have to find a way to get rid of her, too, all for a lettuce farm that is worth, what? A million? Maybe two?"

"Less than that, I think. I'd be surprised if it was. But that's still a lot of money."

"If it was cash in a bag, it would be. But it's not cash right now, it's dry, arid land that you have to farm in order to get the money out of it. Land has value only if you put something into or on it. Manhattan is valuable only because of the buildings and the nearby transportation hubs. Without those, it's an island like most other islands, if not worse … it's Staten Island. Roger Carlson's farm is a farm, it's not a million dollars in cash. And even then, this wasn't just a straight out murder, you had to set Pedro up, pay Sergio to steal Pedro's shovel, have someone murder Sergio—"

"If he was murdered."

"He was. It's too complex for just a simple lettuce farm that the widow may still not want to sell even after all of that. I can't get it straight in my head."

Camilla took a sip of wine and smiled at him. "Maybe you need to think about something else for a while."

He smiled back at her. "If you mean what I think you mean, and I'm pretty sure that you do because I'm fairly well trained in the art of observation, there's not a lot of thought involved in that."

She set her glass down. "We can finish the rest of dinner later."

"We can?"

"Yes." She took his hand and led him toward the bedroom. "We'll eat later. And we'll worry about Roger and Pedro's girlfriend and everything else tomorrow. Because for the rest of the night, we're going to celebrate as tomorrow is quite likely to be the worst day of Ted's life."

34

TED RAWLINGS PULLED his Cadillac into his garage, feeling pretty damn certain that so far this day had quite likely been one of the best days of his entire life. He'd spent the afternoon in a flurry of conference calls with his lawyer and a group of political advisors.

He and his lawyer had plotted and planned for this moment ever since he became sheriff and now what they worked for was about to come to fruition.

He already had a book deal in place, that'd been set up earlier in the year. He was going to be an author and, best of all, he didn't even have to write the damn thing, they hired some kid to do the writing for him. Ted had talked to the kid for a week straight, got his words all recorded and the kid would put all the commas in place, make the grammar work and shit like that. Kid was supposed to deliver a rough draft in a few weeks for Ted to sign off on.

The book would cover his life and philosophy on American government and border security. TAKING AMERICA BACK was the working title. Ted chuckled as he slid his bulk out of the Cadillac.

But the book was small potatoes compared to what was to come. They were thinking governor, the current one was very vulnerable at the moment. They were convinced Ted could take the top seat in the state.

Four years as governor, they figured, buttressed with a couple more bestselling books and carefully selected media appearances, and then they would make the move for the big kahuna—the White House. Four years, maybe sooner if a natural disaster or terrorist strike pushed his presence in the public eye further along. All very doable.

He'd have to lose weight, he was told. A hefty governor is fine, but no one wants a fat president it was said. He'd have to lose at least a good forty or fifty pounds in order to look presidential. He could switch to salads, easy enough, if it meant he'd be the owner and operator of Air Force One. Shit, if he had to, he'd get his fucking stomach stapled.

The other vexing problem, Ted thought as he left his garage and walked through the connecting door into his house, was that if Ted were serious about the White House, he'd have to get married. That's what his team had told him. He groaned just thinking about it.

Ted himself had nothing against married women, not at all. In fact, he was currently juggling sexual relationships with three married women. Married women were perfect for him, they were home during the day, didn't demand too much face time, gave him the space he needed and they were tigers in the sack.

But Ted was no fan of marriage. He'd been married once, years ago, and it had been a miserable experience from day one. Plus, the fucking bitch took him to the cleaners when it was finally over, got half of everything he'd owned at that time. It was ridiculous. Ted had vowed never to put himself through that kind of torment ever again.

But his team had told him that the nation wasn't really ready for a single man as president and he'd have to get his stability established.

Ted walked into his kitchen, still mulling that over as he removed his gun belt and dropped it on the kitchen counter. He opened his refrigerator and pulled out a beer. He didn't really want to get married again, but his team underlined the importance of image when it came to the national stage. They explained that the best candidate for a wife was one who'd been born and raised in Arizona, divorced herself, so they could angle it as they'd simply been searching for each other for their entire lives, and she needed to have a couple of children of appropriate ages, too.

Ted had no intention of stopping his outside sexual activities, so the perfect candidate for wife for him had to be one with some empathy and compassion for the attention a powerful man gets. He would need to find a Jackie Kennedy, a woman who knew her place and would not make waves about what he did on his own time.

Ted didn't think this would be a problem. A lot of women would give their left tit for a shot at being the first lady and couldn't care less how many women their husband fucked on the road to the White House, as long as he got them there.

He'd have to come to a financial understanding with his ex-wife, too. She knew too much about him and would have to be paid off handsomely, but his guys told him that was no problem. Money solved all problems in the end.

President Ted Rawlings, Ted thought as he padded into his dark living room, *I really like the sound of that.*

He didn't realize until he turned the light on that he wasn't alone. Someone sat there, in Ted's favorite recliner in the dark, waiting for him. Ted recognized the man immediately and glowered.

"You!" Ted said. "What the fuck are you doing in here? This is my home."

"Sit down, Ted."

"Why? What do YOU want?"

35

S LICK AND CAMILLA met Doris Carlson early the next morning at the diner, the very same diner that Slick had been arrested in, though he didn't think she was aware of that fact. She looked more haggard than she did before, but greeted both Camilla and Slick warmly nonetheless. They joined her in a back corner booth and Slick noted that the rest of the customers kept a polite and respectful distance from the mourning widow.

"Thank you so much for meeting with us," Camilla said. "I know this is a difficult time for you and I'm so very sorry to bother you."

"It's fine, honey. I'm sorry I took so long to call you back," Doris said. "I just had to get out of the house, off of that ranch. If I stayed there one minute longer I was going to pull my hair out. I have a friend who I know from antiquing, she lives in the mountains and she invited me stay with her for as long as I needed. I went up there for a couple days."

Doris paused as the waitress came by with menus, listened patiently as the woman offered her condolences and told her that her money was no good here. Doris thanked her and asked for tea, nothing else. Camilla and Slick ordered the same and the waitress bustled off. Doris sighed.

"They tell you, the grief experts, that it gets better. That it never goes away, not completely, but the pain lessens over time as one gains perspective and distance. That's what they say. Maybe that's how it works for some folks, but that's sure as hell not my experience. Each day it just gets worse and worse. I miss him so much."

"I'm so sorry."

"I know it's not gonna get better with time, either. Roger and I never got over the loss of Jim. I kept hoping it would get better but it never, ever did. It just got worse. In fact, it put Roger over the edge, that's why he got involved in crazy politics and conspiracy ideas, all that stuff. He'd spend hours on the phone or online arguing about stuff like that. I couldn't bear to listen to it, I couldn't. If I never heard the words nine-eleven ever again, that would far too soon.

"I hope you don't think too poorly of my husband, I'm not criticizing him and his little political squabbles." Doris ran her hands back through her hair, took another deep breath. "He was a good man, everyone liked him. Even in an argument, you couldn't stay angry at him. He just needed someone to tussle with once Jim was gone, he needed somebody to blame for what happened. So he got caught up in all that crackpot conspiracy theory garbage."

"Conspiracy theories?" Camilla asked. "Like what?"

"You know, the usual. How the towers were an inside job, bombs set inside to detonate the towers, by the government, in order to scare folks and get them to do what you want. He had a name for it, I forget what it was called again…"

"A false flag," Slick said.

"Yes, that's it. A false flag operation. He went on and on about it. Mr. Elder, you saw his office, you saw what a mess that was. Notes and scribbles everywhere. I thought it'd go away, after time, but it only got worse and worse. He wrote letters to his Congressmen, he attended rallies. It's how he grieved for our son."

She sighed again. "I'd be irritated, listening to him holler on the phone, but now that he's gone, damn it … it's just too quiet. So quiet that I think I might just bust sometime. Both my men dead and gone and me left with nothing but dust bunnies. So I got out. I only came back to get some personal things and, well, get started on the paperwork."

"Paperwork?" Camilla asked.

"Yeah, I decided to sell the old place after all. I can't stay there without losing my mind and I'm fooling myself to think I'd be any kind of farmer anyhow. That was all Roger's deal, he handled that end of things."

"That's something we wanted to ask you, Mrs. Carlson. Had there been offers on the farm, and if so, from whom?

"Please, call me Doris. There've been offers for it, off and on, over the past year or so. Maybe a little longer than that. Seems like we got a new one every month. That was Roger's thing, he always dealt with the business, not me."

"Was it the same company each time?"

"Uh, no. Of that I'm pretty sure. Because Roger always wanted to know who the company was, what they did and what they were gonna do to the land. I don't know why, I think he didn't want any munitions factories or fracking or anything like that. Roger was dead set against war and very pro-environment. So it was different companies, making different offers. You'd have to ask Del Martin, he handled most them, not all, but at least half of the offers. He'd know more and probably the names of any other realtors sniffing around. I know there were other realtors besides Del. I'm meeting Del this afternoon, he'll sell the place for me."

"Do you remember Roger's reactions to the offers?"

"Other than, 'Oh, hell no'? I don't really, but I have to be honest—" She caught herself here. "I tuned him out over the past few months. Just stopped listening."

"Why the last few months? Was he worse than usual?" Slick asked.

"Well, now that you mention it, there was a bit more shouting than usual."

"Did he say anything lately that you remember? Do you remember any particular arguments with any of these guys about their offers, anything unusual?"

Doris thought hard as the waitress brought tea for everyone.

"Roger … he never discussed any of his political ideas with me. He never said anything, because he knew it just made me angry. I snapped at him because of it once … and he never brought it up around me again. He kept his distance. So I don't know."

"Anything you may have overheard or seen on his desk that was … out of the ordinary for him, anything at all?"

"You think it might have something to do with Roger's murder?"

"We don't know, we're looking at all angles."

"It wasn't Pedro, was it?"

"No, definitely not Pedro."

"I knew Pedro would never do anything like that. But…" Doris closed her eyes. "But you think somebody may have killed my Roger just to get the place from us?"

"It's a possibility. We don't know for sure. Can you think of anything?"

Doris clenched her fists, emotion bubbling close to the surface.

"I'm so sorry to bother you with this," Slick said, "but—"

"No, it's okay. I understand," Doris said. "A day or so before he was … he was shouting at someone over the phone, I was in the kitchen and he was in the yard, I could hear him through the window. I thought it was another offer on the farm, he had that tone he always had when he … talked to realtors, even Del, who he liked. He said, 'Bullshit, I researched it!' and something I couldn't hear and then he said, 'Fifty thousand per year. Per year! It's a factory for profit, not for…' and I missed what he said after that. And then he said, 'I'm going tell them,' and he shouted a bit more about letting the public know and hung up.

"He was smiling when he came in, and went right to his office to write something, but he didn't tell me what it was about and I didn't ask. I didn't want to know. I figured it was another one of his lost liberal causes. He did that, like, once a month, he'd find some terrible injustice on the Internet or something and threatened to tell the world. I never thought there was anything to any of it, never. Oh my God. Oh my God, Roger."

Doris lowered her head as tears finally came through. Camilla's phone rang. She checked the caller ID and excused herself to answer it.

"Did Ted know?" Doris asked. "He had to have known, that's why he was dead certain on Pedro, despite what I told him."

"We don't know what Ted knew," Slick said.

"He had to have known. Damn him," Doris said.

"Yes, I know exactly where he is," Camilla said into the phone. "He's here having breakfast with me right now and … at City Diner. Why? Javier? Javier!"

Camilla looked at her phone then at Slick, concerned. But Slick wasn't looking at her. He stared over her shoulder. Deputies Brower and Collins pushed into the diner, followed by four other deputies. They didn't come in sloppy this time, either. They all had their weapons drawn and aimed right at Slick.

"Hands where I can see them, right now!" Brower shouted.

"Doris," Slick said. "I'd like to read those letters Roger wrote. Can you get his computer and give it to Camilla? I think I'm going to be busy for a little while."

36

"HANDS WHERE I can see them!" Brower shouted again. "What's the meaning of this?" Camilla demanded, keeping her body between the deputies and Slick.

"Out of the way, counselor, we have a warrant to arrest that man. Move!"

Collins and two other deputies fanned out. Diners scattered out of the way. Slick kept his hands on the table and did not move.

"On what charge?" Camilla demanded again.

"Out of the way, counselor! I'm not going to tell you again!"

"Not until you give me an explanation! What charge?"

"Counselor, I'm not going to tell you again—"

"You think I'm going to let you arrest this man on a bullshit charge so you can beat him again in custody? So he can end up like Pedro Garcia? You don't give me orders, deputy! You tell me right now what charge or—"

"You'll either move or I'll have YOU arrested and charged with obstruction!"

Doris stood up. "Then you'll have to charge me, too."

Brower shook that off. "Collins, move them both out of the way."

Collins holstered his weapon, charged forward and

grabbed each woman by the arm. A diner stood up, a big man, a local farmer.

"You got no cause to arrest Doris," the man said quietly. "It ain't right."

A couple more local men stood up. Slick noticed that these men were armed, as was sometimes the custom in these parts. The deputies got still.

"You arrest Doris, you're gonna have to arrest all of us," another man said. More diners stood up and stepped closer, aligning themselves with the others. "And we ain't gonna like being arrested, I'll tell you that much. It ain't American, being arrested without cause."

"Look, everyone, back away. That's an official police order. You're obstructing justice, so move aside. Now!" Brower said. The men didn't move. "Mrs. Carlson, counselor, I'm not going to tell you again. Out of the way. All of you."

The diners just stood there, silent but united against the deputies. Brower swallowed, this wasn't how this was supposed to go.

"That's an order!"

"You gonna beat this man here to death, like you did the other? Doris too?" one of the men said. "Maybe you shouldn't be giving orders, if that's how you run things."

The other diners nodded at that, hands on their weapons.

"This is your last warning," Brower said.

"And yours," said another diner. Their intent was clear. "No one hurts Doris."

"Calm down, everyone, please," Camilla said as she tried

to pull herself out of Collins's grip but he was too strong. "Let go of me!"

"What the FUCK are you doing!" A bellow from the diner doorway startled the deputies and they instinctively turned their heads. *Bad training,* Slick thought.

Javier stood at the door, his eyes burning. He barreled forward toward Collins, knocking tables and chairs out of the way. He grabbed the big deputy by the front of his shirt and shoved him aside. Collins stumbled backward.

"Don't you ever, ever touch her, ever again. You understand me?" Javier said. "You even THINK to put your hands on her again and I will personally take your nuts off and put them in a cup on my desk, you understand me, asshole?"

"Agent Rivera—" Brower said.

"Shut up!" Javier barked at him. "You've fucked enough things up. I've got this. Back off."

"Javier, what's going on?" Camilla said.

"Camilla, we have to arrest this man. Stand back and let the process—"

"Arrested for what?"

"Murder."

"Murder? Who—"

"Ted didn't show up today. They went to his house and found his body. Somebody broke in and shot him. This man here did it. Now stand aside."

37

"T̲H̲A̲T̲'S̲ I̲M̲P̲O̲S̲S̲I̲B̲L̲E̲!" C̲A̲M̲I̲L̲L̲A̲ sputtered.

"It's not, he did it," Javier said. "Just step aside and let these men—"

"Javier, you know what will happen if he goes into custody, you KNOW what they'll do to him once they get him—"

"They won't. I'll be there every step of the way. I'll walk him through it and make sure that he gets to his expensive lawyer in one piece. Any of these deputies here try for any type of payback and I'll eat their lunch, you have my word on that. Now just step back, please. Everyone. Please."

Javier took her elbow, gently, and led her aside. "Mrs. Carlson, you, too."

Slick held his hands up, slowly. Brower and Collins moved forward.

"On your feet, sport," Javier said. "You should have left town when I told you to and left justice to the professionals."

Slick did as he was told. The deputies cuffed him, none too gently.

"Jon Elder, you're under arrest for the murder of Ted Rawlings," Brower said. "You have the right to remain silent, the right—"

"I understand my rights," Slick said.

"Javier, it can't be, he didn't do it," Camilla said. "I know he didn't do it!"

"And I know that he did. Ted was shot three times with a pistol. Twice in the chest, once in the forehead. The weapon was left at the scene. It had fingerprints on it. This man's fingerprints. Now step aside, Camilla. These men have a job to do."

"Two in the chest, one in the head," Slick said. "Classic double tap, pretty professional. But then you wonder what kind of professional shoots a man so expertly and then leaves the weapon behind, with his fingerprints on it. Who does that?"

"I don't know, sport, lots of smart people do stupid things all the time. You have the right to remain silent, I suggest you take advantage of it."

"What time?" Camilla glanced at Slick, who shook his head.

"Don't, Camilla. Melvin will iron it out," Slick said. "Don't say anything else."

"What time what?" Javier asked. "What are you talking about?"

"What time was Ted murdered?"

"There's no coroner's report yet, they only just found the body—"

"What's the earliest it could have been?"

"Camilla—"

"Just tell me, Javier!"

Javier glanced at Brower, nodded.

"Ted was at a dinner meeting until ten or so then he

went home," Brower said.

"Then he couldn't have done it," Camilla said.

"Camilla, don't—" Slick said.

"He was at my place the entire time. I was home before ten, and he was still there. You didn't leave while I was gone, did you?" she asked him. Slick shook his head.

"He didn't leave," she continued. "You can check the security cameras at my condo. There's no way to get in and out of there without being caught on camera. It's not possible, check the cameras. And I was with him after I left you and George. There's no way Jon could have murdered Ted, because he was with me the whole night. He didn't do it, Javier."

Javier took that as well as could be expected, conscious of the eyes of the witnesses watching, but it cut him deep. He took a deep breath and let it out.

"They still have to take him in. His prints were on the murder weapon. Let the system do what it does. They'll take him in, process him, get him his lawyer and you can give your official statement. If the cameras back your statement, then he'll be cleared. Until then, he's still a murder suspect. You've done this before, you know the song."

Javier turned to Brower. "This man had better be in the exact same condition that he is now the next time I see him, or you won't be, is that clear?"

Brower nodded. Javier spun around and walked out without looking at Camilla.

38

I T WAS ACTUALLY all over before Slick's lawyer Melvin even got there. Brower and Collins took him back to the station, booked and printed him and stuck him in a cell without a word or question. He cooled his heels in there for a few hours and then they took him out again, this time without handcuffs. They returned his personal items, stuck him in the back of a squad car and drove him downtown.

They didn't speak and neither did he. He just waited them out. At least he wasn't handcuffed. But he had time to think while he was in there. Something Doris Carlson had said had tickled his imagination, but he couldn't quite put the pieces together in his head.

The squad car pulled into a parking space at an office building and the deputies climbed out, their faces coldly professional. They opened the back to let him out of the car. Slick stood and stretched the kinks out.

"So you gave me my shoes and my belt, does this mean I am I free to go, or what?"

Brower shook his head, not saying a word, and gestured to the entrance. Navajo Joe stepped out of the front, nodding gravely to Slick.

"Joe," Slick said. "Fancy meeting you here."

"Slick. I'll take you on up."

Slick turned to the deputies. "Well, it's been real. Don't buy any wooden nickels."

Brower and Collins, glaring hatred at both men, climbed back into their squad car without a word and drove off, squealing tires the whole way.

"I don't think they got that joke," Slick said.

"I don't think I got it."

"Now that you mention it, I don't quite get it, either. I just remember it from a Bugs Bunny cartoon and for some reason it always made me laugh. Still does."

Slick followed Navajo Joe into the building. They stepped inside an elevator.

"Your lawyer on his way?"

"Am I going to need him?"

"From what I hear, no. But you got pretty damn lucky last night. And I'm not talking about being invited into Camilla's inner sanctum, though that is ultimately what saved your ass."

"There's a saying amongst card players. It's good to be good, but it's even better to be lucky."

"Well, you got more than your fair share last night. If not for Camilla, you'd be a dead man walking, easy. You had motive, weapon and opportunity. They could have just as easily shot you in the diner, too, if you didn't have an alibi for last night. They checked the cameras in her building, they got you going in and not coming out until this morning. That, plus Camilla's testimony that she was with you at the exact right time, pretty much gets you off. And things look bad, real bad for the sheriff's department right now."

"Good, because the entire department stinks of corruption and you know it. Who's taking Ted's place?"

"Ordinarily it'd be Brower, but that's sort of up in the air now, given that he hit you on the head and beat you while you were in custody and perjured himself in his report. And, well, it looks like the whole department is rotten to the core. That's probably what's going to be discussed with you at this here meeting."

The elevator doors opened and they stepped out. Navajo Joe leaned close.

"The gun, I figure you took off them rednecks outside that roadhouse, stuck it in your motel room and somebody broke in and stole it."

"I can't honestly answer that without incriminating myself, but that would be a good operating theory, if I were in your shoes. I've got a better one prepared, though. You set troopers up to watch Camilla, yeah?"

"Yeah, they got on her place at about nine yesterday morning."

"They weren't there this morning."

"Our orders were to go after we saw her home safe from the office, which we did, so they went off when she got home a little after nine. Verified it all. They were supposed to pick her up again this morning at eight."

"And we left before that."

"You know that Javier and Camilla—"

"Used to go out some time ago, yeah, she told me that."

"Yeah, they were an item and I'd say he's none too happy with you. Though the thing that pisses him off the most, you spending the night with her, just gave him a huge career boost gift-wrapped with a pretty bow on top. But don't expect bro hugs and happy birthday cards from the man."

"I'm not too happy with him or most people in this town, so we can call it even."

Navajo Joe nodded and a secretary welcomed and escorted them into a large corner office. Camilla and Javier waited for them inside, along with an older, silver-haired man who Slick recognized from the pictures in Camilla's condo.

"Mr. Elder"—the man held out his hand—"George Hanson, District Attorney."

Slick shook hands without a word. George turned to the big trooper. "Thank you, Joe, for helping us out with this situation, I really appreciate it. I'll be in touch later on to coordinate things, as we discussed."

Navajo Joe nodded. "Have a good rest of the day, folks." He left the office. The secretary closed the doors so they had privacy.

"Mr. Elder, first let me begin by saying that I've spoken many times to your lawyer, Mr. Hayes, and have been upfront with him that we are not charging you with the murder of Ted Rawlings or for any crime. You are not being charged, you are not obligated to speak with me or be here, but I'd appreciate it if you could give me a few moments of your time. Nothing said here will go beyond this room or be used against you at any time. I've prepared an affidavit to that effect, and you can also speak to Mr. Hayes if you wish, he's waiting by the phone for your call, if need be."

Slick glanced at Camilla and Javier. The latter sat stone-faced, not moving. Camilla looked exhausted. He nodded.

"No need, please proceed."

"Thank you," George began. "First things first. Here is the bail money that your friend put up for you, I took the liberty of getting that back. Sign here, please."

George gestured to a satchel, unzipped and filled with cash. Slick signed and zipped it back up without a second look. George nodded.

"Second, do you have an explanation for how your fingerprints ended up on the murder weapon? You don't need one, but we've been unable to answer. It's clear that you didn't commit the murder, but—"

"The gun was registered to Jason Brogans," Javier broke in. "Who is not a suspect, either. He's in the hospital with a broken wrist and jaw. Apparently, he and a few of his buddies got into a fight with a large black man in the parking lot of a bar somewhere outside county lines. He's not talking, he can't with his jaw wired shut, but in writing he confirmed that the weapon in question was stolen from him. We showed him and his buddies your picture and they all swear that whoever it was they fought with it wasn't you, but some OTHER six foot four black man who knows how to break bones."

"Imagine that," Slick said.

"Yeah, imagine that. We asked him when his pistol was stolen and he doesn't remember," Javier said. "He don't know a whole lot, nobody's ever gonna give him a genius grant, but maybe you can explain to us how your prints got on the stolen pistol that ended up killing Ted Rawlings."

"No charges will be brought, you understand. You don't have to answer these questions, of course—" George began.

"No, it's fine. I've spent a little time in a few bars since visiting Arizona, and on occasion some of the locals want to impress me by showing me their firearms. I guess it's how they get off or something, I don't know. They bring it out, ask me to hold it and what do I think of it, so on and so forth. I wouldn't swear to it under oath, but it's entirely possible that, while I was in a bar, some white guy handed me his gun and asked me what I thought, I held it up, said I thought it was fine piece of hardware and handed it right back. And left it at that. I don't know why white guys do that, but—"

"You expect us to believe that?" Javier said.

"You can believe or not believe, I don't care. I didn't kill Sheriff Ted, why would I? He was on his way out of office anyway, right? I had no motive."

"Of course you had a motive, he beat the hell out of you," Javier said.

"And he was going to jail. You know I didn't do it, what's your beef?"

Javier stared at Slick, steaming. Both knew what the real beef was, though it couldn't be spoken aloud.

"It is plausible, Agent Rivera," George said. No one spoke for a moment. George walked around his desk and sat down. "Mr. Elder, we have a rather complex problem to solve in our county here. Obviously there are people who need to be questioned and removed from the positions they currently hold in law enforcement, and a rigorous house cleaning is in order. Ted was a friend I grew up with, I'll be honest with you, and I'm shocked at his death. But I didn't agree with the direction Ted had gone as of late, and it seems clear to me that he's also guilty of crimes that perhaps got him killed. Whether it was retribution for the killing of an innocent undocumented laborer or for something else, we don't yet know. But we will find out."

George cleared his throat. "Agent Rivera has put me in touch with a federal prosecutor and, in conjunction with the State AG's office, we will work together to get to the bottom of everything. Heads will roll as a result. Of that you have my promise and the promise of Agent Rivera here. You have been mistreated and discriminated against ever since you set foot in town and I offer my deepest, sincerest apologies for that and my word that those responsible for that treatment will be held accountable to the fullest extent of the law. You have my word as an officer of the court and as a family man who once marched and campaigned for civil rights. My word, sir."

It was a fine speech, Slick thought. A pretty classic political stump speech. But Slick expected there to be a 'but' somewhere in there and he wasn't wrong.

"But I need your help, Mr. Elder. I've no right to ask you for help, you are a free man who can choose to do what you please. I'll say that up front. But we could really use your help here."

Slick glanced at Camilla but her face was impassive and for the first time he couldn't read her. He looked back to George.

"What is it you need from me?"

"Well, to put it frankly, we need you to take a leave of absence from the area for a period of time. I realize that I don't have the right to request that of you, but I ask it nonetheless. Obviously someone tried to implicate you in capital murder, unsuccessfully thank God, and in light of the digital video you gave to Camilla, it doesn't take a great leap of imagination to note that there is a great deal of ill will toward you from the law enforcement community. Until we get the sheriff's department straightened out, there will be a period of flux and I would not be able to guarantee your safety if you stay. There are going to be wholesale changes made and some will blame you exclusively for this. They are wrong to do so, of course, but that will matter little in this time of turmoil. For your sake, and, in all honesty, for the sake of our community, I humbly request that you give us time to fix what's broken and to heal from the damage that has been done. I've no right to ask that of you, but I ask you regardless."

"What about Roger Carlson?" Slick asked.

"We will, of course, re-open the case on Roger's murder, that investigation has already begun, I've got some of my best prosecutors and their staff on it. They will work night and day until we have a resolution. Again, I give you my word on that. Roger was also a friend, too. I want to bring whoever killed him to justice."

Slick glanced at Camilla. Her face gave away nothing.

"You will be welcomed back once everything is re-solved, of course," George said. "I hope to get to know you better, even, on a personal level. Camilla … uh … clearly thinks highly of you."

"You got very lucky," Javier said. "You can't count on luck to save you every time. Take a break and let me clean up the mess here."

Slick saw that Javier badly wanted to glance at Camilla, but controlled himself. The fed took a deep breath and stared Slick right in the eye. "Once we got everything straightened out then you can come back."

Slick thought about that and finally nodded.

39

CAMILLA WALKED OUT with Slick but didn't speak and he stayed quiet, waiting her out. They left Javier in the office with George, walked down the hall and took the elevator, the whole time she didn't speak or glance at him. Slick felt it coming, however, and set the satchel with his bail money in the back seat.

When they got outside and into her car, she put the keys into the ignition but didn't start the engine. Just sat there and stared forward. Slick waited.

"Did you use me?" she finally asked.

"Use you how?"

"As an alibi? Did you plan this, plan to get me to provide you with—"

"You know I didn't kill Ted, so who—"

"Your friend Thumper could have. Or someone he knows. He's mixed up in organized crime. Javier showed us pictures of him consorting with known criminals—"

"Christ. He runs a BOXING gym in Chicago. Boxing. In Chicago. You can't work the fight game in that town and NOT meet gangsters. It's impossible not to run into them. The fact that he's had some pictures taken means nothing, they also get their pictures taken with all sorts of celebrities and athletes. Gangsters love to have their picture taken. And

Thumper's in training camp right now anyway, you can verify it."

"Javier showed me pictures of you with criminals, too."

"I'm a professional gambler, I spend a lot of time in casinos. Again, it's inevitable that one will run into people like that. They're just pictures, nothing more or less."

"What about the gun? I don't buy that bullshit story you gave them—"

"Yeah, I did take the gun off of that redneck, he was pointing it at me and I didn't like it. I took it and broke his jaw and wrist and walked away. That gun was stashed in my motel room in a vent. I forgot about it. Someone broke in and took it to set me up. Camilla, look at me."

She turned to him.

"You invited me to your place, that was your choice," Slick said. "I didn't use you, I had no control over what you were going to do or not do. You asked me to stay that night, remember? You were going to take me back to my motel and changed your mind. If you hadn't done that, I'd be in jail or dead right now. Ted was going to jail, you know that. I wanted to see it. I didn't want the man dead, I wanted his ass publicly humiliated and in prison. Someone set me up and it's only because of you that I'm a free man right now. I didn't use you. I'd never do that."

Camilla stared at him, her eyes filling, until finally she smiled. She started the car.

"I knew that, in my heart, I did," she said. "But Javier—"

"Is very hurt and pissed off about you and me and everything. Are you in the weeds with your boss because of this situation, because of me?"

"I'm a grown woman, I can take home who I please."
She put the car into gear and pulled out into traffic. "But
George, while he's not saying anything, clearly disapproves.
And Javier isn't really speaking to me. He showed the
pictures to George while I was there, but, just as you pointed
out, there was no way you could have known that I'd decide
to take you home and keep you there. I didn't know myself,
at least until you told me about Pedro being at the park."

"If I was going to arrange it, I for sure wouldn't leave a
weapon with my prints at the scene. So what's their operating theory on who did it?"

"They have no idea. Javier suspects Angel Martinez, and
George likes that because it takes pressure off the sheriff's
department—"

"Bullshit."

"Yes, I agree. But I do agree with them on one thing.
You must leave town."

"You want me to go?"

"Jon, you very nearly ended up on death row. Someone
murdered our sheriff and targeted you for it. This will be in
the headlines for months. I'm taking you to the airport now.
You have to leave."

"What about Roger Carlson? What's their take on that,
now that Pedro's out of the picture?"

She sighed. "They have a tip about Pedro's friend Sergio, they think maybe he's responsible."

"Again, bullshit. Bullshit squared."

"I know, but—"

"This all hinges on Roger, whoever killed him used Ted
to set it up, and then when Ted became vulnerable because

of the video evidence we found, they killed him. Otherwise, he might talk to get a deal. That's why he's dead. And they set me up as the murderer because I'm here, convenient and poking around."

"All the more reason you should get out of town, at least for now. I'm going to leave, too."

"You are?"

"Yes, I can't leave today, I have to reassign my case files and some other busywork, but George convinced me to take a leave until everything here is sorted out. By tomorrow afternoon, I'll be on a plane as well."

"Really. Where are you going?"

She glanced over at him. "I've heard New York City is a nice place to visit."

"It surely is."

"Can I come visit you?"

"That would be my absolute pleasure."

Slick thought about that as Camilla drove. Spending a week in New York with Camilla promised to be all sorts of fun times. Walk away and get out while the getting is good, that was the smart play. But the situation still tickled at him.

"We'll go to your motel and get your things," she said.

"No need, just leave them. It's only clothes and the room is probably trashed. You speak to Doris about Roger's letters?"

"Yes. Doris had a break-in and, well, the computer was stolen."

"Convenient. That's been going around, hasn't it?"

"She said she's not selling the farm, not right away. She sounded very angry."

"I'll bet."

"It bothers you, doesn't it?" she said. "Leaving it un-done."

"It's the smart play, leaving, but yeah, it's bothersome. And there's something else, too."

"What?"

"My moms used to watch game shows back when I was a kid, you know? She was big on them. One of her favorites was this show called Name That Tune, you know it?"

"I've never heard of it."

"Basically, they'd have contestants bet money that they could name a song based on a small number of notes that they'd play for them. I can name that tune in five notes, and so on. The fewer the notes, the harder it is to figure out what the song is, right? And I kind of feel that way right now, we got some notes that fit together, and it feels familiar and I'm sure I know the song, but I can't quite figure out what the exact tune is. A lettuce farm with an owner who won't sell. Fifty thousand per annum. The farmer, something of a known conspiracy crank, says he'll expose them. What could it be, what would he be exposing and why would they need his place?"

"Drugs? They wanted to use his place for drugs?"

"Why, if you're a drug dealer, would you do that when you have this entire desert to play in? No, that's not it. It's the 'per' part that's tripping me. It feels... Wait. Okay. Can we go to the county clerk's office?"

"What? Why? I don't..."

"I just had an idea I want to check out, it's out there,

and I can catch a plane right afterwards, but you can get us in, right?"

Camilla looked at him a moment then immediately turned her car around.

40

"SO WHAT ARE we looking for?"

"Land sales, focus on the area around the Carlson place, dated the past two years if not longer. Doesn't matter who bought what or why, just the sales."

Camilla nodded and tapped into the computer. The staff at the county clerk's office didn't say a word when she flashed her ID, just showed her to a spare office and a desktop computer to work on. Slick roamed until he found what he was looking for, a pull down map of the entire county on a wall. It squeaked as he brought it down and stared at it until he found the Carlson ranch. Camilla exhaled suddenly.

"Oh. Wow."

"There's a few, I'll bet, right?" Slick said.

"Yes. Nearly every tract of land northwest of the ranch has been purchased, going back the last three years. Different companies. I'll print them out."

Slick studied the map as Camilla picked up the printed pages from the front office and handed a copy to Slick when she returned. "The purchasers are all different companies."

"We'll Google them in a minute, first let's take a look at the big picture." Slick picked up a pencil from a nearby desk, glanced around and then began marking the county map. Northwest of the Carlson ranch, which Slick had circled, the recently purchased land, when added up together, formed a near rectangle.

"This is nearly the entire northwest corner of the county. That's a lot of land. Missing a chunk on each bottom side. Here on the Carlson ranch and here, on the other side, near the river," Slick said.

"Oh my God, I know that spot, that was big in the news last year," Camilla said. "It was undeveloped public land, but when the county tried to lease it to someone, the Navajo tribe sued to get it back on the basis that it covered part of their reservation. The court awarded it back to them."

"Do you remember who they were going to lease it to?"

"I don't, that wasn't really the main hook of the story, it was a battle between the local government and the tribe, a huge fight. The county maintained it was their land and there was talk of an energy company, but no one knew for sure. I'll have to look."

"Odds are it'll be a name you've never heard of, just like every single one of the other companies on this list. They're all shell companies, I'll bet. And look at the timeline, here. Most of this land was bought two years ago. They had most of it and then they hit a snag."

"When the tribe sued to stop the sale of land they think belongs to them."

"Yeah, and the tribe wins and whoever it happens to be is screwed, they needed a certain size of land and they lost a big chunk. The only available nearby land is a lettuce farm but it's owned by a bleeding heart liberal conspiracy theorist who wants to know exactly what you're going to do with it before he'll sell, and even then he'll probably say no."

Slick looked at her. "I've been an idiot. I only looked at it from the angle of what does someone want a lettuce farm for? They don't want a farm, they want the land as part of a bigger piece of a pie. They needed a certain size of land and when the county lost the court battle for a significant chunk that was supposed to be sold to them, Roger's place was the only one nearby that fit."

"Needed it for what?"

"Something that netted fifty grand per annum."

"Per what?"

Slick didn't answer, just stared at the map, deep in thought.

Camilla gathered up her things. "I'll get a subpoena and find out who those shell companies belong to right away."

"It won't do any good. Most likely each one is a PO Box in Costa Rica, it'll take forever and a day to even get a non-answer."

"What else can we do?"

"Who brokered these sales? It's not on this printout."

Camilla went back to the computer and tapped away. She stopped when she found it and looked up at Slick.

"Same name for every single sale," she said.

"Del Martin?"

"Yes. But that doesn't mean he—"

"That he knew? How could he not know?"

"We have to go." Camilla stood. "I have to take this to George and Javier right away. We'll get a warrant for Del's office, we'll subpoena his records, everything."

Slick again didn't answer, just stepped closer to the map.

"Jon?"

"Just a second."

Slick stared hard until he felt something click in his head and an unconscious smile spread across his face as he stepped back.

"I think I know what the fifty thousand per annum is," he said. "But I need to borrow your tablet first, to check something. I'll do it on the way."

41

"BOTH YOU AND Joe Stormcloud have mentioned federal money coming into the county for different projects, I mean that's how the cameras in the park got set up, right?" Slick asked as he typed into Camilla's computer tablet.

"Yes, but that's hardly abnormal, all counties do," Camilla said. She drove fast, heading back toward her office. "What does that have to do with—"

"I'll bet your county's arrest numbers have skyrocketed in the past three years, too. And your conviction rates as well. Brower told me they have the best arrest-conviction rate in the state."

"I don't know the exact numbers, but we're certainly busier and, yes, our arrest-conviction rate is one of the highest in the state. Both George and Ted ran for office on platforms that emphasized being tough on crime."

"That's the thing though," Slick said. "You look at national numbers on crime, you'll see that violent crime has actually gone down across the board. Yet everyone's afraid of crime, and all the politicos promise greater and greater punishments for those caught and to keep their promise, they have to keep arresting people. Did you know that Arizona is number three in terms of incarcerated people, just behind Texas and California? Even though population-wise it's far smaller, it holds a greater percentage of prisoners than nearly anywhere else, according to numbers online."

"So?"

"So what do you think that land is for? It's for a prison, a big one. Seeing it on the map, that's what clicked for me. I named that damn tune."

"It can't be, if it was to be a state or federal prison, they could just appropriate the land, they wouldn't need to go through Del—"

"Not if it's privately run. Prisons aren't built by the government anymore, they're now privately owned and operated—for profit. That's what the fifty thousand per annum that Roger was screaming about stood for. That's what he meant by a factory for profit. You go the private prison route, it can cost the country fifty grand per prisoner."

"Oh my God."

"It's the only thing that fits, and it's a good scam. They convince the average taxpayer that private businesses are the only way to run something like a prison in the most efficient way, and since most people distrust the government, they buy into that bullshit. They get state or federal contracts to do so and it actually ends up costing the taxpayer more money per prisoner than it would if it was run by the state."

"And state and federal prisons have to follow set guidelines in terms of the incarcerated care and rights. Private prisons don't, they can cut corners," Camilla said.

"Yeah. Walmarting incarceration. And looking at the

size of it, we're talking about millions of dollars of state and federal money, not to mention local jobs. I'll bet someone's lobbied and landed a sizeable state contract, for THIS county, that's why that area was so important. It's the only one the right size in the county. If they don't get that land, the prison and the money go elsewhere. To another county."

"There's something else," Camilla said. "We arrest and convict a lot of undocumented people in this county. Ted and his boys are infamous for it. Even families simply driving through the county are at risk. We're on a hub of a major highway and he was taking advantage of it."

"And?"

"And if we just arrest someone for being here without papers, they simply get sent back. But if an undocumented person is arrested and convicted of a crime, any crime—"

"Like resisting arrest, assaulting a police officer. Drugs."

"Right, or if they're arrested and confess to a crime, they're not sent back, not right away. They're sentenced and sent to jail and after they've served the entirety of their sentence, only then are they sent back to their country."

Slick whistled. "Now that's a moneymaker, right there. You're a sheriff and you have a piece of private prison profits. You nab an illegal, plant drugs on him or just beat him in custody until he confesses to a crime, any crime, and send him to a prison where he'll make money for you just by being there, courtesy of the American taxpayer."

"Yes. I've had issue with a lot of Ted's arrests and convictions for a long time, had many an argument with George about it, but George is a politician, he knows what plays well, he doesn't care about specifics, especially when voters respond to it. And voters did respond to Ted's song on crime and illegals. That's a whole other tune that the crowd responds to."

"If the crowd is too stupid to pay attention to the lyrics."

"So someone brokered a deal from a private company, one that had the contract already, promised them the land in this county, and then, when things got complicated, they used Ted to remove Roger."

"They used Ted to cover it. Ted wasn't smart enough to take Roger out, someone else did that. They gifted Ted with a prime suspect for Roger's murder and he still fucked that up. He killed the kid in the diner and then he arrested me, too, which gummed everything up. If he'd just let me go, chances are I'd have left town, made it to the airport, gotten on the plane and never even looked in the rear view. Instead, I stuck around out of pure spite and started asking questions. And so did you."

Camilla didn't say anything for a bit, just drove.

"It's all just conjecture at this point," she finally said.

"Yep. Entirely conjecture."

"We have not a single piece of evidence to support any of that, none."

"True. Not yet, anyway. At least until you lean on Del and Javier gets his teeth into it. You know what he's going to do once he gets hold of this."

"Yes, I know."

"We drop this in his lap, we go to New York City and see the Empire State Building, eat lots of great food, catch some shows and sleep in late in the morning."

Camilla pulled into the parking garage of her office, not

replying right away. Slick could feel the steam building up inside her, however.

She parked her car, turned it off and just sat there.

"Or don't we?" Slick finally asked.

"Are you comfortable just walking away now?"

"I could now. Ted's dead, I know what the scam is, we can sic your friend Javier on whoever is responsible and he'll chew them up and shit them out again. You and I can be drinking mimosas in the East Village by tomorrow morning. I say we walk away."

Camilla didn't say anything at first, just sat there.

"I don't think I can do that," she said. "I can't."

"Okay."

"I can't … walk away. Not now. I could have before, but not now. I'm too angry. I'm the angriest I've ever been in my entire life. All this … killing. For money. For a prison. A private prison!"

"Love or money, this time it was money."

"It's stupid and evil and … it infuriates me. Infuriates me! Our law enforcement officers involved in this! And I can't stop thinking about that poor girl, Pedro's girlfriend, who was the happiest she'd probably ever been the night before the man she loved was killed. I want to find out who she is and I want her to know that I found the people responsible for his death and brought them to justice."

She glanced at him. "I can tell you don't agree. You want to walk away."

"I want us to walk away. Together."

"Don't you care about the girl?"

"I cared about cracking it and getting justice done.

We've done it, it's over. Javier will carry the ball into the end zone. We got it to the five-yard line. Nothing is going to change the girl's situation, once he does that. You're not going to bring Pedro back."

"I know, but I can't walk away from her now. I can't. And I don't want to just hand this over to Javier and George, to the men, and let them deal with it. I need to finish it. I want to do this for her and for myself and for my community. It's my job. I can't walk away, not now. I'm going to make George give this case to me, he owes me and knows it, and I'm going to see this all the way to the end."

"Okay."

"You think I'm being silly."

"I think you're caring too much about the wrong thing, but we're all guilty of that. You need to do what you need to do to be you. I get that. Stay if you have to."

"You should go, though." She turned to him. "Go back home and I'll come see you when it's all over. You're in danger here."

"And you won't be?"

"I'll have Javier and George and Joe looking after me. I'll be fine. I'm going to find the girl and—"

"You stay, I stay."

"After what just nearly happened to you, you want to stick around? No, if something were to happen to you, I don't know what I'd do—"

"I'll stay in your condo the entire time … if I'm welcome there, that is."

That brought a smile to her lips. "You mean I would get to keep you at home, full time, like a pet? I think I like that. I like that a lot."

"I'll be your household pet and kept man until everything is said and done. Won't even go outside without you. Cross my heart."

She stared at him, her smile growing. She leaned forward and kissed him hard.

"Take my car and my condo keys, drive back to my place. George and I will be busy for the whole afternoon, so I'll have Javier drop me off when I'm done. I need to have a heart-to-heart talk with him about us anyway. It may be late when I'm back, but make yourself at home."

"Will do. And I'm warning you right now, I'm a good cook."

Camilla's eyes widened and she kissed him again. She climbed out of the car and Slick slid over to the driver's seat, got settled. Camilla leaned in through the window.

"I'm warning you right now," she said, "I may be falling for you, hard and fast."

She kissed him a third time. Slick smiled at her then nodded to a nearby security camera.

"We're putting on a quite a show for the powers-that-be."

"Let them watch," Camilla said. "I don't care."

She stopped as a thought struck her.

"What is it?"

"You just gave me an idea. I'll tell you later." She leaned in and kissed him a final time, gathered herself together and walked away.

42

SLICK DROVE THROUGH the city in Camilla's car without incident and pulled into the garage at her condo. He parked in her reserved spot, grabbed the satchel with his bail money, locked the car up and headed for the stairs.

He always preferred stairs to elevators whenever it was a reasonable amount of steps. Camilla lived on the third floor, so it was doable. His cell rang as he hit the second level. He saw it was Camilla and answered right away.

"Listen, I don't have much time," she said. "I'm sending you a video, you have to send it to your cloud to save it for me, okay? Don't let anyone else have it."

His phone dinged, indicating an email message.

"Okay. What is it?" he asked.

"I surfed all the traffic and bank cameras in town on the night of the murder and found additional footage of Pedro and his girlfriend. I know who she is now."

"Great, who is she?"

"I can't say right now, it's not private enough here. I'm going to leave as soon as I can get a ride. Just save that video for me, okay?"

"You want me to come get you?"

"No, just stay there, it's not safe. I'll come to you."

"Did you tell your boss or Javier?"

"I don't know where Javier is, he's not answering his phone. And when you get to my condo, you'll find out why I can't tell George. Just look on my mantel."

Slick reached the third floor. "What does that mean?"

"It was love AND money, in the end. You'll see. I have to go," she whispered. "I hear George. Jon, I know we've moved very quickly, you and I, and I know it's only been two days, but … I wanted you to know that, no matter what happens, I think I'm in love with you. I know that I am."

"Camilla, I—" he began but she'd hung up.

He stopped, clicked on his messages and downloaded the video. He watched it as he went through the stairwell door to the third floor hallway. It was security footage from a camera near the edge of the city. Pedro and his girl appeared in the darkness, holding hands. She had her hood down now. They walked toward the camera, closer and closer. Her face came into focus. She was blonde, pretty and most certainly white. Her face was familiar but Slick couldn't place it right away, not at first. He reached for Camilla's condo keys.

"Mr. Elder, or can I call you Slick?"

Del Martin leaned against the wall opposite Camilla's apartment.

"No, you may not."

"I feel like I know you so well already, so I will anyway." Del straightened up. "I checked you out, you know, I know who you are. You're not just a poker pro. You do freelance murder for money on the side, you and your little boxing buddy … Thumper, that was his name, right? You are 'hit' men. Here I thought you were just a general pain in the ass, but it seems not. Hit men. I'm still chuckling about it.

"You're not really connected, you do the occasional gig for different syndicates here and there in Chicago and New York, but freelance is freelance. Live or die by the gig. I mean you guys do all right, but you're strictly ham-and-eggers, really. Which is why I can't understand why you're still hanging around here. I mean, seriously, did you even look in that bag?"

"Nope. Why should I?" Slick closed the video he was watching on his phone and emailed it to his home server. He struggled to place the girl's face, he knew he'd seen her somewhere before but it was eluding him.

"Because there's a lot more money in that bag than there was when your little buddy handed it in. An incentive for you, seeing as you're a man of this business, to pick up and leave town. One would presume that after the close call you just had you wouldn't think twice, you'd just take the money and run. But you didn't even LOOK in the bag. I mean is she really that good in the sack?"

"You don't know her or me well enough to ask that, friend."

"Why, what are you gonna do, beat me up—like you did those five guys outside of the bar? I don't blame you, I mean, any man who's ever met Camilla had to have fantasies and you're living it, my man. I get it. But here's the thing…"

Slick assessed the situation. There was no one else in the hall except for Del and himself. But something didn't feel right. The salesman kept talking as he strolled closer.

"You have been a big pain in the balls, ever since you

came to town. I mean, really, it's astounding to me how one guy could fuck things up for us so badly. I know you went to the county clerk's office today, and I know what you found there. And after the mess of your arrest this morning, Doris Carlson won't even speak to me now, she's holed up at her place, cursing up a storm. It's a huge clusterfuck. So here's my question. How much?"

"How much what?"

"How much do you want? I will pay you to work for me. Hell, I'll pay you to go away just so you're not working against me."

"I don't think so."

"You realize how big this is? We're talking millions. Tens of millions, more than that, even, for decades to come. It's a very big pie and there's even more of it to go around now that Ted's gone. How can you say no?"

"Pretty damn easily. There's a reason I work independently. I don't like to do things I won't want to do. And I don't want to work for you in any capacity."

"Well, that's too bad."

"Too bad for you."

"Even worse for you."

Slick sized Del up. He didn't seem to be carrying a weapon.

"You going to kill me like you did Ted?"

"Me? No, not me, I don't get my hands dirty, that's not my game. And how could little old me handle such a big strapping buck like you? I'm not stupid. You'd go right through me like a hot knife in butter. But, see, I don't need to, because I've got an ace in the hole."

The door to Camilla's condo opened and a pistol came out, pointed right at Slick.

"I was praying you'd turn down that money," Javier said. "So I could do this."

"My ace in the hole," Del said. "And he's very, very unhappy with you. But not to worry, we're not going to kill you right away. You're still potentially useful."

Javier clubbed Slick across the head with the gun. Slick went down to his knees.

Javier clubbed him again and again, cursing in Spanish, until Slick lost consciousness.

43

SLICK DRIFTED IN and out of consciousness for quite some time before he finally woke up, unable to see because nearly everything was black. He knew he was in the trunk of a moving car and it was driving on gravel. He knew his hands were cuffed behind his back with plastic ties and he knew that he was hot and thirsty. And it was dark outside.

He was bruised and aching and also fairly certain that he'd been Tased at some point in the afternoon. He had that specific metallic taste in his mouth that comes from that and it would also account for why he'd been out for so long.

He could hear men arguing in the car, one of them was Javier. He couldn't make out what was being said, however. He wiggled his arms, getting his circulation going again. He felt for his phone. It was gone. He did a quick mental evaluation of the situation. It didn't take long. The short version, he was fucked.

That was, ironically enough, also the long version of the situation, too. Slick took a deep breath, centered and calmed himself. He'd prepared for this moment for a long time, his eventual death, and wanted to be ready.

For some reason he couldn't get the image of Pedro's pregnant girlfriend out of his mind. Her face floated before him like a ghost. Slick was certain he'd seen her before.

The car finally came to a stop and the voices inside climbed out. They were still arguing. Slick heard another vehicle pull up. And another. He counted at least eight voices, maybe more.

"Turn the lights off, we don't want her to know we're here," Del said. "Not yet."

"She's probably in bed, old people go to bed early around these parts."

Slick didn't recognize that voice. He knew Brower and Collins, Javier and Del, but there were at least four others. He listened as the men waited and smoked.

"Where's the nig?" said one of them.

"Hey," Javier said. "Stow that shit."

"What?"

"I don't want to hear any of your racist bullshit, understand? Keep it to yourself."

"Agent, we're pretty far off the reservation, and the FBI ain't calling the shots here, last I checked." Some of the other men giggled.

"You keep it up," Javier said, "and I'll put my fist so far down your throat that I'll be able to yank your brains out of your ass. Is that completely clear, deputy?"

Everyone got silent and still until Del spoke up.

"Easy boys, Agent Rivera is right, let's act professionally here. Our man's in the trunk, pull him out and we'll get this show on the road."

The lid opened and hands reached inside, lifted Slick out of the trunk. They dumped him on the ground face first into sand and dirt and shined their flashlights on him. Slick spit and cleared his throat. Rolled to up to a kneeling position, testing how much play he had in his hands. He didn't have much at all.

Del stood before him, smiling. Behind him, Brower, Collins and a couple of other deputies. Javier stood nearby. In the distance behind the men, Slick recognized the Carlson ranch, all tucked in for the night.

"Why are we here?" Slick asked.

"Well, I must admit, I've got a touch of OCD," Del said. "I came up with this perfect solution for getting rid of both you and Ted, I mean it was a thing of beauty. It really was. And had Camilla Leon been able to control her urges, it would have worked."

"Hey," Javier said. "You don't talk about her."

"My apologies. Just telling it like it is, Agent Rivera. But I hear you." Del kneeled down next to Slick. "See, Slick, I don't like to waste a good idea, and that one was as good as they get. It itches at me, bothers me so much that mere chance fucked up a perfect plan. So I'm going to use it again. Doris Carlson has been particularly stubborn, she was all set to sell and now she's said she won't sell the farm under any circumstances. So you're going to break in and kill her."

"Oh, I am? And why would I do that?"

"Because you're a killer, that's what you do. We'll make the story stick, trust me. And you'll be shot dead on your way out. You'll have powder burns on your hands, finger-prints on the weapon, and you'll be shot dead exiting the scene of the crime—it'll be a slam dunk. We'll blame the Ted murder on you as well, we'll say that you forced Camilla to lie for your alibi, so on, so forth. It'll take a bit of finesse, but that is what I do, I finesse situations. I'll have a federal officer and a district attorney telling folks what to believe and they will believe it. I don't know if you realize this, but black people aren't trusted a whole lot in Arizona."

"I have noticed that, yeah. And not just in Arizona."

"Yeah, white folks tend to think the worst of your people, it's a shame, it really is."

"A damn shame. Well, okay, what are we waiting for? Give me the gun and let me go cap her sorry ass."

Del laughed. "I like this guy, I really do. In spite of himself. Sorry, Slick, you're not getting a firearm. One of these fellows will take care of the soon-to-be-departed Doris Carlson and then Javier here will take care of you immediately afterward. Both Brower and Collins wanted to do it, but Javier, seems he's got a bit of a bone to pick with you."

"I've got one of my own to pick with him. Where's Camilla?"

"She's somewhere safe, not to worry. George is taking good care of her." Del rose to his feet. "Okay, boys, stand him up and let's get this show on the road."

Collins and another deputy grabbed Slick under his arms and yanked. Slick resisted at first. They pulled harder and Slick pushed into it, butting his head into the deputy's chin. He kneed Collins but was stopped with a punch to the kidneys from Javier. Javier hit him again and they bent him face first over the hood of the police car.

"Country, career and Camilla, I thought those were your big three, Javier. That was all bullshit then? You're all about the dollars after all, I guess, and fuck everyone else, including Camilla," Slick said. "Right?"

"Shut up. This is for her own good, you're a fucking professional killer."

"And now so are you. The only difference is who we work for. I work for myself. I ain't all about the money like you. You're taking orders from this fucking asshole."

Javier bent Slick's bound hands up high behind his back until Slick grunted.

"Nobody orders me to do shit."

"We have a huge investment in Agent Rivera," Del said. "He's going places. He's a much better political prospect than Ted could ever be. Ted couldn't control himself, couldn't rein in his natural biases. Javier is a lot smarter. He'll be the first Hispanic director of Homeland Security, maybe even president. The sky's the limit, especially after he resolves this whole situation here. A career like that takes money and connections and now he has both. We'll all be taking orders from him someday."

Slick felt someone place a gun in his hand. He resisted but they made sure he gripped it tight.

"Put your finger in there or I'll break it," Brower said. He and Collins forced his index finger into the trigger guard.

"They're going to kill her, Javier, they have to."

"Shut up," the fed said. "She'll be fine."

"No need to kill her," Del said. "It'll all be explained. You're a professional killer, we've already put together a portfolio to explain it all. You're the one who really killed Roger Carlson and set Pedro up. You were hired to do so by a company that will soon go under. I've got a bunch of shell companies set up solely for that purpose. You used Camilla for cover once you got busted by Ted. You lied to and seduced her. And you came here to the Carlson place to finish business, but Agent Rivera was on to you and stopped you, although sadly just a touch too late. It's a very compelling story."

"Clear, fire in the hole," Brower said.

They forced the weapon in Slick's hand to fire three times. The shots echoed out over the desert. They removed the pistol from his hand, spun Slick around. Collins handed the weapon to Brower, who wore plastic gloves.

"She'll never believe it. She knows too much and she won't stop digging," Slick said.

"She won't be able to dig too much, George will regretfully have to ask for her resignation. I mean she did consort and sleep with a known murderer, that just can't be done. But she'll go into private practice and be fine. Okay, Brower, Mrs. Carlson next."

Brower nodded to Del and disappeared into the darkness, two deputies behind him, heading for the ranch house. Slick blinked, because Del's comment about George triggered something in his mind. He just remembered where he'd seen that girl before.

"Javier, they have to kill her. She won't stop, you know she won't."

"She'll stop. I'll make her believe it."

Slick switched to Spanish. "*It's too late, she knows who the girl is.*"

"*What girl?*" Javier replied in kind.

"*She knows who Pedro's girl is,*" Slick replied, his Spanish just barely good enough to be understood by the agent.

"*So what?*"

"What's he saying?" Del asked.

"*She knows the girl. That girl is her boss's daughter. She found video that shows the girl's face and recognized her. She sent it to me. It's on my phone,*" Slick said, thankful that he finally remembered. He'd seen her face in the picture on Camilla's mantel and in the pictures in George Hanson's office. The girl was his oldest daughter. "*You can see it for yourself. She'll never believe that story because she knows the girl.*"

"Agent Rivera, what is he saying?"

Javier didn't answer, just stared at Slick.

"*They have to kill her now, because she knows too much. She knows the only reason that Pedro was chosen was because he was involved with George Hanson's daughter. Pedro got her pregnant. They're lying to you, they have to kill her now, if they haven't already. I bet they killed Father Jose, too. They're going to kill her, Javier. I don't care what happens to me, I care about her. Where is she?*" Slick asked.

"Javier, what is he saying about George?"

"What happened to Father Jose?" Javier asked. "He wasn't supposed to be harmed, that was the deal."

In the distance, Brower pounded on the front door of the Carlson house.

"He wasn't, he's upstate with some contacts of mine, like we discussed—"

"He's lying, Javier," Slick said. "Look at him, listen to him, you've done this long enough to know when someone's lying. He just lied to you, right there."

"Come on, Javier, this man will say anything right now

to save his life—"

"Where's Camilla?" Javier asked.

"I told you, she's with George—"

"Get her on the phone. Now."

"Javier, that might be difficult, because—"

Javier pointed his weapon at Del. "You have five seconds."

Collins and the remaining deputies pulled their weapons and aimed at the agent.

"Javier. Calm down. She's fine."

"Four seconds."

"Oh shit, he's lying," Slick said, reading Del's face. "Goddamn it. Shit! Motherfucker. I am going to KILL you for this. You motherfucker!" Slick pushed forward until a deputy shoved him back against the car. "You killed her already!"

"It is true?" Javier said, his face tight with fear.

"Lower the gun and we'll discuss it."

"We'll discuss it now. Three seconds."

In the distance, Brower kicked open the door of the Carlson house.

"Two seconds."

"Javier, there are ... certain ... unavoidable realities that we have to face in an endeavor such as this. Certain sacrifices we all have to make. I was going to tell you—"

"No. No ... no, you didn't—"

"Javier—"

Javier shot Del where he stood. The deputies opened up on him and he ducked out of the way, swung his pistol around at one of the deputies and fired back at him.

Slick lashed a foot out at a deputy who had the drop on Javier, catching the man with a kick right to the joint of the knee, breaking it. The man screamed and went down. Javier shot him. The rest of the deputies dropped their flashlights and scattered, firing wildly at Javier as he shot back at them.

Slick rolled back over the hood of the car behind him, landing on the ground on the opposite side. He sat down on his ass, scooted his hands under his butt and over his legs and feet. Now his cuffed hands were in front.

He crouched down as bullets flew overhead. A deputy ran around, his flashlight bobbing up and down. Slick leaped on him, dropping his cuffed hands over the man's throat. He turned his body and twisted. The man's neck broke. Collins popped up from behind a car and fired at Slick. Slick twisted the dead man's body around, shielding himself from the shots, which thudded into the corpse.

Slick brought his hands back off of the dead man and rolled forward as shots whistled close by him. He kept rolling right to the firing deputy. Slick came to his feet when he got close and elbowed Collins on the chin. He brought his cuffed hands down on the weapon. He knocked it out of the deputy's hands and it disappeared into the darkness.

Collins batted Slick away with a backhand. Slick went down again and bounced right back up. Collins stalked him, his fists high and his shoulders bunched up tight. He swiped at Slick with a big, meaty paw. Slick ducked under it and rolled again, this time staying on his back. He got his knee behind the plastic cuff ties binding his wrists and pushed. The plastic ties snapped and his hands were now free. He rolled again just as Collins tried to stomp on him. Slick got to his feet and squared off with the big man.

Shots echoed as Javier cursed somewhere in the darkness.

Collins swiped at Slick again. Slick blocked this one with his forearm and it stung, numbing the entire arm. Slick countered with a head butt right on the big man's nose. Blood spurted. Slick followed that with a vicious Muay Thai kick to the inside of the deputy's knee. It cracked and Collins went down on one knee.

Slick unloaded a barrage of punches and kicks and the big man just covered up and absorbed them. He grabbed Slick's leg and tackled him. Slick allowed himself to fall backward and got one leg up and over the deputy's shoulder, trapping one of the arms inside and cinching a jiu-jitsu triangle choke, Slick's legs now locked tight and cutting off the blood supply. The bigger man fought it, got to his feet and picked Slick's whole body up.

He slammed Slick's body down hard on the ground, trying to shake loose of the chokehold. Slick just hung on tight, grabbing the deputy's outsized head and pulling on it. Collins picked him up and slammed him again. And again. Slick gritted his teeth and hung on. Finally Collins went to his knees and then fell over on his side, slowly losing consciousness.

"Fuck you, nigger," Collins said right before he went lights out.

Slick released the unconscious deputy and got to his feet. Looked down at him.

"Fuck you right back, friend." Slick stamped on the bigger man's throat, crushing it. He spun when a flashlight behind him lit him up. Javier stood there, blood pouring from a wound in his chest, aiming a pistol at him. After an instant, he lowered his weapon, breathing heavily.

"Is that all of them?" Slick asked.

"Yeah, except for fucking Delbert, he's still alive—but not for long."

Javier limped over to his car. Del was stretched out on the ground next to it, his belly open and splattered. He was pale and gasping, trying to talk.

"I'm going to make him tell me what they did with Camilla," Javier said.

Shots echoed again in the darkness, this time coming from the Carlson house.

"That's a shotgun," Slick said. "Doris Carlson is fighting back."

"Here." Javier handed him his pistol. "You go, I'm not gonna be able to make it that far in this condition. I'll take care of fucking Del, you get them."

Slick jacked the slide. "When this is all finally over, I'm going to kill you."

"If Camilla really is dead then I'll welcome it."

44

SLICK RAN HARD and fast for the ranch house. Shots echoed again, this time both pistol shots and shotgun shots. He made it to the front door. One of the deputies was sprawled out on the kitchen floor, his chest cratered by a shotgun blast. Slick moved past the kitchen and through the living room.

Brower and the other deputy stood at the hallway leading back to the bedrooms, leaning around the corner to fire at Doris, barricaded somewhere in the back. A shotgun blast took out a piece of the wood paneling near his head. Brower stayed calm and assured as he reloaded.

"Brower!"

Brower and the remaining deputy saw Slick in the kitchen. Each man brought their weapons up simultaneously and opened fire. Brower took a shot in the shoulder and in the chest. Slick dodged, still firing. He hit the other deputy in the head and dropped him. Brower stumbled forward, bleeding, unloading almost his entire clip at Slick, who dived behind a kitchen counter. He dropped his pistol when he hit the floor and it skittered away. Brower raced around it to take his shot, but before he could even gloat, a shotgun blast turned Brower's entire head into a big, red mist.

Brower's headless body went to its knees and then collapsed.

Doris Carlson stepped into the kitchen, her face white with shock and determination. She looked to Slick, who raised his hands and got to his feet.

"They broke in with bad intentions," Doris finally said.

"They certainly did."

"I had to do it, I couldn't ... I had to—"

"You had to. They were the ones who killed Roger, Doris. They wanted the farm, that's why they killed him and why they were going to kill you."

"It was them that did it, murdered my Roger?"

"Yeah. They murdered your husband and you flat out killed both their asses."

Doris looked at him for a moment, her eyes blinking and emotions welling. She stuffed it back inside and finally nodded.

"Good," she said. "For Roger. Good."

45

THERE WAS A state trooper SUV parked near the police cars and carnage by the time Doris and Slick made it back to Javier. Del lay on the ground, now dead and sporting considerably more damage than he did when Slick left him. Javier sat with his back against his car, blood pooling on the ground near him. Navajo Joe crouched near him and raised his gun when they approached. He lowered it when he recognized Slick.

"Joe," Slick said.

"Slick, Mrs. Carlson," Navajo Joe said. "Good to see both of you in one piece. Mrs. Carlson called me when she first heard the shots. Quite a mess we got here. Javier was just filling me in on the whole sordid scheme and voluntarily confessing to a number of crimes he's responsible for personally."

"I have evidence, in my car," Javier said, his voice weak. "There's a flash drive with the goods on all of them behind it—George, Ted, Del, the board of directors. It was my insurance policy in case they tried to double-cross me. Take it, burn the whole shithouse down. Do it."

"He won't let me call in an ambulance for him," Navajo Joe said.

"No, don't. Slick's gonna take care of me. He promised,"

Javier said.

"You get answers from Del about Camilla?"

Javier didn't speak, just nodded.

"Tell me."

"I can't—"

"Fucking tell me, Javier."

"Brower and Collins picked her up at the office this afternoon, after we secured you. George called them. They took her out to the desert." Javier swallowed. "They made her dig a hole, shot her and buried her out there."

Slick had known that intellectually, he'd known it ever since he caught Del's first lie, but hearing it out loud hit him harsh in the gut. He turned away and screamed at the desert. He screamed and let it all out. Navajo Joe and Doris just stood there.

Javier didn't hide the tears streaming down his face. "It's all fucked up, I've been such a fucking idiot. I got greedy. It should have been me, not Camilla. Anyone but her."

Slick took a deep breath, let it out and turned back to Javier.

"You promised me something," Javier said. "Keep your promise. End it for me, right here and right now."

"Hey now, hold on—" Navajo Joe said.

"Do it, Slick. I've been a fool, put me out of my misery."

"No."

"Slick—"

"You'll be dead any minute as is, way you're bleeding out. You lived as a fool, true, but you didn't go out like one. You stood up at the end. Not everyone can say that. Take that with you as you go."

Javier thought about that and finally nodded to Navajo Joe. "Don't call this in until I'm gone, understand?"

The trooper nodded. Javier sighed as if finally unburdened and, after a few moments, died where he sat.

"You can call it in now," Slick said.

"I will, as soon as I figure out how the hell I'm going to explain this tale of woe and sorrow to my bosses."

"You open to suggestions?"

"Why not?"

"Here's how it can play. Camilla collected evidence on Del and the deputies and gave it to Javier and let him know they were coming after Doris. He got here just in time to stop them, killing them all but dying from his wounds. His gun killed most of these men. He's got powder burns on his hands. He told you what they did to Camilla. I was never here. She's the hero."

"You were never here?"

"Just fucks everything up, me being here. You probably have a good idea of what I do for a living besides playing cards. I don't want my name public and, besides, it's a lot simpler my way. I left when I was told to leave. Camilla kept on the job, cracked this criminal conspiracy, she gets the credit for the evidence on the flash drive and for tipping Javier off, everything, and I walk away. Local papers will eat it up, it works into the narrative that had already been going on with Ted, it's a much better story than the reality. You got your villains, your dying heroes, it'll play."

"I can't argue with that." Navajo Joe took his hat off and rubbed his head. He looked to Doris.

"Would you be all right with that, Mrs. Carlson?"

"Is that what you want?" she asked Slick.

"Yeah, it's what I want."

"If it's what he wants, then I'm fine with it. If not for him, I'd never have known who really killed my Roger. I'll say whatever he wants me to say."

"Camilla's name comes out of this all good, but are you comfortable with Javier also being the hero, after all he's done?" Navajo Joe asked.

"He knew what the truth was before he died, so I can live with it. But I want something in return," Slick said.

"What's that?" Navajo Joe asked.

46

"KEEP DIGGING," SLICK said.

He sat on the hood of Doris Carlson's truck. The headlights lit up the desert as George Hanson dug a hole in the sand and begged for his life. Slick had borrowed her truck, driven back to town and snatched George when he came out to investigate a noise he'd heard in his garage.

Slick had tied him up, stuffed him into the back of the truck and driven out into the deep part of the desert. Slick tossed him a shovel and ordered him to dig. Told him if he didn't he would kneecap him and leave him for the coyotes. He fired a few shots into the ground near his feet to motivate the man. George cried and dug his hole. It was nearly chest high and the older man was slowing down, trying to prolong the inevitable.

"Okay, George. Out of the hole."

"Please, don't do this. I have money, I'll pay you anything—"

"I don't want your money. Out or I make this very painful."

George crawled out of the hole, blubbering.

"Turn around," Slick said. George did as he was ordered.

"Please, I'm begging you, I have a family—"

"Camilla Leon had a family. She had a mother and father, brothers and sisters. She had a family and now she's dead because of you, she was brought out to the desert and forced to dig a hole just like the one you just did. She did that and she was killed by your men."

"Please, I had no choice—"

"Everyone has a choice, George. You know who else had a family? Pedro Garcia. He had a mother and a girlfriend he loved. Your daughter."

"Listen—"

"And he had a child on the way. Your daughter was pregnant and because the father was an undocumented Mexican, you set him up to be killed."

"What?" George turned around. "Jenny's pregnant?"

"You didn't know?" Slick lowered his pistol as he examined the older man's face. "How about that, you really didn't know."

"She didn't tell me," George said. "I had no idea. I knew who she was seeing, yes, she told me finally. I admit that I him set up so he'd leave my daughter alone, but Ted wasn't supposed to kill Pedro and I had no idea she was pregnant. I sent her away up north, away from this mess, when it got out of control. She took off the morning after … after he died, and I don't even know where she is. I've called and called her and she won't have anything to do with me."

"Can you blame her?"

"Please—"

"Turn back around. Do it!"

George did as he was ordered. Slick put the pistol to the back of his head. George sobbed for what was to come.

"You killed the father of your unborn grandchild, George. You also killed a woman I could have loved forever."

Slick pulled the trigger and the pistol hammer fell upon an empty cylinder. George cried out loud when he realized he was still alive and soiled his pants. Slick shoved him into the hole with his free hand. He stood at the edge of it.

"This hole is too good for you. Going out the same way Camilla went out, far too good for you. I ain't gonna do that. You're going to do life in a federal prison, a prison like the one you sold your soul for, and you're going to die cold and miserable and publicly humiliated. That's what Camilla would've wanted."

Slick turned back to the truck, got inside, started it up and drove away, leaving George there alone in the desert. Either George would find his way back or he wouldn't, but Slick had a feeling the old man would.

JENNY HOPED BEYOND hope that she was done throwing up for the day.

She'd puked at least five times before noon as it was, twice since coming to work and she still had at least eight hours of her ten-hour shift to go. She hadn't eaten anything since the previous night, so hopefully there was nothing left inside that could some out. Nausea rose again as she cleared a table and wiped it off. She swallowed it back down and hurried to the front.

Her manager, Rob, had already made a couple comments about her trips to the bathroom, but the other girls told her that he did the same thing to them when they started out, too. He was just an asshole, especially to new girls.

Rob dressed like a hipster, mostly to fit in with the collegiate ambience that was common not just in coffee shops like this one but throughout the city of Portland. Rob even had the man-bun and pierced tongue, but Jenny quickly found out that his heart was as cold and hard as any capitalist robber baron. He'd sack her in a second if given any excuse, the other waitresses had warned Jenny. He liked firing new girls and he was at his most dangerous when he acted nice.

Jenny used to love the smell of coffee, too, especially in the morning. Now it just made her ill and she didn't think she'd ever be able to drink the beverage again. The smell was in her clothes, her hair, everywhere and followed her home at night, staying with her even after a long shower.

She caught a glimpse of herself in one of the mirrors. She had new wrinkles around her eyes and her face was harried, her blonde hair a perfect mess. It'd only been a few weeks and she thought she already looked ten years older. She wondered how long she'd be able to keep this up.

Rob snapped his fingers at her and Jenny rushed to pick up an order of coffee. "This has been here for at least a minute already. Move faster. And you have someone at table four, he's been waiting," Rob said. "We don't let our customers wait, we're the wait staff, not the customers. We wait, they don't, understand?"

"I understand, I'll take care of it," she said.

"I've got my eye on you," Rob said as she balanced the coffee on the tray and threaded through the maze of tables to deliver it to a group of college students, who took it without even saying thank you. Jenny remembered when she was just like them. If she ever got out of this place, she'd never look at a waitress in the same way ever again.

She sighed and hurried to the man sitting in the back. She couldn't believe she'd missed him, he was a very large, very black man dressed in a loud pink shirt. He tapped away on a computer tablet. She took out her pad.

"Hi, what can I get you?"

He stared at her for a second, and then put the tablet away. "A moment of your time, Jenny Hanson, nothing more or less."

Jenny froze for a moment, shocked, but then she figured it out and glared at him. She put her hand on her hip, indignant.

"Nice pink shirt. Since when do private investigators wear pink?"

"I'm not a PI and this shirt was a gift from a very special lady."

"Yeah, right. Sure you're not a PI. Listen, I don't know how you found me, but tell my father that I'm not interested in his help or even hearing from him—"

"I'm not here on behalf of your father. I'm a friend of Pedro's."

That stopped her. "You knew Pedro?"

"Briefly, yes. I'm here on his behalf. Have a seat, please."

She glanced over her shoulder at Rob, who glared at her.

"Don't worry about your manager, I'll take care of him and make sure to tip big. I just need a minute, that's all. For Pedro."

Jenny gave in to curiosity and sat down.

"Who are you?" she asked.

"My name is Jon Elder, friends call me Slick."

"What do you want?" she asked.

"Did your father find out about you and Pedro, or did you tell him?"

"I told him, I had to tell him. He was furious. I didn't tell him that I was—"

"Pregnant, I know. This was a couple days before—"

"Before Pedro was arrested, yes."

"And you left town when you heard—"

"No, my father sent me away the next morning. I didn't know why, exactly, I only heard Pedro got arrested and that my father was going to try to help him. He said he didn't want me to get into trouble too, it was a legal issue, he said, and I ... I believed him.

"I shouldn't have. I thought he'd just get sent back to Mexico, and I could see him there, at the very least. I didn't even know Pedro was in the hospital until it was too late. I sent him text messages, but ... when I heard ... when I finally heard that Pedro was dead, I ... ran away. From my father's friends, from everyone. Ran here. I had a friend who let me stay with her, helped me find a job. This job."

She looked up at Slick. "We were going to be married."

"I know. Your father's in jail."

She started at that. "I didn't know. For what happened to Pedro?"

"And other things. That bother you?"

"Not if he was responsible for what happened to Pedro."

"He was. I guarantee it."

Jenny closed her eyes, bit back more nausea and tears.

"I somehow knew he was, in my heart."

"You planning to keep the baby?"

"Not so loud," she said. "My boss doesn't know. If he finds out I'm pregnant, he'll fire me now so he won't have to pay for maternity leave. I have fifty more days before I get any benefits."

"So you're keeping it."

"I want to. I really want to."

"You were in college, right? This fall was supposed to be your junior year. You were pre-law, too, right? You thinking about going back?"

"I'd like to, but … I don't know, with the baby and everything—"

"You can, if you want. Here." Slick reached down, picked up a satchel and plopped it on the table.

"What is it?"

"Take a look."

She unzipped it and glanced inside. It was filled with money. She shoved it back at him. "I told you before, I don't want my father's help."

"And I told you, this money ain't from your father. This money is from me, because I considered Pedro a friend in need. Now it's yours, take it. It's enough that you can quit this shit job, go back to school and take care of the kid without slaving away, hoping you get enough tips to pay the bills. This is for you, from Pedro, not from your father. I helped put your father where he is. For Pedro. He'd want you to have it."

She glanced over his shoulder at Rob, who was steaming and now walking over to their table. Slick turned and stared at the manager, gave the officious prick his prison yard stare and that did the trick. Rob stopped in his tracks and found something else to occupy his attention.

"Okay." She sighed. "I'm not going to lie, I could really use the help."

"Take this and walk out of this place now, get yourself set up in a nice apartment and go back to school. I only have two conditions, if you take the money."

"What conditions?"

Slick slid a card over. "This is the lawyer who represented Pedro, Melvin Hayes, he's suing the city, and your father I might add, for wrongful death on Pedro's behalf. He'll want to talk to you. There will probably be a big settlement, though those things take time. Melvin also has the name and address of Pedro's mother in Mexico. I want you to call and introduce yourself to her and explain that she's going to be a grandmother. I know that you learned to speak Spanish in school. She's your family now, she'll need financial help from you as well, but mostly I want her included in the life of her grandchild. Pedro worshipped his mother and it's what he'd want."

She took the card. "Yes. I'll do that. Definitely. What's the other condition?"

Slick stood and headed out. "If it's a boy, you name him Pedro."

"I'd already planned on that. What if it's a girl?"

Slick didn't stop, just kept going.

"If it's a girl, name her Camilla."

Elijah Drive was born in the Midwest with a large chip on his shoulder, one that he still carries with pride to this very day. Currently based on the east coast, among his many interests are literature, politics and martial arts. He doesn't believe in murder for money, but he does believe in karma and kicking ass, big time.

Bullets is Elijah's first novel.

Follow his Facebook Page for more information: Elijah Drive – Author

If you enjoyed this novel, please leave a REVIEW wherever you purchased it from. Every review and every reader counts. Thank you and remember … karma is a boomerang.

58581962R00177

Made in the USA
Lexington, KY
13 December 2016